ELEMENTS OF THE FLOW: The Exile

Ross Salwolke

Dedication

This book is dedicated to the woman, without whom I never would have completed this. Elizabeth LaRocque, soon to be Elizabeth Salwolke, without your undying support, faith, and love I would never be able to achieve what I can with you. I love you! Never ever stop being who you are!

Special Thanks

There are a number of people that I would like to thank in addition to the one noted above. My sister, Athena, for always being my sounding board and supporting me and telling me I'm being stupid when I'm being stupid. My parents, Ross Sr. and Cathy, for raising me to hold myself to a higher standard than society does. My best friend, Will, for listening to me and encouraging me when I put myself down and said I couldn't finish this book. My friend, Brandy, for being the voice of reason and guiding light through the darkness of just what it takes to write a novel.

To Elissa McMurrain, thank you for your help and hard work in creating the amazing cover art for this book.

To all of those who were a part of the test read group and had a hand in the editing process, thank you so much for your help!

ELEMENTS
OF
THE FLOW
THE EXILE

Prologue

I could be cliché and say once upon a time, or a long time ago, but I don't think it appropriate in telling my story.

My name is Kane Malacor and, at one time, I was a normal Atrethian; Well, as normal as Atrethians are compared to you humans. We resembled humans in just about every way. From our diverse hair color to the color of our skin. Though our eyes were very different from yours. We don't have pupils like humans.

You see, on Atrethia, there was this power that we call the Flow. It's an energy that encompassed everything in existence. Everything living and dead was a part of the Flow. Every rock; every blade of grass, every leaf on every tree; every person; you get the idea. We could manipulate what you call the "Laws of Physics" and we could even create physical objects just through the use of our power. At least the more powerful of us could.

One thing that all Atrethians had in common is that before we were born, this power filled us with academic knowledge. Our only explanation for that is that our ancestors, specifically those that passed of their own choice, were passing on their knowledge to keep our society moving forward.

Like with all abilities, there are varying degrees of skill. Some could merely light a candle with their thoughts while others could make an entire town disappear without a trace. Now, back to how this pertained to our eyes.

Our eyes were one solid color. There were the common colors like green and brown and blue. Some of us had silver eyes. Some had gold eyes. It all depended on your energy and how strong it was. Each person's energy had a primary element. The element of our energy is what it best manipulated. We could manipulate other elements of course but to lesser extent.

Those of the fire element that were more powerful could control it and some could even create it. Those of the wind element could control the direction and strength of wind and some could create wind storms. The water element, as you have probably guessed, could control the flow of water. Most of the earth element could not, however, control the earth to a large extent. At the most, they could move loose dirt. Some stronger in the element could do much, much more.

Our power and element determined our eye color. Platinum was the strongest of all or at least that's what they thought. I was born with platinum eyes but my sister, she … she was born with pure white eyes. That had never happened in the history of our people. At birth, every Atrethians eye color was recorded, and as far back as our records go none showed anyone born with white eyes. Many a powerful figure watched my sister grow. We were born on the same day in the same year but we were not identical. I believe you humans have a word for it but on our world it was unheard of. A medical mystery if you take it as such.

Our laws forbade the use of our abilities in destructive manners, unless we were defending ourselves of course, but even then we may not defend in excess. Our civilization grew much like yours did until what you call the Medieval Era. We had our energy to support what we needed. We didn't need technology. Why create a telephone when you can project yourself into someone's home?

We were a great and moral people. There are always the occasional bad people, but as a whole, we were good. We cared and we always worked towards the betterment of

all Atrethians. At least I thought we did.
    This is my story...

1

A small home sat on the edge of an immense city. A modest, one-story home with a thatched roof stood out as a pleasant welcome to the bustling city. The walls were light blue with a window on the front near the door. The door slammed open suddenly and two young children bolted through. A boy about three feet tall with short black hair wearing brown pants and an off-white shirt. His feet were bare. His twin was a girl wearing a flowing off-white dress with the sleeves pulled up. Her feet were also bare.

"Kane! Aerika! You be careful!" Their mother, Liana, called after them as they ran out of the house. Her light pink dress seemed to shimmer in the summer sun. Her gold eyes shone through her long brown hair. Her hair hung loose over her chest. She couldn't help but smile watching her children play. She would enjoy this day with them, once they finally caught up with them that is.

It was early morning. The smell of the breakfast they had just finished still lingered in the air. The farther they ran from the door the more it mixed with the morning air until it had disappeared altogether. They were finally five years old and would soon start their training at The Academy. The Academy was where all young Atrethians went to learn about their power and the responsibility of having it. The Academy put you through thirteen entire years of training on "The Flow." What it was, how it worked, how to find it and how to use it. But perhaps the most important part of their training was the discipline they taught. Morality with The Flow was key to education at The Academy.

Atrethian Law determined what the most severe

crimes were but offenses were judged largely by the Atrethian High Council because the only limitation on the use of "Flow" is the user's imagination. This led to many wonderful and very dangerous outcomes.

At one time, all of Atrethia was at peace. Then a man named Terrei emerged. He later came to be called the Malicious One. He created horrific beasts. Unnatural creatures designed specifically to defend him in his home as he wrought destruction upon the world around him. The Atrethian High Council could not stand for his crimes so he was forcibly brought before them and put to death. After his death, peace returned to Atrethia and life has remained that way ever since. Though such things were hardly on the minds of the twins.

Kane and Aerika ran across the hills into the fields outside of Mi'Tiya, the capital of Atrethia. Grass and small yellow petals shot up into the air behind them as they ran through the fields. They raced past trees, past fields of grass and small ponds towards the Barean Cliffs. Kane and Aerika slowed to a walk as they approached the cliffs. The scarlet red Barean Halos, flowers native only to these cliffs, appearing over the final hill as they reach its peak. They stop to take in the sight and to catch their breath.

"I can't believe we start training tomorrow." Kane said still trying to catch his breath. "We won't get the chance to come out here until next year."

"I know. We will have our memories of this place though. We can just close our eyes and we're here again." Aerika replied. She pushed her bottom lip up into a pout and said, "And don't want to think of it that way. It's so sad when you say it like that."

Aerika looked over at her brother and smiled once again. Kane's eyes met hers and he smiled back. "You're right. Let's just have fun."

Aerika ran towards the cliffs laughing as she made

her way towards the edge. Kane started laughing too. He started after her running hard to catch up with her. Aerika entered into the field of flowers their scarlet petals standing out against her off-white dress. She raised her arms brushing her hands against the silky flower petals as she ran through their bed.

Kane stopped at the edge and stared at the flowers. He loved them. Their beauty and complexity. The strength that they possessed. These flowers didn't break apart when you ran through them. They didn't die when it didn't rain for weeks on end. They survived no matter what happened.

He grabbed hold of one turning it to face him. A thin blue halo near the center of the flower for which the flowers were named stared back at him. He took a long drag of the flower's aroma. The scent always made him relax. Always made him happy. This was his favorite place.

Aerika ran up next to him and wrapped her arms around him. "Kane ... come run with me in the flowers. Mom and Dad will be here soon and we'll have to spend the rest of the day with them."

He pulled his eyes away from the flower to look at his twin sister. He smiled and nodded. He gripped her hand tight and they ran off into the flowers laughing.

Liana came to the top of the hill before reaching the cliffs. This sight always took her breath away. It seemed to do that to everyone that saw it, but the scenery was made even more beautiful by her children laughing and playing amongst the flowers. She looked back down the hill behind her.

"Sinal, look at our children play." Her husband joined her at the top of the hill. Sinal was a tall man standing at over six feet. His white shirt bulged from the muscles of his chest that came with his job as the primary combat instructor at the Academy. His large arms holding a white blanket and basket of food for their lunch. A sudden gust of wind made his cropped black hair dance around his head.

Liana wrapped her arm through his helping to carry the blanket and they walked together towards the cliffs. They reluctantly parted from each other when they got to the flowers. Sinal put the basket down and began to lay out the blanket.

"Children! Join your mother and I!" Sinal called out while straightening out the blanket for them to sit on. He finished just as Kane and Aerika joined them. They all sat down on the blanket. Liana smiled at her children while Sinal got their food out for the picnic.

"Did you two enjoy your morning?" she asked.

"Yes, mother!" they said in unison.

"Very much!" Aerika continued.

"I am glad." She smiled a sad smile at them. She wasn't ready for them to go off to train or for them to stay at the Academy until the next summer. They stay in the school so they have no distractions from learning. Sinal passed a salted meat sandwich to his wife and children and grabbed one for himself. The children started into their sandwiches without a word. Liana and Sinal's eyes caught each other's. Liana took a bite of her sandwich and smiled lovingly at her husband.

They sat and ate their lunch enjoying the feel of the breeze passing over the cliffs and the sound of the waves crashing against them far below. It was a pleasant moment for the family before the children began their training. The rest of the day was pleasant enough. The children running and playing in the field just outside their home while Sinal and Liana prepared for the change in their lives that would occur just the next day.

They all hardly slept that night. Liana and Sinal because they worried how their children would take to starting their training and Kane and Aerika out of sheer excitement. The next morning was a quick one. Kane and Aerika were up and ready to go quickly. So was Sinal. Liana had gotten an early start on breakfast to make sure they would have full stomachs when they went to The Academy. The walk through the city was a quiet one. There just wasn't much to be said.

Sinal and Liana approached the Academy with their children. Kane and Aerika had the wide eyed wonder that is typical of children their age when they go to a new place. Sinal and Liana were very proud of their children.

The closer they got to the school the more people were taking notice of the two very special children approaching. Aerika drew her white eyes across everything with the wonder of exploring something that hadn't been seen in ages. Kane looked around only a little. He was more interested in his sister's reaction to the Academy.

People stopped to stare in wonder at the twins that approached. After a while, everyone outside the Academy was staring. Aerika's pure white eyes even at age five pulsing with the power that lie within her. And Kane's platinum eyes seemingly reflecting more light than the sun gave off.

After a few moments, Sinal placed a hand on each child's shoulder. "Say goodbye to your mother. We have to go." When he said this, Liana squatted down and held her arms open for her children. They turned to their mother and pushed themselves against her. She just held them tight and let them lean against her. She knew they were sad to be leaving for a year and that the excitement of the morning had kept them from thinking about it. She was sad too but she was already looking forward to them returning from school. She closed her eyes and imagined the reunion that would happen when the year of training ended.

"OK kids. It's my turn to say goodbye." Sinal said. Liana let the children go reluctantly and stood back up. She wrapped her arms under her husbands and buried her face against his chest. She melted into the warmth of his loving embrace. He just smiled and closed his eyes enjoying the moment. She pulled her face out of his chest after a while and looked into Sinal's eyes. A small smile pulled its way across his lips before he leaned in to kiss her.

The children went back to taking in the scenery of the Academy's entrance. The pitch-black doors standing five men tall were framed by stark white marble walls standing taller than any building the two children had ever seen. The walls went as far as the eye could see in either direction with pillars standing before them holding up an overhang. The pillars were carved with images of great battles, the creation of the most amazing monuments in the world and some very horrible acts.

"I love you, Liana."

"I love you too, Sinal."

They hugged each other tightly one last time before Sinal took Kane and Aerika in through the black doorway into the long entrance hall of the place that would be their home for the next year. The children looked back over their shoulders to catch one last glimpse of their mother, but the light of the sun raining in through the open door blocked everything outside from them.

As they strode through the halls of the Academy, they noticed things. The hallways seem to go on forever in every direction. It seemed that the building was larger inside than it was outside. Sinal led his children to a door very near to where they had entered. At least they thought it was near. They weren't quite sure how far they had gone.

"This is your room. I was able to get the both of you in the same room. Two doors down this way," he pointed to his right, "is the stairwell. My room is just up the stairs to the left. So if you get scared or you want to see me, I will be right there. Alright?"

The two children nodded up at their father. He bent down and kissed both of them on the top of their heads.

"Pay attention and, more importantly, have fun." he said to them smiling proudly at his children.

With that, he turned and walked to the stairwell, disappearing into the doorway. Kane and Aerika looked at each other and walked into their room. When they entered their eyes shot open wide.

"How?! This … how is this possible?! We left all of this at home!" Kane exclaimed shocked.

The room had their beds with their blankets. Their pictures on the wall right where they would be in their home. The dressers and wardrobes were the same as the ones they had left behind. Everything looked in place. They locked eyes with each other and ran into the room further to check out what was going on.

Kane pulled open his dresser and laughed aloud at the sight of all his clothes already being in it. He looked across the room at Aerika who just found the same of her clothes in her wardrobe. This might not be as difficult as they had thought. If the Academy could do this, maybe it would be an easy year.

2

"Take your seats children!" The kids all rushed to their seats. Kane and Aerika were sitting in the front center of the room. These had been assigned to them do to their special eye colors.

A gaunt man stood before them. He was a very unassuming man with short cropped light brown hair. His skin was pale but not so much so that you thought he never got any sun. His light-green eyes stood out nicely against the light tone of his flesh. You could tell upon first glance at this man he was an intellectual.

"I am Instructor Koel. I will be your trainer for the next five years during primary school." he stated. "Today we will focus on teaching you what The Flow is. Once I feel that you all have a firm grasp on this, I will start teaching you how to see it in yourselves and then eventually to see it in others if you are able. Keep in mind that some of you will not be able to do some of the things I teach you how to do. Do not get discouraged by this! It just means that you are not tuned in that way. Very few can do everything that is taught here at the Academy."

He paused for a moment to let them take in what he had just told them. "Are there any questions about who I am or what I do here?" No one said anything or even moved for that matter. All of the children sat perfectly still and silent. He smiled just the slightest little bit. Nobody ever had anything to ask.

"The Flow is the energy that makes up all things. It controls everything from the wind that ruffles your hair to the birds that use the wind to hold them up when they glide. We use the Flow to do just about everything."

The students listened intently. They had all seen the effects of use of the Flow and some had even felt the Flow affect them when it was used on or around them. They were all very interested in learning how to use it themselves. Koel continued his explanation of the Flow.

"The Flow is used most often by those more powerful with it as they have more effect with it on the physical. This could mean it is used to maintain certain aspects of our world's infrastructure. Basically that means they ensure we have what is essential to our continued comfort and survival.

"Within the Flow are elements. These elements are Wind, Fire, Water and Earth. Each one of you is stronger with one particular element. Some of you are strong with two or three … maybe even all four." He looked to Kane and Aerika when he said this. Kane wondered to himself if he was implying that they were that strong or was it just that he was looking around at all of the students.

"Those strong with the element of fire are commonly used to control fire to protect people, to enrich soil for use in farming, or to fight. Few of you will be used for the last purpose as we have not had a reason to fight for many thousands of years.

"Those strong with the water element are commonly used as assets for controlling the flow of water for irrigation at the farms. Those that are stronger are used to control the weather so we do not have any naturally occurring destructive storms hitting a populated area.

"Those of the earth element are commonly used to control seismic activity to prevent the quakes from occurring or are used to keep volcanoes from erupting near populated areas.

"Those strong with the element of wind are perhaps the most versatile of all. They can use the power of wind to lift, push, pull and do just about any other physical activity you can think of. They can create and control wind storms to an effect of moving naturally occurring storms to bring rain to lands suffering from droughts."

His gaze became very serious suddenly.

"Those of you who prove to have a great propensity for the use of any or all of the elements will be taken for special training after your fifth year. Keep this in mind as you progress as I will be evaluating you constantly."

His mood became lighter just as suddenly. It was almost like he had just switched personalities.

"But, my how time has flown. It is time for lunch and then you shall all be tested to see what your element is. So if you would all follow me I will show you how to get to the dining hall and you can make your way back here when instructed that lunch time is over."

He made his way to the door and all of the students followed him. Kane had a bad feeling about how he had changed so suddenly to talk about this 'special training'. Aerika hung back behind everyone else with him. She put a hand on his shoulder as they followed Instructor Koel.

"What's the matter Kane? Something is bothering you." she inquired.

"Yes. I just feel like something is odd about how he changed all of the sudden. I don't know."

He just walked in somewhat of a daze trying to figure out why he had this bad feeling about it.

"Hey you two! What are you doing all the way back here?"

Kane shook his head to break his daze. Two boys had broken from the pack of children and stopped to wait for them. One boy had blonde hair cropped short and parted in the middle. His deep blue eyes seemed to have a current to them like they were filled with water. The other boy, his exact duplicate, save his hair being down past his ears rather than cropped short, had blood red eyes that seemed to beat as if with his heart.

"Just thinking about something Instructor Koel said. I am Kane Malacor and this is my twin sister Aerika. I didn't know there were any other twins in the class."

"Yes there are. I am Magus Deium." said the boy with red eyes. His tone was very harsh.

"And I am Tieg. Pardon my brother. He can be very competitive." the other explained. His tone was very soothing.

These twins were exact opposites which were usually how twins worked. But Kane and Aerika were exactly the same as one another. Their personalities did not differ at all. In fact, they seemed to think with one mind at times.

They made it to the dining hall and after getting their food the two sets of twins sat together. They talked the whole time they were there just getting to know one another. Tieg and Kane became fast friends but Magus seemed to be a little put off by this boy with platinum eyes. He put on a happy face though it didn't hide his already apparent desire to compete with this other boy.

Aerika quietly ate her food seeming content to just be near her brother and his new friends. Tieg explained that their mother was some special instructor at the Academy but he didn't know what she taught.

According to Tieg, he and Magus had been born in the town just like Aerika and Kane had and they were living somewhere near the center of town in a place called Molara's Crossing. They didn't know who Molara was or why he had an area of Mi'Tiya named for him.

"I've never heard of twins that were different gender before." Tieg stated quizzically.

"Our father says we are the first ever." Kane replied proudly.

"Wow! And you're eyes?"

"Well, father says I am to be in a special class. And Aerika is to be evaluated for the same because her white eyes are different from any they've ever seen before."

Tieg seemed very interested in this. They talked about what they liked and disliked. Things they enjoyed together and things they enjoyed separately. It seemed that Tieg and Magus did things separately a lot but Kane and Aerika never did anything apart. This seemed odd to Kane. He had always thought all twins were as close as he and Aerika.

"Students will now return to their classrooms!" A voice sounded throughout the room. Everyone rose from their seats and started making their ways back to class. Koel was sitting at his desk waiting for the children when they got there. He waited for all of the children to sit down before moving. He stood as soon as they had all taken their seats.

"As I said you will all be tested to see what your element is. We have a man outside that will be escorting you to the test area. Some of you will be separated for testing elsewhere." Koel explained.

He turned towards the door, "Come in the room please!"

A man stepped silently into the doorway, his face was shrouded by the dark brown hooded robe that he wore. His hands were interlocked in front of him within the sleeves of his robes.

"Magus Deium, Tieg Deium, Aerika Malacor, Kane Malacor, and Raven Mataius, remain seated. All others follow this man to the testing area."

The five named sat still while the hooded man led the others out and down the hallway. Kane looked over his shoulder and saw Magus and Tieg sitting near the center of the room. Behind them, on the very back row, sat a thin but muscular boy.

He seemed unnaturally muscular for the age they

knew he was. His black hair, for which he was obviously named, hung down to his shoulders. His solid gold eyes emitting an eerie shine from behind the hairs that hung before them.

"The rest of you will follow m ..."

"Not so fast!" he was cut off by a man wearing a shiny suit of armor.

The armor looked bulky and cumbersome while at the same time appearing flexible and light. The man's face was hidden behind a helm both frightening and beautiful. On his hands were thin black gloves that seemed to reflect light that wasn't even there. In the center of his breast plate, a circle of six different color pairs of eyes; one set, gold, one set, silver, one set, red, one set, blue, one green, and the last set, brown; surrounding one rich violet eye in the center, the symbol signifying the council. This man was a member of the Enforcers, the right hand of the Atrethian High Council.

"Raven Mataius! Come with me!" the voice came from beneath the helm but didn't sound muffled by it at all.

Raven stood up without showing the slightest ounce of fear at this strange armored man coming for him. He followed the armored man out of the room. Kane somehow knew he would see Raven again but wasn't sure how he knew that. That didn't matter though. He hadn't been taken by the Enforcer so it didn't matter to him.

"Fine. The rest of you follow me." Koel turned and started towards the door. Kane, Aerika, Magus and Tieg followed Instructor Koel into the hall and towards their testing area.

After twisting and turning down different hallways throughout the Academy, they finally came to the testing room they were going to. It awaited them at the end of a small corridor with two Enforcers standing guard outside.

"Greetings Instructor," came the voice of one of the Enforcers, "Four this year? Never seen so many from one class."

"Well," Koel replied, "We had five but your prestigious order took one."

Kane thought he saw the Enforcer nod but it was difficult to tell with all the armor they wore.

"Raven Mataius. Yes I'd heard we were taking him. He will be a great addition to our order."

"Anyway, I should get the testing underway. With four students, I can't be sure how long it will take."

"Of course, Instructor. We'll be right out here if you need us." he slapped a clenched fist to the violet eye in the center of his chest.

Instructor Koel nodded and pushed the door open for the kids to enter. It was a rather small room. Big enough for everyone to fit comfortably within its walls but it wasn't wasted space. Or at least that's how it seemed. Though when they walked through the door there seemed more space to move around then they had initially thought.

In the far corner of the room, there was a black chamber, if you could call it that. The stone appeared devoid of any light at all and so too did the air around it. It was only a half box though; two of the walls weren't complete. Against the wall to their left sat a row of 4 chairs. They were carved out of a beautiful, dark-shaded wood with runic symbols carved into them.

Koel motioned towards the chairs, "Take a seat."

Magus ran to get the first seat. Tieg followed him and sat in the second chair from the door. Kane sat down next to Tieg and Aerika sat down last.

"Alright children. This is the test chamber." He was motioning towards the structure in the corner, "This will test your power and tell us where your affinity with The Flow lies and any other information that it finds important for us to know. It will talk to you when you enter but it is merely to help keep you calm. Tieg, we will test you first."

Tieg stood up and walked slowly towards the black chamber. He was obviously nervous. He jumped when a hand landed on his shoulder. He looked up at the Instructor. "Go on. Everything will be alright. You have nothing to worry about."

Tieg nodded and walked a little faster towards the chamber. When he entered it, the walls suddenly closed around him completing the chamber and isolating Tieg from the rest of the room. The walls seemed to grow from the rest of the chamber rather than just extending out from it.

His heart felt as if it had jumped up into his throat. He started to push frantically at the walls trying to get out. A soft voice called into his mind. He heard it but not with his ears. "Calm yourself Tieg. There is no need to be afraid. I will not hurt you." Tieg thought the voice belonged to his mother but it was different somehow. Tieg calmed down none-the-less. He let his arms fall to his side and took in a few deep breaths to calm his nerves.

"Close your eyes. Let your body relax completely. The test will begin shortly and will be over before you know it." the voice whispered.

Tieg did as he was told. He closed his eyes and took in a deep breath to relax. As he let out the breath, he was overcome with a weightless sensation. Like he was floating only he knew he wasn't. He could still feel the pressure of the floor against the bottom of his feet.

Outside the chamber the light began to retreat from the room away from the chamber. Once all light was gone, a soft white glow seemed to grow from within the chamber walls. The light focused to two small points and shot out into the room. The beams flew about the room for a while. It seemed like they were relishing their new-found freedom and dancing happily.

The lights turned suddenly and caught the eyes of Instructor Koel. The instructor was lifted from his feet though he appeared relaxed. His arms and legs hung loosely towards the ground and the expression on his face gave the impression of peace.

He was returned to ground after a moment of suspension and the light retracted into the chamber once again. As soon as the beams returned to the chamber walls, the room filled with light once again. The walls of the chamber opened and Tieg was standing within. He stepped off a bit uneasily but seemed renewed when he found his legs had the strength to hold him up.

"Tieg, you are of the water element. You will receive special training." Koel said to him as he walked back to his seat. "Magus you are next"

Magus stood and hurried into the chamber. He seemed almost excited. The chamber closed as it had before. Magus felt panic rise within him but he stifled it quickly. "Close your eyes. Let your body relax completely. The test will begin shortly and will be over before you know it." the voice whispered.

The light retreated from the room again. The beams danced like they had before and Koel was once again lifted from his feet. Once complete the chamber doors opened and Magus walked out confidently towards his seat.

"Magus," Instructor Koel seemed almost angry with him. The boom of his voice made Magus jump. "You are of the fire element. You will not be in the special classes." This struck Magus' ego harshly. He almost fell flat on his face it stunned him so much. "Heed the lessons of morality with regards to use of the flow or you will cause harm to those you care about."

Magus walked back to his chair. He was completely taken aback by this. He couldn't imagine what it could mean. He sat down and just stared at nothing.

"Kane. You are next." Koel said. He didn't sound angry anymore. Aerika grabbed Kane's shoulder when he went to stand up. She was very obviously frightened for him. He placed a hand reassuring on hers. "Don't worry. I'll be back out before you know it. Everything will be fine." Kane smiled at her and she nodded and pulled her hand back.

Kane walked into the chamber. The doors closed around him like they had around Tieg and Magus. He took in a deep breath and let it out slowly. When the chamber closed, Aerika stopped feeling Kane. Their connection had been halted for some reason. She grew even more worried than she was before.

The voice came again. "Close your eyes. Let your body relax completely. The test will begin shortly and will be over before you know it." He did as he was instructed. He drew in a deep breath and was about to exhale when he was struck with a sudden and excruciating pain. It hurt so bad a loud ring screamed in his ears. His muscles tightened and he opened his eyes wide. He tried to scream but he couldn't draw a breath enough to make a sound. The voice came back, this time sounding very sinister.

"DESTROYER! YOU SHOULD NOT LIVE! YOUR EXISTENCE THREATENS ALL THAT IS!"

Outside the chamber, all of the rooms light disappeared almost instantly. This time, two pure black beams shot out from the chamber. They're lack of light seemed to rip the very life from the surrounding air. The beams did not dance around the room. They went straight for Koel's eyes.

When they caught his eyes, his arms and legs shot out rigid and his face contorted in pain. His mouth dropped open in what appeared to the children as pure terror. He floated up from the ground slowly. The flesh on his face began to pull tight against his skull. The color drained from his skin. And just when the sight became more than the children could handle, Koel let out a wracked scream. The unnatural sound that escaped his open mouth kept Magus, Tieg and Aerika frozen in horror.

Just as suddenly as all of this had started, it ended. The beams retreated into the chamber. Koel fell to the ground and collapsed to his hands and knees and then fell flat. When the beams had fully retreated into the chamber, it opened and Kane was thrown screaming out into the room. He flew clear across the room and crashed against the wall. When he hit the wall, he fell silent.

Aerika was terrified. She looked from Kane to the Instructor. The silence within the room was almost deafening. Aerika's eyes became clouded with tears but the silence was broken before she broke into sobs. "None of you move!" One of the Enforcers said as he ran into the room. He moved to Instructor Koel to check him. "Go get the boy!" he barked at the other. The second enforcer nearly made the distance to Kane in one step. He knelt down by Kane and started examining him.

Kane moved a bit; not much but enough that everyone noticed. "The boy is alive. We need to get him to the doctors." the Enforcer said. "Alright bring him! I'll get the Instructor! You children stay here. Someone will be along for you shortly." The two Enforcers ran from the room with Instructor Koel and Kane.

Aerika watched in silent horror. Once Kane was out of the room she burst into tears and fits of sobbing. The terror of what just happened threatened to steal away her sanity. Tieg got up from his seat and pulled her up against him out of hers. He hugged her tight trying to comfort her as much as he could, but he was just too frightened for his new friend and their instructor. Koel hadn't moved or made a sound since that scream. It all just seemed so unreal to him.

Magus just remained where he was. Between what was said to him and what had just happened, he wanted it all to be a dream.

Word traveled quickly to Sinal that there had been an incident. His friends within the Enforcer ranks had at least gotten him that much. He pushed his legs as hard as he could to get to the test chamber. Sinal rushed into the room now guarded by two new Enforcers. The two Enforcers clapped clenched fists to the violet eyes on their breastplate as he passed. They had been expecting him, but he barely even noticed them standing there.

"Aerika?!" he looked over where the children were sitting. She was sitting now, crying silently to herself. She didn't even move when she heard her father's voice. He visibly calmed when he saw she was unharmed. He had already seen the state Kane was in but his daughter needed him now. Sinal stepped in front of her and knelt down. He placed a hand on hers which were resting on her legs.

"Aerika." He spoke softly as if he didn't really want to disturb her, "Aerika, it's me, your father. Everything's going to be fine. Kane is alright. He's resting now."

Aerika finally looked at him. She watched him for a moment through her tears and then whispered softly to him. Her voice seemed wracked with pain. "I can feel him. He's in pain daddy." She broke into fitted sobs once again.

He was rather confused now. He didn't know how she could possibly feel her brother. And he had just seen him and he didn't appear to be in any pain. The doctors had said that aside from hitting the wall there seemed no other trauma. The only thing they could say for certain was that his energy was odd. But her statement made his need to know what had happened even greater.

Shadows swirled around him. The pure unadulterated hatred that he could feel emanating from this energy that swirled around him kept him frozen in terror. Kane stood as still as he could, trying to keep from touching this blackness. But every so often it would touch him. When it did it scorched his flesh.

He couldn't remember what happened. He couldn't even think of how he had gotten here; Where-ever here was. Nothing was familiar. And it didn't even feel like he was actually there. The shadows pulled away from him as if clearing the way for something new. An image appeared around him.

He was in a completely new environment. It didn't feel any different to him but there were people there. At least, he thought they were people. He was standing in a cave of some kind. But the stone was strange. The color was all wrong. Each one seemed to contain an ever changing rainbow. It was beautiful, but it couldn't make his fear dissipate.

Standing in the cave were two members of the Atrethian High Council, a group of very mean-looking men standing around a creature that appeared to be female and another creature that he thought he recognized but he couldn't place it. Kane couldn't see the "female" if you could call it that but he got a good look at the other creature.

The creature stood almost two men high. His jaw not wide but also not narrow. His nostrils like that of a skull with no cartilaginous extension. He had no lips. Instead fangs continued from what Kane first thought flesh. The jagged protrusions looked sharper than any blade a man could create. He had no eye brows but boney protrusions that took their place. Just below them his deep blue eyes pulsed with the power within him and actually gave off smoke of an almost platinum shade.

He carried a head of black hair down to the middle of his back. His hair came to a point just above his pronounced brow and curved down to near his ears. His ears came to two points, the top one just a few centimeters longer than the bottom with no lobe dangling at the bottom. They seemed an extension of his jaw.

His wide shoulders and strong arms sporting muscles that were much larger than seemed possible for his frame. At the end of his arms, his hands appeared almost normal save for the elongated razor-like talons that took the place of his fingernails. This powerful and frightening abdomen sat atop equally powerful and frightening legs. His feet resembled talons with a claw like stem to replace his heel and three sharp claws on the front.

One of the members of the High Council was the Grand Magistrate, but was a female. That didn't seem right to Kane. As far as he knew, there was a man in that position at the moment and had always been a male in the position. Nothing of what he saw made sense to him.

The men flanking the female creature dragged a very sinister looking knife across her throat without provocation. Kane wanted to look away but something would not let him. The male creature stood helpless obviously very upset by what was just done. Kane couldn't blame him. He wanted to shout out at the outrage of killing the helpless creature, no matter how imposing she was.

"Why have you done all of this?! We just wanted peace!" the familiar-looking creature screamed! He still couldn't place how he could know something that looked like that. The councilman laughed and replied, "You abominations could never be at peace with us! You must be eradicated! It is the only way!"

The Grand Magistrate took a firm step forward dropping her hood from atop her head. "That's enough! You cannot do this! He is helpless! It is a clear violation of our laws!"

Kane's mouth dropped open in mute shock. He couldn't believe who it was that was standing there as the Grand Magistrate, the leader of the Atrethian High Council. Aerika, his sister, even at the age she was, was completely unmistakable to him. He would know her anywhere. The councilman pushed her to the side and, with a knife he pulled seemingly out of nowhere, stabbed the creature Aerika was defending.

Aerika screamed and dropped down to her knees beside the creature crying. Her cry sounded pained to him but she brushed that aside. She pulled the creature's head into her lap and brushed her hand over his hair. "I'm sorry," she said, "I'm so sorry I couldn't protect you."

It opened his toothy maw and whispered in a peaceful voice despite what had just occurred. "It's alright … it's not your fault. No one could have prevented this from happening. Aerika, please … please don't bl- … blame yourself."

Kane watched as life left the creature. Even though he had never seen that happen before it was very obvious to him that he had just died. He fell limp in her arms. Aerika just sat there for a moment crying to herself. Then the energy he knew lie within her began to rise from her eyes as though she weren't controlling it any longer. Just as this happened, his vision went black again and he could feel the shadows closing in around him once more.

Kane seemed almost peaceful lying on the bed in the infirmary. Sinal couldn't see how he could possibly be in pain. He seemed so at peace despite what had happened. But then, Sinal didn't know what actually had happened. All they had really said was his children were involved in an incident. None of the children could seem to recall it when they were asked. It was as if what had occurred was too horrifying for their minds to recall. He could only hope that Instructor Koel woke up.

"You should go get your wife, Sinal. She would want to be here when Kane wakes." Sinal turned to see a man walking into the room wearing a deep blue robe. "Councilman Doe'n! I … I only just arrived to see my son. Do … do you know what happened sir?"

"No, Sinal. I wish I did. But be at ease old friend. I have been sent to investigate this incident. I promise I will find out what happened and I will do it as delicately as I can so as to not harm your children."

"Thank you, Councilman."

"Sinal … Call me Doe'n. We've known each other since we were children."

Sinal turned to look back at Kane. He hadn't moved. "Of course, you are right, Doe'n. I'm going to go get my wife. She needs to be here." Sinal started walking towards the door, but stopped just short of the threshold.

"And Doe'n …" he said, "Thanks…for everything."

Councilman Doe'n just nodded and turned to look at Kane as Sinal walked out.

"Come on, Kane," Doe'n said. "What happened in that chamber?"

Intense pain stabbed into Kane's mind. His senses weren't dulled … they were completely paralyzed. A sharp whistle blew continuously in his ears keeping him from recovering his hearing. His eyes felt glued shut and he didn't mind that so much. Even the darkness beneath his eyelids felt like needles were pierced straight into his eyeball.

His muscles ached and burned as if strained beyond

the point of any normal exhaustion. It felt as though acid were pumping through his veins burning everything throughout his body as it went. He hurt from the tips of his toes to his fingertips to the top of his head. He imagined that if he could feel his hair that might hurt right now too.

Suddenly, relief began to wash over him starting at his chest and crawling its way down to his toes and up to his head. The pain was being washed away, though it didn't stay away long. Kane achingly pulled his eyelids apart. He quickly shut them again when the light hit his eyes causing a shock and pain to shoot through him again.

He groaned softly and turned his head trying to get away from the light that had caused floating circles to appear under his eyelids after he shut them again.

"... Brother ..."

It was Aerika but something sounded different. The word sounded forced as if it were pushed through unwillingly. Despite this, her voice seemed to push more of the pain away. He groaned again trying to open his eyes once more. This time he opened them much more slowly letting the light in in waves to get used to it. It still hurt but he wanted so much to see his sister. He had to make sure that she wasn't like she was in his dream ... or was it a vision. He didn't know, but he had to be sure that she was still her.

" ... ..."

He couldn't manage to muster his voice. Nothing seemed to come forth. He could feel his lips move. At least he thought he felt his lips move. But the pain was still excruciating.

" ... Brother ... I ..." she hesitated for a moment as if something was giving her pause, "I feel it too. You have to fight it."

Now he knew why her voice sounded different. For the same reason he couldn't bring his own to bear. She was feeling the pain he was feeling. He had to push it back. He had to swallow it and protect his sister from it. He had to get the pain away from her … get it away from him.

He gritted his teeth and balled his fists trying to push back the pain. He tried to swallow it down and ease Aerika's suffering. He felt the pain falter. It was waning. He opened his eyes just enough to confirm what he somehow already knew … Aerika was indeed her normal self. She smiled through the pain she was obviously feeling when she saw Kane's eyes open.

"Hello brother." Her voice seemed less strained than it had before. He could see a shadow standing over her but he couldn't make out more than a silhouette.

"Very good, Kane. Now, let the Flow wash over you. Open your mind to the energies around you so the healing can take its full effect." The voice was familiar but he couldn't place it. He felt put at ease at least that someone was taking care of Aerika while he was in this state. He managed a pained nod and closed his eyes trying to envision what he had just been told.

"Think of a place where you are most comfortable. The place you feel the safest. Bring it up in as much detail as possible. Every piece of dust and dirt needs to be in its proper place."

He tried to bring it together. He built it up piece by piece. He imagined the walls to his and Aerika's room. He brought the pictures to the walls. The beds to the corners. He even managed to get the little wooden dolls that their father had carved for Aerika to keep her company at night. He brought together the room with every single detail intact. He didn't miss a beat. It felt so easy to him. Once he had envisioned this place, he sighed a breath of relief. He indeed felt better, but the pain was still there, that much he knew.

"Kane … I want you to open the door to your sanctuary. I want you to breach that safety that you feel.

Allow the world in."

But he didn't want to. He liked being in here. All alone. But he knew something was missing. Seeming to read his thoughts, the voice came again. "Kane … Aerika is outside … you must open to door to let her in."

Kane didn't hesitate a moment when he heard this. He grabbed hold of the door knob and pulled it open. He had to let her in. But once the door had breached … once he had broken the serenity of that place, it collapsed. And it did so violently.

The walls seemed to erupt outward carrying the pictures with them. The beds melted through the floor in a flash and the ceiling blew away on a wind that was not really there. The floor beneath his feet heaved tossing him into the air and then shattering beneath him like glass when he slammed down upon it. He fell, it seemed, forever, but for some reason fear never bit at him.

He just wanted to find Aerika again. That's when he realized it. The pain … it was gone. He shot open his eyes and sat upright on the bed. He took in the room. He washed his eyes over Aerika and the Councilman standing behind her. It was Doe'n, his father's friend.

Doe'n smiled and nodded his approval. "Good job Kane. Well done. You have done in minutes what it takes second year students weeks to accomplish."

Kane just looked at him puzzled. He wasn't sure what had just happened. He couldn't seem to bring his thoughts together.

"You found your sanctuary … and broke free from its boundaries. You're a fast learner. However, we have much to discuss and I am afraid I must have Aerika escorted out of here. You will be able to join her soon in your chambers."

Kane nodded and Aerika locked her eyes on him. "But I don't want to leave him. I'm worried for him."

"Do not worry, young one. I will take good care of

your brother. This I promise you."

She blinked away some tears that tried to find freedom and she smiled at Kane. "I will see you soon, dear brother. Be well until then." After she said this she stood up and walked out of the door glancing over her shoulder just before exiting the door.

"Now, Kane … we must discuss what occurred inside that chamber. What did you hear? What were you told? What … what did you see?"

He gaped wide eyed at Doe'n. He knew … he didn't know how but somehow he knew. Kane thought that maybe Instructor Koel must have told him what had happened. He thought he'd ask anyway. "I … how did you ..." Doe'n cut him off.

"It's happened before, but not in many thousands of years. This is not something that occurs often and it is almost never a good thing. So you must tell me. What is it that you saw so that we may prevent it?"

"The chamber … it showed me something …" Kane thought it best to avoid telling him what it had called him. Maybe he could block the thought from his mind if he focused on the vision. "I saw a … a creature getting killed … by a councilman. I saw Aerika … she was … she was the Grand Magistrate. She tried to save the creature. But that's all I saw." Doe'n thought for a moment and then continued, "What did this creature look like?"

Kane described the creature in as best detail as he could but it all felt inadequate. As though no matter what he said, it wouldn't stop what he saw. That he couldn't relate it well enough to give any clues as to what was happening.

"I see … Well, we may never see this come to pass. I know Aerika will be powerful but there has never been a female Grand Magistrate and I don't foresee that changing anytime soon. Such are just the customs of our people." Doe'n seemed to relax a bit as if his own words pushed the fears from his mind. I shall report what I have discovered and see if further investigation is necessary. For the moment, you shall return to your training and we will see how this progresses from here."

Doe'n turned and started for the door stopping just short. He half-turned back and locked eyes with Kane, "Tell no one what you saw within the chamber. Not even Aerika."

With that Doe'n made his exit and passed out of sight and soon the sound of his footsteps disappeared as well. He had to talk to Aerika. He had to find out if she was alright. Kane slipped his feet down to the floor and started towards the door. Just as he was about to exit someone stepped into the doorway and Kane was knocked flat.

" ... Ow ..." Kane said rubbing his lower back.

"Kane?! You're awake!"

He looked up when he heard the voice though he didn't need to know who it was. His father was now kneeling before of him. He was smiling almost ear to ear with obvious relief.

"Hello father."

"My Son!" Sinal hugged him tight. "I'm so glad you're awake. We were worried sick. I brought someone to see you." Sinal pulled Kane up to his feet. He stepped off to the side.

"MOTHER!" Kane ran into his mother's arms. She had obviously been crying. "Kane! I'm so glad you're alright!" She held her son tight against her as though if she let go he would fly away.

"Mom ... Dad ... where ... where is Aerika?" He had to find her. Despite his parents being there now he wanted only to find her.

"She's fine son. She's asleep in your room. You're mother and I saw her before coming here." Did you finish with Councilman Doe'n?" Sinal was curious as to what had occurred inside the room but was ordered to silence as to what had happened. All that Liana knew was that Kane was involved in an incident and that he had been injured.

Kane looked up at his father. "Yes father. He asked me some questions and then left. He said I can't talk about it." "I know son. I was told the same thing." Liana glared at her husband. She didn't like that he couldn't tell her what had happened but she was sure that if he knew anything he would have told her anyway. It was her son after all.

"Come along Kane. We'll take you back to your room so you can get some rest. You must be exhausted." Liana grabbed onto her husband's arm. She obviously didn't want to leave the building but now that Kane was awake she would have to.

Kane nodded to his father. He didn't care about sleep yet. Not until he saw Aerika with his own two eyes. He knew she had felt his pain. And he wanted to know that she was not hurt badly. They stepped out of the infirmary and started down one of The Academy's many corridors.

"Son ... there is something I'm curious about. How is that you woke up so soon? The doctors said you wouldn't wake up for days, if not weeks." Sinal looked quizzically at his son. Liana followed suit. She was curious too, despite her worry.

Kane just kept focused on getting to Aerika while he answered, "Councilman Doe'n said that I did something. He said I found my sanctuary and broke free from it. Or something like that."

Sinal and Liana stopped dead in their tracks. Kane had done that already. He hadn't even gone past the first day. Sinal looked to his wife. They couldn't fathom the potential their son had if he could do that on his first day. Kane didn't stop. His focus was unrelenting. He would find Aerika and see she was alright with his own eyes. He barely noticed that his mother and father had stopped moving.

Aerika lay sleeping soundly in her bed. Her eyes moved frantically beneath her eyelids. Her mind seemed to be working overtime on the dream she was having. Her eyes shot open despite this and she sat up. As if on cue, Kane walked through the door. Before he even looked at her she was on her feet and running towards him.

She threw herself against him so hard she nearly tackled him to the ground. "It's alright Aerika. I'm fine now. But you know that now don't you?" He was right, of course. She just nodded against his shoulder. She couldn't help but cry. She was still frightened of what had happened in the test chamber.

Sinal and Liana just smiled at how close their children were. Liana brought her gaze upon Sinal. She wanted so badly to stay in the school; to make sure Kane was unharmed and to spend more time with her husband. Sinal pulled at her shoulder seemingly reading her mind.

"Don't worry my love. I will make sure Kane is safe. I promise he will be just fine."

Kane and Aerika turned and ran to their mother. They both knew that she had to go. They hugged her one last time before going to their beds to get some sleep. It had been a very trying day and they had another big day ahead of them. Their training, at least the bulk of their training, would actually begin the following day. They would finally learn how to access The Flow. They would finally start to learn their strength.

It was amazing that Kane had done what he had done

already. Sinal wondered what power lie within Aerika yet to be tapped. If Kane were powerful enough to find his sanctuary that quickly and break free from it, how much must be within his sister. Sinal pulled the door closed and walked with his wife towards the entrance to the school.

Just a few corridors down, Councilman Doe'n stood over Instructor Koel's body. He shook his head silently. Another man stepped into the room. His shining plate armor seemed to light up the room. "Councilman ... I have been instructed to take the Instructor's body to his family. Do you have any further need of it in your investigation?"

Doe'n shook his head before answering. "No. Do as you must." The Enforcer clapped a fist to the violet eye in the center of his chest and went to grab the body as the image of Councilman Doe'n shimmered and disappeared.

Doe'n stood and walked out of the door of the Council's meditation chamber. It was where they went to focus on difficult tasks individually, though, like in this case, was primarily used to project themselves to different locations. He walked without pause to the Mythril Hall, the place where the Atrethian High Council met. Doe'n approached the tall, black stone doors to the hall.

Each door was adorned with carvings depicting the most severe of Atrethia's laws. The worst of which at eye level so anyone who enters for this reason may know what they shall suffer.

The first image on the left door showed a man standing over another. The man on the ground was cowering; holding his arm up to block what he knew would come. The man above held a club raised above his head to strike down upon the other. It was the act of physical violence upon another without just cause.

The second depicted a despicable scene. A man holding a woman by the arm and ripping her clothing off with the other; the act of rape.

The last on the left had a man using the forces of nature to tear a home down at its foundation while another man begged him to stop; the use of The Flow to destroy another man's property.

The first on the right side had a man standing with his arms raised out to his sides. Lightning arched from his fingers to a creature crafted from the earth itself. The creature's eyes burned with the fire of life. This image depicted the use of The Flow to create unholy abominations.

The second on the right bore the image of a man standing before a vast army. The army, committing atrocious acts at the behest of their commander. The act of commanding others to commit heinous acts.

The third on the right and final image was a depiction of a man standing with his hand outstretched towards another, flames rolling from the man's hand and crawl over the other. This showed the use of The Flow against another.

All of these acts, if proven, were punishable by the image depicted at the top of the doors. A vast, barren landscape with strange, foreign creatures spanned the top of the door. A land unfriendly to the living. The punishment for these crimes was exile to the Terrei Desert.

Doe'n pushed the doors open to enter the hall that he found himself in more often than anywhere else on Atrethia. The rest of the Atrethian High Council, including the Grand Magistrate, stood in place with Doe'n's place amongst them open.

"Councilman Doe'n. What have you to report?" The Grand Magistrates voice echoed within the hall, amplified by The Flow to fill the chamber. It wasn't something he was doing intentionally. The Mythril Hall did this to all of the Council members voices when they spoke from their positions of authority.

"Yes, Grand Magistrate. It would appear we have another prophecy on our hands. The details are scant but this child, Kane, it seems he is destined for either a great good or a great evil."

An uneasy silence fell upon the hall. The Council members all seemed to ponder this for a moment. The Grand Magistrate was the first to break this silence.

"What do you propose we do about this prophecy, Doe'n?"

"Absolutely nothing, Grand Magistrate."

The High Council looked puzzled at the suggestion of the councilman. "Explain yourself Doe'n."

"Fellow Council members, this is a good child with good parents. It is my distinct impression that Kane will be the catalyst for a great good in the world or a great many good's in this world. I doubt highly that he will be the cause of any harm."

The Grand Magistrate nodded. "I shall take your suggestion under advisement. Council members we shall recess while I deliberate on this matter. Return to the Buorthian Chamber until I summon you."

The Buorthian Chamber was home to the Atrethian High Council. When each member entered the door to the chamber, he would be transported to his residence which, if they chose, existed in a realm of greater existence far removed from the physical world. If someone were trying to visit a council member, they need only think of who they desired to visit and enter the door to be brought to them, though you must be welcome and expected for the door to even open for you.

The council members bowed to the Grand Magistrate and exited the main doors to the Mythril Hall. Councilman Doe'n remained for a moment longer then made for the door.

"Doe'n." The Grand Magistrates voice halted him at the door. "The boy shall be placed in the normal classes. If he has even the potential to cause as much harm as you think, he must not be allowed to progress as he would in the gifted class."

Doe'n turned back. "But Grand Magistrate! He is a good boy! He wi..."

"ENOUGH! I have made my decision and you shall carry this task out without a word more! Do you understand?!"

Doe'n paused a moment and prostrated himself to the Grand Magistrate. "Yes Grand Magistrate. I shall do as you command."

"Very good, Doe'n. Very good. You are dismissed."

Doe'n turned and pushed open the heavy doors. His deep blue robes fluttered around his feet as he walked making his way back to the meditation chamber. He would carry out his orders as he had sworn to do. All Council members swore an oath to do as the Grand Magistrate commanded in an instance like this, though none of them ever thought it would actually happen. He was not pleased with the decision but such was his duty.

Doe'n sighed heavily. Burdened by the task at hand he sat, crossing his legs as he did. He placed his hands upon his knees, took in a deep breath and closed his eyes. A moment later, an image of Doe'n appeared in the office of the headmaster of The Academy.

Sinal shook his head ... more in disbelief than disappointment. "I just don't understand how they could think my son would be the cause of some great evil. He's a good boy."

"I know how disappointing this is Sinal. I know how you must feel. But you have to understand that my hands are tied here. This order came from the Grand Magistrate himself."

"I ..." Sinal conceded. "I know. You are one of my oldest friends. You would fight this to the bitter end if you thought there was even a chance of winning. I just hope Aerika will be alright through all of this."

"She's a strong girl Sinal. I'm sure everything will work out in the end. I must return to my duties however. I just thought you should be made aware of this development. And Sinal. If you need anything, absolutely anything at all, don't hesitate to ask me."

"Thank you Headmaster. I appreciate it."

Sinal stared blankly at the wall still hardly believing what had occurred. The Headmaster turned and walked out and down the hall before disappearing into a stairwell.

Sinal had to figure out a way to break this news to his children. They would be crushed he knew but he had to help them prepare for it. That Kane and Aerika would not be in class together, it had never occurred to him that anything like this would happen or even could happen. Although, a lot had changed in the week since the incident. It seemed all the children that had seen it happen were more mature at least then they had been. He would have to tell the children, but 'how' was now the question on his mind.

Kane and Aerika sat silently on their beds. They had been back together a week already and had not spoken a word about the incident or what had happened. Kane didn't know how to address it. He was terrified of what she might already know. Aerika never once took her eyes off of Kane though. It was as if she somehow knew he wanted to tell her something. She just seemed to be waiting for him to find the words.

Kane finally lifted his eyes from the ground to meet hers. "Aerika, I … The chamber it …"

"I know." Her words cut him off.

"You do?" Kane blinked and shifted uneasily. Somehow he had already known that she knew but to have it confirmed like this. He felt their connection to but he didn't think it went that far. But no one knew everything that occurred. He hadn't shared everything.

"I heard it too. After you came back out. I think … I

think the chamber told me."

He fidgeted nervously before asking his next question. "Did you see the vision too?" She looked away for the first time since it had happened. She just nodded her head the slightest bit in affirmation. She obviously knew it was her in the vision.

"I wonder what's going to happen … Because of all of this, I mean."

"You are going to be trained in the normal classes, Kane." Sinal walked in but he didn't appear to have heard the exchange.

"Father?"

"Aerika will be undergoing the special instruction and you will be in the normal classes."

"But … why?"

"I don't know son. It's just what they decided upon."

Kane just stared at his father. He couldn't believe that he and Aerika would be split up. Aerika buried her face in her pillow. Kane knew she was in pain because of this. He could feel it. He couldn't stand to be apart from her either. He wasn't sure how they would survive being apart for so long. At least they had time to prepare for it. They still had four and half more years before that happened.

"You know where I am if you need me." Sinal continued. "Try to get some sleep. You have a lot of training left before the year is done."

Kane lay down on his bed but he couldn't sleep. He knew Aerika couldn't either. His own thoughts were racing so much he imagined she could hear his brain at work. It would be a tough day the next day for them without any rest. But they would get through it together; like they always did.

Kane, Aerika, Tieg and Magus all took to their training rather well. They progressed much faster than the other children. Some of them were angry about it, while others just accepted the differences of these four other students.

They had surpassed all expectations and were well beyond the normal pace of the class. They were all already sensing even the smallest changes in the flow of energy around them. Though they had not progressed beyond the room they were in, their instructor knew they would continue to grow.

They would have to practice more and more until they could sense changes around the entire planet. The instructor pushed the other students to take note and follow in their example as they meditated and practiced daily to improve their skills. The other students just worked and worked and never seemed able to even gain any ground on the four.

The training went on for months and months. Finally as the year drew to a close, Kane, Aerika, Magus and Tieg were able to detect any and all uses of The Flow around all of Atrethia, even without meditating. These four would be powerful indeed, even before their specialized training, of that much the instructor was sure.

Kane clapped his hand into Tieg's as they prepared to bid each other farewell for the short break. "See you next in the harvest, Tieg."

"We'll be back here before long Kane. And then we can learn even more of what we are capable of." Magus just glared at Kane from behind Tieg. "Until then Kane."

Aerika just stood silently as she usually did. Content merely to be near Kane, at least for now. Her quiet demeanor was disconcerting to many, but those that knew her and her brother were used to it, at least somewhat.

Sinal approached the group and placed a hand on Kane's shoulder. "Are we ready to go? Your mother is waiting."

Kane nodded up at him. "Yes father. We are."

Kane and Aerika fell in step with Sinal. They made their way down the winding corridors of The Academy until they finally made it to the large doorway that made up the entrance to the place. Liana rushed forward as they came out and took her children into her arms. She hadn't seen either of them since the day she was allowed in after the incident. Her children looked well enough considering how the year had started. Maybe, she thought, they had gotten past it.

She kissed both of them several times on the head. They squirmed when she did this. "EW … mom! Let us go!" Sinal laughed. The happy scene was a nice reminder of how things could be. The children hadn't let that year away get to them. Liana let the kids go and practically fell up into Sinal's arms. He just held her tightly relishing in the feeling of being near her again.

"Let's go home my dear. I am wary of this scenery. I could do with a change at least for a little while." They would be back soon enough and the training would progress even further. Things would be very interesting during the years to come. Sinal feared what would happen when the children were split up, but they had time to deal with that issue. For now, it was time for them to be a happy family again.

5

The break from training seemed shorter than it should have. Kane thought maybe the anticipation of the coming year and the coming lessons had made the time at home seem to pass more quickly. But the day had come when they were to return to The Academy. He only hoped that this year would be less intense than the last.

They approached the entrance to The Academy and were still awe struck. Sinal gripped the shoulders of his children. "It never ceases to amaze." Kane and Aerika nodded their heads in agreement. The building still seemed to climb endlessly above them and the halls went on forever when they entered. They still shared the same room as they had the last year. Sinal parted from his kids to attend to his duties prior to the beginning of class. Kane and Aerika settled in and prepared themselves mentally for the next day. They would need to be at their best if they wanted to continue with the same momentum they had the previous year.

Kane and Aerika settled in nicely and prepared for their training the following day. They even found Tieg and Magus when they went for dinner that evening. They picked up as if no time had passed at all. Tieg was still his normal friendly self and Magus was still cold and quiet. Everything seemed as it should. In the following days they had met with their new instructor and begun learning to focus their energies to try to manipulate their surroundings.

Kane sat on his heels next to Aerika. She was cross legged. They were told to sit in whatever way would bring them the most comfort for concentration. Instructor Naarell had replaced Koel as their Instructor. At first, he was supposed to be a temporary replacement, but the kids took to his methods well so they kept him on.

Kane took in a deep breath and held it for just a moment before letting it out. He found himself in his bedroom as he had many times before. And as he had before he opened the door and the room exploded around him.

His eyelids slide up slowly releasing a heavy platinum mist from beneath them as though they were being forced open. His power had found its release. The other children did the same though not all did as quickly. As they had learned in the few weeks since their arrival this was how you found your peak of energy.

Though not all of the students had achieved this level of concentration yet. Aerika was following right along with Kane; as were Magus and Tieg. It seemed these four would stay together through it all. They never seemed to part from one another for very long if they did at all. Instructor Naarell always found himself in awe of the speed with which they took to the training.

"Alright children. I want you to focus on the block in front of you. You have felt for yourselves that it is far too heavy to lift with physical strength. I want you to try to lift it … without touching it."

Naarell smiled as some of the kids locked their eyes on the object and some even began sweating they were concentrating so hard. He knew none of them would be able to do it but he had hoped maybe one of the four would at least move it a little. He watched them very closely.

Magus was the first of the four to try. He closed his eyes for a moment and drew air deep into his lungs. He held in the breath until it began to burn at his lungs and he pushed it out slowly between his lips. He opened his blood red eyes and drew them down to the heavy metal block before him.

He concentrated for what seemed to him like hours but it did nothing.

His twin brother, Tieg, was the next to act. He drew in a deep breath and as he exhaled the dust around the block began to stir. Naarell perked up when he saw that hoping maybe this was it. But it didn't move. He wasn't disappointed. He had already resolved that it wouldn't happen, but he still had some hope left with Kane and Aerika.

He could feel the power growing within Aerika and Kane as they concentrated pulling in the energy from around them. It was what he had taught them to do. Aerika locked her pure white eyes on the block. Her slow even breaths continued unabated by the obvious effort she put forth.

The edges of the carpet she sat on curled up. The dust around the object pushed out and away from it. The block stirred. It shifted right a little and then back left. She eased up and took in a deep, frustrated breath. Naarell had seen student do that before but it was few and far between that they did. He looked to Kane, the last of the four, preparing himself once again for disappointment.

Kane closed his eye for a moment. He listened to the frustrated exhales of the students around him. The sound of his own heartbeat echoed throughout his body. Suddenly, he could see again. He could see himself sitting on the carpet. The rest of the world stood perfectly still. Aerika sat next to him, her eyes fixed on the object before her. Magus was glaring at the back of his head. Tieg was watching Kane in awe and wonder. He seemed to idolize him for some reason.

The softest sound begged for his attention. It came as a whisper so soft he couldn't make sense of it. He looked around the room trying to find the source of the hushed noise. Naarell was watching him as he sat on the carpet. Kane could move freely around the room without anyone so much as moving an inch. Some of the other kids were still straining with droplets of perspiration frozen on their cheeks and foreheads. The sound had come from seemingly nowhere.

Then, it came again. The disembodied voice was louder this time, but he still could not make out the words. He thought he heard his name. All he did know for sure was that he had heard something. He could feel the power coming to his aid from everything around him. The stones that made up the floor, walls and ceiling all giving to him. Even the metal block before him was giving energy for his purposes.

And the voice returned, this time with enough strength to be heard; and heard loudly. So loud in fact that Kane jumped and turned to the source standing in the doorway. It was just a silhouette but obviously a man. The person's eyes seemed to be orbs of solid gold. He had seen eyes that shade before but he couldn't quite place where. Something about the man seemed wrong to him.

"Kane … you must grow stronger! Call on the wind! It is your ally!" The words made sense to him but he couldn't figure out why. He thought for a moment staring at the man. He was trying to make eye contact but he could scarcely tell if the man was even looking at him. He focused for a moment reaching out with his energy, as if by instinct. He beckoned for the wind to help him in his task.

Kane's eyes shot open. The world had gained motion again. He was back within his body. Suddenly, the room filled with a powerful gust of wind. The loose papers on the Instructors desk flew around the room in the torrent. The edges of each carpet and the loose robes the children wore whipped around as the wind blew about the room.

Naarell jumped in the shock of this occurrence. His eyes locked open wide at Kane. This torrent was incredible for someone Kane's age. Naarell couldn't imagine how he had learned to call on the elements. He hadn't taught them that just yet.

Kane's focus fell on the object before him. Everyone attention had locked on him as he was the only one still concentrating on the task at hand. The shiny silver block before him didn't shift left or right. It didn't wobble or tilt or even levitate slowly. The block leapt from the ground where it once lay to the ceiling. It moved with such force that embedded itself in the stone blocks built above them as if its only desire were to become one with the building itself.

"Oh my! Kane!" Naarell was struck dumb by this. He couldn't figure out how Kane had done that. Not only did he lift the object but he catapulted it into the stones above. Aerika only smiled. She admired her brother's strength. She looked down at her own object and mimicked exactly what he had done. Though there was not a torrential wind storm in the room this time. A metal block just seemed to desire being in the ceiling with Kane's block.

Magus was visibly angered by this. He scowled at Kane and Aerika both. If looks could kill, the twins would be stone dead at that moment. Tieg, like all the other students and the instructor, sat with his mouth agape. None of them could believe what they had just seen. "Kane … Aerika … That was incredible. Bravo. Well done."

The next four years continued much like that one moment. They continued to grow with similar intensity. The instructor grew more and more elated with every feat they achieved.

From moving objects to commanding anything with energy of its own to do something. From sensing changes in the energy around them to finding something and even someone as far as the other side of the world. The four prodigies had even begun to gain access to their elements as Kane had that first day. He, it seemed, had paved the way in their learning. In fact, all of the students that had witnessed Kane launch the block had progressed much faster than others with their level of power.

Aerika, Tieg and Magus all followed suit with him. Only Magus seemed more determined to surpass him, though he could never gain the upper hand. Kane was always able to take the necessary steps to stay ahead and he seemed to do it without effort. Tieg and Aerika were content to follow Kane's lead.

Kane and Aerika showed proficiency with all of the elements. Both seemed exceedingly powerful in all fathoms of the use of The Flow, while Magus and Tieg could only access their own elements with great skill and general uses of the others.

They would soon move into their advanced course where they would learn further specialization. Naarell could only begin to wonder if they would continue to grow with such speed as they had over the past four years. He hoped they would. Maybe he would try to find the time to check on them in a year or two to see if they had.

Perhaps he could make time to watch their progress in the coming years. He could even use their story as inspiration in his teachings for years to come. He would have to wait and see how it all turned out for the pair of twins.

The student all sat in their desks. Instructor Naarell walked into the room with a list in his hands. He smiled at the trainees before him. He had watched them grow over the past five years. Each one learning and evolving and finding themselves as they progressed.

"Hello children. It is finally time to place you in your advanced classes. As you know, some of you will be placed in special classes as you are a bit more skilled than the others, but do not think that just because you are not in this special class that you are any less special. Each one of you will have an important place in society once you complete your training."

"Now … if I call your name you will be going to the special training course." He looked down into the list of names and his expression changed. He now looked puzzled. "This must be some sort of mistake."

"It's no mistake, Naarell. Kane will not be entering the special training course. He will be trained alongside everyone else." Councilman Doe'n had entered the room to ensure the Grand Magistrates wishes were carried out.

"But Councilman this can't be right. He has shown himself to be of higher skill and speed of learning than even his sister."

"This is the wish of the Grand Magistrate. If you think you know better than he, than feel free to try to convince him to change his mind. I too would like nothing more than to have Kane stay with his sister."

"Of course, Councilman. But if I may make a suggestion, I would like him to go under Malious' instruction. He is the best instructor I know that isn't teaching the special courses."

"Yes, Naarell. I think we can arrange that. Now given the events of four years ago which many of you are already aware. Some things have changed. Magus and Tieg will attend training with Kane under Instructor Malious. Aerika shall attend specialized training."

Kane had known this was coming, but he really hadn't been prepared for it. He had been all too absorbed in his training. His heart sank. He knew that Aerika was sad as well. She hadn't been able to prepare either. Magus and Tieg both seemed shocked by this turn, as did the other students within the class.

He remained strong though and nodded, graciously accepting his situation. "You will all wait here until your instructors come to get you." Naarell said this watching as Councilman Doe'n made his way out of the room. "I would like to say that it has been a pleasure to instruct all of you.

You all have great potential and I'm sure will go on to serve Atrethia very well in the future."

With that, Instructor Naarell made his way out of the room. The children obediently remained in there seat. Hushed whispers crawled across the room as they debated the reason for Kane's predicament. Kane just sat silently waiting for this Instructor Malious to come to retrieve him, Tieg and Magus. They didn't have to wait long before they were led to their new classroom. Once all of their fellow students were situated, their instructor spoke.

"Children! I am Instructor Malious and you are in my class because you either need discipline or you have shown great promise and need someone very structured to help your learn more quickly." Malious was a small man. His arms seemed feeble beneath his robes and he was barely taller than the children he taught. By the sound of his voice though, Kane could tell he would not be very nice. "As you can see, this is a small class."

The students all looked around the room. He was right. There were only eight students in the class. "This happens so that I will have ample time to work with each of you individually to help you progress with your use of The Flow. Today, you will meditate and focus on feeling everyone around you for most of the day. If you work at sensing the world around you, it will eventually become second nature to you and will just be an additional sense, like sight and smell and taste."

Kane, Magus and Tieg did as they were told. They took their positions for meditation and began to feel the world around them. This was something they knew well. They had become very adept at do that through the past few years of training under Naarell. Instructor Malious walked out of the room as they began their meditations.

Three of the other students walked up behind Kane. The leader of the group standing close to him. "Hey kid!"

Kane was finding his way into his sanctuary and hardly heard the other boy's words. The child became visibly angry at the fact that Kane was ignoring him. He raised his hand up and slapped him hard across the back of his head. Kane fell forward, smacking his head against the floor. His head throbbed and the room began spinning wildly. The sound of Kane's skull cracking against the floor brought Tieg and Magus out of their mediation.

Magus was shocked by the already apparent violence of the situation. Tieg shot up to his feet as soon as he saw what had happened. One of the two boys flanking the leader held Tieg at bay. The leader leaned down towards Kane. "Aw … did that hurt? Well too bad. I noticed you have those special eyes. So, what are you doing in my class?"

Kane pushed up from the floor with one hand and cradling his forehead where his head had hit the floor. His head was still spinning and he hadn't even regained his bearing enough to stand let alone come up with an answer.

"ANSWER ME!" he screamed as he slammed his foot into the Kane's abdomen. Kane was lifted off of the floor by the force of the kick. He gasped hard with the power of it. The kick had knocked the wind from his lungs. He lay hunched over with his arms wrapped around his chest trying to regain his breath.

The kid got a smug look on his face. He was pleased with what he had just done to him. "You remember who's in charge here. The names Janus and don't you forget it. Come on guys before the Instructor gets back." He and his friends returned to their places in the room. Tieg went to Kane's side and helped him up to his feet. Kane was finally able to catch his breath just as the Instructor came back in the room.

"What are you two doing?! Didn't I tell you to meditate?!"

"But sir! That boy Janus just assaulted Kane."

Janus looked at Tieg from his spot in the back of the

room. "No I didn't! Liar!"

"I highly doubt that what you say actually happened! Return to your meditations now!"

"But ..." Tieg tried once again to plead Kane's case for him since he didn't seem to want or be able to himself.

"NOW!" Instructor Malious interrupted Tieg. Tieg jumped at the harsh sound of the command and hurried back to his spot. There was nothing they could do at this point. They would just have to wait. Kane and Tieg both returned to their meditations.

6

Kane sat silently on his bed. He couldn't think of what to do. This boy Janus had been giving him a hard time for months and it wasn't getting any better. To make things worse, Instructor Malious had told his father that he was making up stories about being bullied by Janus and his friends.

No matter how much he, Tieg or Magus spoke up about what was happening no one ever believed him. The one person that did believe him was his sister, Aerika. And that's because she could feel what he felt. She felt every hit, every scratch, everything. She felt it all.

He knew he had to do something to stop this but he couldn't come up with any ideas. Nobody would believe him and if he retaliated he would get in trouble and then it would probably only get worse.

Aerika pushed the door open and stepped inside. She went straight for Kane's bed and sat down next to him. Neither said a word. They didn't need to. Kane knew she felt his pain and Aerika knew how much pain he was in. Kane was just glad that she didn't have that pain actually inflicted upon her.

He just needed to hold strong. Maybe Janus would get bored and leave him alone eventually. Or maybe he would slip up and Kane would finally have proof that this was going on. Either way it went, they only had a few more months until this year was over and he would get a reprieve from this torment. He could only hope to hold out.

Kane and Aerika lay down on Kane's bed. He

couldn't help but feel responsible for her pain. Had he been good enough, maybe he would have been in the special training with Aerika and she wouldn't be feeling what was being done to him. It was eating him up inside. He was that cause of her pain.

The twin's father wasn't having an easy time of it either, though for far different reasons. Sinal let out a heavy sigh. He sat at the desk in his office with his face in his hands. He wanted to believe his son but Instructor Malious had said nothing was happening. And Sinal could do nothing without proof. He couldn't think of why his son would lie. It didn't make sense. And for Aerika to not only confirm it but know exactly what his injury claims would be before he claimed them. None of it made any sense to him.

Whatever the case may be, he had to figure out what to do about this situation. Kane couldn't continue going on lying like this and getting Aerika to lie for him, if that was truly what was happening, wasn't helping the situation. What troubled him more was Kane's friends, Tieg and Magus, were standing with him saying it was happening. For four children, all known for their hard work and integrity, to lie about the same thing seemed impossible. Yet there was just no proof. Sinal wanted to see for himself what was happening, but he just couldn't spare the time.

They would wait. It was all they could do. Maybe the truth would show itself in time, whatever it may be. He could only hope that it did. The year was almost over anyway. Just a few months left and they would leave this year behind and go on to the next.

Councilman Doe'n moved wordlessly through the Vi'jal Temple. This was where they housed the group of prophets, known as The Twelve since there were never more than twelve prophets at any one time. Prophecy was something that the Atrethian High Council took very seriously and since the incident with Kane, Doe'n had been assigned to monitor all prophecy.

This was a difficult thing to do as most prophecy was very vague. Rarely did it specify a person and even more rarely did it specify a specific time. And prophecies were becoming more and more scarce. It was as though there wasn't a future to be predicted.

Doe'n entered the Chamber of Visions, named for what it used to show. Visions of the future didn't actually happen in there, except by chance on occasion, but it was instead where the prophecies were shared with whoever was sent to listen.

Doe'n approached the prophet that had sent word. "I am Councilman Doe'n Iaren."

A man stood in the only light in the chamber. His black robes flowed down and appeared to become one with the shadows of the floor of the chamber. The prophet's deep red eyes gave off an uneven glow from beneath his drawn hood. His hands were interlocked inside his overlapping sleeves. "A prophecy has been shared and you shall hear it. Listen close and hear my words for they portray a future that cannot be avoided."

Doe'n was given pause for a moment as he'd never heard of a prophecy that was this specific. "Wait … This is a path we can't change?"

"I'm afraid not. But all will be revealed once you hear the prophecy." The prophet seemed almost impatient to tell this prophecy, but Doe'n thought it better to just listen than to comment.

"Then, I shall hear it."

The glow from beneath the prophet's eyes shifted its hue. The color began to mix as though his eyes were changing color. The glow suddenly held a myriad of colors ranging from yellow and red to blue and green. Every color eye that Doe'n had ever seen mixed with the color of this man's eyes. When the prophet spoke his words sounded as though a dozen people were speaking all at once.

"A warrior will be forged by events set into motion ... Grand Magistrate Kis'tohl's decision will drive this man ... His decision ... has condemned this man. A period of peace will end."

The many voices fell quiet. The glow from beneath his hood returned to its blood red shade. The prophet shrugged his shoulders as if the act of relating the prophecy was uncomfortable, though Doe'n could somehow tell he was quite accustomed to this act. The word of the prophets was the only word that held more power than the Grand Magistrate's.

Doe'n couldn't remain silent any longer. "What does this mean?"

"Bring in the two Enforcers standing outside of the chamber and I will tell you." The cryptic command from this prophet, coupled with his particularly foreboding tone, sent a chill down Doe'n's spine.

Doe'n did as he was told. He had to bring word back as he was ordered. He stuck his head out into the hall leading up to this chamber. The two Enforcers stood rigid in the hall. "You two ... The prophet has requested you witness their command."

The Enforcers clapped their gloved fists to the violet eye on their chests. They followed Doe'n into the room and stood at his flanks.

"Alright. What is it that The Twelve command?"

The Atrethian High Council had been in session since Councilman Doe'n had been summoned by The Twelve. This was the custom when it came to prophecy. The doors to the Mythril Hall swung up with more force than normal, startling the council members. Doe'n entered with two Enforcers at his flanks. His face held a stern and determined expression. He had prepared himself for what must be done as ordered by The Twelve.

The High Council stood on bated breath. They would hear what The Twelve had to say and, if there was one, what they demanded. The Grand Magistrate stood at the center in his deep violet robes.

"Well Councilman Doe'n ..." The voice of the Grand Magistrate echoing through the hall with the power of the Mythril Hall raising its volume. "What word do you bring from The Twelve?"

Doe'n stopped short of entering the half-circle formed by the Council. He glanced over his shoulder and motioned for the Enforcers to do as they were commanded. They moved to the flanks of the Grand Magistrate. He looked from the two Enforcers and back to Councilman Doe'n. The Enforcers took hold of the Grand Magistrate's arms.

"What?! Doe'n! What is the meaning of this?!"

The other Council Members stood in mute shock. None but Doe'n and the two Enforcer's knew what had been commanded. They dared not move for fear that they were next.

"Jerek Kis'tohl! You are hereby removed from your position as Grand Magistrate for crimes against the people of Atrethia. You will be stripped of your post as Grand Magistrate and the new Grand Magistrate will determine what your punishment will be. Until that happens, you will be held in the custody of the Enforcers until such time as a decision is made."

Kis'tohl starred into the eyes of Councilman Doe'n. He couldn't believe what was happening. The entire room was tense. Kis'tohl's words broke through the growing silence and even caused a few councilmen to jump. "What do they claim I have done?"

"The prophecy named you specifically as the man who condemned an innocent man and will cause our period of peace to end."

Hushed whispers came from the rest of the Council.

It was a disturbing prophecy to claim that this time of peace that had lasted for over 2000 years would end. The thought that it could end had never even occurred to anyone.

The Grand Magistrate stood silent. He didn't know when this had happened. He'd been Grand Magistrate for more than a hundred years. He'd passed judgment more times than he could remember, but no one judgment stood out in his mind as the one that was possibly 'unjust'.

"Doe'n …" His words came barely as whispers. "The Enforcers are not necessary. I resign my position as Grand Magistrate. If The Twelve say it is so, then I have committed these crimes. But before I leave the Council I have one request ... if you will all permit me."

The members of the Council merely nodded. They had served with the man for his entire time on the Council, save Councilman Doe'n who had replaced Kis'tohl when he took the position of Grand Magistrate. That and the fact that none of them could find a word to say at the moment.

"I would like to make a recommendation for the position of Grand Magistrate. It is a position that will have to make decisions that may be unpopular at times and may even conflict with your own beliefs. The position requires a love for our society and its ways that must be unrelenting. The person must have the strength to make a choice that could harm people he cares about. This person must also have the heart to care for the people he serves."

He paused for a moment letting the Council Members drink in his words. "Council Members … I recommend Councilman Doe'n Iaren as my replacement."

Doe'n took a step back. He and the rest of the Council were baffled by the recommendation. He was the youngest member and had the least experience on the Council.

"Doe'n, Members of the Council. I do not make this recommendation for personal gain. I make this recommendation because I believe it will benefit our world. Councilman Doe'n has time and time again shown a love for our society, a love for our laws and, most importantly, a love for our people. He has shown compassion as well as good judgment. I believe he will give everything he has to serve Atrethia as best he can."

"Jerek … I …" Doe'n couldn't manage a complete sentence. He hadn't planned for this and could come up with no response.

"I agree." The voice of another member of the council broke the silence.

"So do I." "And I." Agreements resounded throughout the hall. The entire Council was in agreement for the first time since Doe'n had joined it. Everyone agreed that he should be the next Grand Magistrate.

Doe'n found his words. "Members of the Atrethian High Council. If it is your wish that I continue to serve Atrethia as the Grand Magistrate … than I would honored. As my first act, I call for a short recess so that I may deliberate on the situation. When we return I shall pass judgment and then I shall hear your recommendations for my replacement."

The Council left Doe'n standing in the Mythril Hall. He couldn't believe how things had happened. He couldn't even wrap his mind around how he had come to be the Grand Magistrate. It all seemed to happen so fast. But now he had responsibilities to attend to and he had decisions to make.

Only a short time passed before Doe'n had recalled The Council. They had reassembled quickly with Doe'n now wearing the violet robes signifying his new position as the Grand Magistrate. One spot on the Council stood open and two Enforcers stood just inside the Mythril Hall as was customary. Doe'n spoke testing the power of the volume increase from the energy of the Hall itself on his position.

"Bring him in." His voice came a little softer than he thought it would but it was still easily heard.

One Enforcer clapped a gloved fist to the violet eye on his chest plate. "By your command, Grand Magistrate." The new titled would take some time to get used to. The Enforcer turned and stepped out the door, returning just moments later with Jerek Kis'tohl on his heels. Behind Kis'tohl were two more Enforcers that took position at his flanks once he had found his position before the Council.

"Jerek Kis'tohl … you have been convicted by prophecy of the crime of breaching peace on Atrethia. This is not something that is taken lightly in our society and the normal punishment for this crime would be banishment to the Terrei Desert for all time."

Kis'tohl bowed his head. "I understand, Grand Magistrate."

"However, you did not commit this crime knowingly and have many years of dedicated and distinguished service to the people of Atrethia. I must submit at least some form of punishment. Therefore, I hereby sentence you to twenty-five years of hard labor in the Natulla Mines under the Hidden Peaks. But before we send you off for your punishment I would like to query the Council to see what they think about an idea of mine."

Kis'tohl was puzzled. This was rather unorthodox but that was exactly why Doe'n was chosen. He was a new fresh mind to the Council and would push for some much needed change in their customs.

"Council Members, I submit to you that, due to Jerek Kis'tohl's extensive service to Atrethian society, we call it Time served. What do you all think of that?"

Silence fell across the hall and they obviously pondered this for a moment. Then, seemingly in unison, a resounding 'Agreed' echoed within the Hall.

"I thought as much. Jerek Kis'tohl. You have been

sentenced to a period of twenty-five years hard labor in the Natulla Mines with time served. You are free to go."

"Thank you, Grand Magistrate. Thank you all. I would like to add one more thing if I may."

"Go ahead."

"It has been an honor to serve with you … all of you."

With that, Jerek Kis'tohl took his leave of the Mythril Hall for the last time. He would not return to this place for a very long time, if ever he did. He had seen it for far too long as it were. The thought suddenly crossed his mind that maybe his time on this planet was complete. He had thoroughly served Atrethian society and he felt he had no more purpose. He would find a nice quiet place to go spend the last of his days as he prepared his family for his passing.

Some months later, the twins had returned to The Academy. Aerika sat in deep meditation. Her training was progressing extremely quickly and she took to all her lessons as though she were merely remembering something she already knew. Her classmates were in awe of how quickly she learned and they seemed inspired by her progress and were only steps behind her.

She stared into the colorful world that was The Flow and all it was. It was no longer strange to see with her eyes closed. She no longer felt that way. In fact, she saw things in both ways with her eyes open now. She could see how people looked physically and how they mixed with the energy around them. The world she saw was beautiful and full of color. She felt at peace with everything. Then, suddenly, it all went black and a scaring pain shot through her body. She let out a wracked scream and rolled onto her side from her seated position. The scream jolted her classmates from their meditations and even pulled the instructor from his. They all gathered around the girl as she cradled her arm.

Aerika was groaning in pain and gripping her arm.

She moved as though it were broken though it appeared there was nothing wrong with it.

"Aerika! What's wrong?!" the Instructor asked. "Children, stay back! Don't touch her!" He continued as they children drew in closer to see what was happening.

Aerika just bit hard trying to hold on to consciousness. The pain was almost too great and suddenly it ended. The pain was gone. Kane was in trouble. She knew this but there was nothing she could do.

Janus stood from beside Kane. Kane's arm was now right once again, where it had just moments before been bent the wrong direction. Janus had taken to healing any wounds he inflicted on Kane after doing so to remain in the clear. He wouldn't get caught if he could help it and this just ensured there was no evidence at all. Not even a bruise.

"Poor little Kane. Your platinum eyes can't save you from a physical beating can they? You really should fight back. That would make this much more fun."

His voice sounded almost evil though Kane knew it was just jealousy and anger. He just lay there in mute agony. He knew that Aerika had felt that and that hurt him more than the broken arm had. His mind went to the only solace he could find. Just two weeks. Two more weeks and he would be leave Janus and The Academy behind for a short time and he could breathe easy. At least, he could until he came back for the next year of training. Then, he knew, it would all start again.

7

Kane and Aerika couldn't leave the school fast enough. They didn't say a word to anyone until they had gotten home. It wouldn't be a long enough break before going back. Neither of the two really wanted to go back.

"Kane … Aerika. Why are you two being so quiet?"

Liana had no idea what her two children had gone through this year. She didn't know why they had insisted on leaving The Academy so quickly but she could easily tell that something was wrong.

Aerika looked into the eyes of her brother. If they said anything they would get into trouble for 'lying' but she had asked. "I … I just had a bad year is all mother." Kane's reply was so very deliberately vague that he knew it wouldn't satisfy his mother. He could feel his father staring at him.

Liana looked about the room curious as to what was known by everyone except for her. She shifted her weight to one of her feet and looked to Sinal for answers. He looked right back at his wife and knew that he wasn't getting away without explaining.

He let out a heavy sigh and answered her silent question. "Kane claims to have been the subject of ridicule and several physical assaults throughout the year."

"What do you mean he claims? You don't believe your own son?" Sinal's answer had obviously made her angry and that anger was directed at him which made him nervous.

"Liana, I want to believe him but there is never any

proof. This other boy is always in meditation when the teacher comes back and Kane makes his claims. As he claims it, Kane is making these accusations to get attention since he was placed in these classes away from Aerika."

Liana looked disappointed at her husband. "I can't believe you would listen to this other person over your own son. You raised him. You know him as well as I do. He would not lie. He just doesn't have it in him to lie. It is not in his nature. If something is wrong, he will tell the truth. It is a part of who he is."

Sinal nodded and looked to the ground. He knew. Kane was a good kid and would definitely not lie about such things. Especially not just to garner attention. Both of his parents knew that it wasn't in his character.

"I want you to find out what is going on Sinal. And when you go back to The Academy next year, you will tell this Instructor ..."

"Malious."

"You will tell this Instructor Malious that he will stay with Kane and this other boy at all times otherwise he will know the anger of a Mother."

Sinal smirked a bit. He knew she was serious and he knew that 'the anger of a Mother' as she put it was not something anyone could hide from. Their children just stood silently watching their parents talk. This was something they were not accustomed to. They're mother had never scolded their father before and they were both engrossed. It was interesting to see it happen this way.

Liana walked to Kane without another word, knelt before him and gathered him up into her arms. He pushed against her and wrapped his arms around her. "Everything will be alright, my son. I will put a stop to this. Don't you worry."

The time until they returned to their training went quickly. Kane walked into his class for the first time that year. Instructor Malious was waiting inside and, by the look he cast upon Kane, he had received the not-so-veiled threat from his mother.

"So you finally got some attention did you?" His voice filled with an air of spite.

"I wasn't lying instructor. Janus was careful to avoid getting caught."

"More lies. Do you ever stop?"

"I'm not lying!"

The Instructor stood from his seat in a huff. "You dare raise your voice at me!"

Kane bit his tongue. He had spoken out of turn. "I apologize, sir. But I am not lying."

"Take your seat and be silent. I will not have such insolence in my classroom again. Do you understand?"

A silent nod was all Kane gave in reply. This year may prove to be more difficult than the last. He could tell already. And he knew for certain that Janus would find a way to do what he wanted. Just as it was in Kane's nature to not lie, it was in Janus' nature to get what he desired. Much to Kane's dismay, what Janus desired was Kane's misery.

Sinal walked into Malious classroom. The class was in deep meditation save for Kane, Tieg and Magus. All of the students were positioned roughly 3 feet from the floor with a particular element holding them up. Some sat with fire beneath them. Others water. Some had a sheet of rock on which they sat.

Magus sat staring at Kane with a jet of fire beneath him holding him up. Tieg had a fount of water spitting up around him from the pillar of water beneath him. It was dancing around him in some of the most beautiful patterns Sinal had ever seen. He was rather impressed. Tieg's eyes were locked straight ahead. Though he wasn't meditating he was concentrating very hard.

He then looked to Kane and felt instant pride. His son

sat on a seemingly nothing and everything all at once. Every so often a jet of water would swirl around him. Cinders and burning embers were rising from where he sat in the air. Wind would gust around him occasionally disturbing the embers. And the rocks that floated around him seemed to dance to a tune that Sinal couldn't hear. Kane's eyes locked on to his father when he came in. He smiled the softest smile at seeing him. Kane was taking to his training with greater skill than he had heard.

Malious stood up when Sinal entered the room. "Sinal. As you can see. I am keeping this ridiculous promise that I made."

"I know Malious and I'm sorry. But my wife is insistent that our son is telling the truth."

"Well despite your sons constant grabs for attention, he is taking to his training rather well. Too well to be in this class if you ask me but I am not the one to make those decisions."

"I know you aren't Malious. And I thank you for indulging my wife. I know it is not easy to do. We have far too many tasks to complete in a day to have to stay in the classroom while the students meditate."

"My class will be practicing all day tomorrow Malious. Why don't I come and watch your class for you so you can get some of you duties done?"

Malious smiled and nodded. "Thank you Sinal. That would be most helpful." He clapped his hand into Sinal's respectfully. It almost hurt Kane that his father had this much respect for a man who so clearly hated him, but he imagined that he must remain cordial given they work together.

Weeks passed without any encounter with Janus and Kane had almost thought nothing would happen again. But one day it all started again. Kane was first in the classroom as happened on occasion, only this time it wasn't for very long that he was alone. Two hands slammed into his shoulder blades sending him tumbling to the floor. His jaw cracked down against the stone floor causing him to bite hard onto his tongue. A warm, iron taste filled his mouth.

He turned quick to face his assailants though he knew who it was. "So Kane. You got your daddy to protect you? You know better than that." The rest of the class was in on it now. It was Kane against Janus and five others. Even if he fought back he could do nothing before he would be overwhelmed and then it would only be worse.

But at least Kane knew now that Janus had indeed found a way to continue the punishment. It was almost as much to wonder when it would happen. Now he knew. His misery would continue though it would not happen as much. It would be confined to the early morning when and if no one was in the classroom when he got there.

That day seemed longer than the rest. Kane looked at his sister when they returned to their room. She knew that it had started again. They only had to endure for a short while. A few more months and they would have another break. Then one more year and Janus would no longer be a part of his life. He would move on to a different more specialized class for him and Kane would move into one for him.

Aerika put on a strong face just like her brother. They had to appear happy for their parents. It was their twelfth birthday. They would share this happy occasion with them and then continue their training.

Sinal and Liana entered the room smiling ear to ear. Liana all but ran to her kids. She picked them up. This was the one day each year she was allowed into The Academy to see them unless something was wrong.

Sinal laughed as the kids squirmed trying to get away free from their mothers squeezing grip. This would be a good day. And it was. The rest of the year was one torment after another for Kane. If Janus wasn't pummeling him,

Instructor Malious was glaring at him or verbally assaulting him. The very last day of class couldn't come fast enough for Kane. Only one more year and he would be free of Janus. But for the moment …

A fist slammed across the side of Kane's head. The room spun from the impact. Janus still had one more day this year and he would make use it seemed.

"So you think you're going to be free of me after next year? Well, let me tell you. I will find a way. You deserve torture and I will be the one to provide it. This I promise you."

Kane gritted his teeth and clenched his fists before he noticed the other five were standing around him. He eased up a bit. He couldn't do anything. He stood no chance.

"Take your seats students!" Malious said it before he even got into the classroom. The six were in their seats in an instant. They had gotten very good at hiding their activities.

At least it was over for now. A short break and then one year before he was away from it for good. At least, he hoped he would be.

Another short break and Kane once again sat alone in the classroom waiting for class to start. Another year of torture before he would be free of Janus. Seemingly on cue, Janus and his five lackeys strolled into the room and up to Kane without skipping a beat.

"So Kane! The last year, huh? You ready to get this started? Ready for it to be over with? You know, you're a coward. You really should fight back. It would make this much more interesting."

Following with his form, he raised his fist to begin the beating. Kane flinched and waited for the first hit but it never came. The wait seemed to drag on and on but it never came.

The sound of a beating echoed in his ears but he didn't feel it. The grunts of physical exertion and of sudden and intense pain clawed their way into his ears. Desks and chairs broke and fell over from the scuffle that Kane heard. The crashing sounds stopped as suddenly as they had begun and was followed by a heavy silence.

Kane opened his eyes to see what had happened. Janus was beaten and bloody. Cuts had ripped at his clothing and flesh. Blood streamed from each wound. His face didn't even resemble him any longer. It looked to have caved in on itself. A broken leg from what Kane assumed a desk was rammed through his chest pinning him to the wall.

The other five were all on the ground, beaten and bloody, but in far better condition than Janus. Their limbs contorted in ways they most certainly should not have been and gashed had been torn into their flesh. They at least looked like they might still be alive.

Kane wondered if he had done this. He looked around to see if anyone else was there. That's when he saw her. Standing in the doorway, hands tightly clenched at her sides, though she seemed oddly relaxed. Her eyes were still pulsing with the power she had just used in his defense. Aerika had just used her power to harm another and she had killed Janus.

Kane was on the verge of panic. If he couldn't gain control of the situation his sister would be sent into exile for protecting him. He rushed to her to calm her down. Maybe he could keep her from getting into trouble. Maybe he could bruise himself up a little bit to make them think it was a physical altercation.

Kane took her by her shoulders and pulled her tight against him. She was breathing heavily still in the heat of the moment. Her muscles tensed when he grabbed her.

"Shh … Acrika … It's me, Kane. You must calm down. It's over. Please just try to relax. It's over. I'm alright."

At the sound of his voice, she fell limp dragging Kane

to the ground with her. She had passed out. Kane wondered just how much of his torture she knew. It must have been far harder on her for her to have done this. He held her head in his lap and ran his fingers through her hair. He could hold them back no longer. Tears streamed down his face. He was afraid for her now. She had broken one of the most severe of Atrethia's laws and he had no idea how to protect her from the punishment.

Despite what had just occurred she looked so peaceful. Aerika had thrown everything away to protect him. Kane knew she had done it for him. Any pain he felt seemed to hurt her more than pain she felt. That's just how she was. Kane thought for a moment of what he could do for her. And it suddenly came to him.

"Whoa! Kane?! What happened here?!"

It was Tieg. He and his brother had just shown up. A little too late though. If only they had been there a few minutes earlier. Maybe none of this would have happened.

"I ..."

The word had barely left Kane's lips when, "YOU DID THIS?!"

Kane's heart jumped up into his throat. There was no time. Not anymore. Behind Magus and Tieg, stood Instructor Malious. His deep gold eyes fixed upon Kane as if he were looking at his bare soul and seeing all that had happened. Kane couldn't even get another word out before he fell unconscious. Forced into sedation by the well trained power of Malious.

Muffled voices began to seep into Kane's mind. He grabbed onto the sounds trying to use them to bring himself back to reality. The muddy sounds finally broke into words, however unintelligible, but he could at least make out distinct sounds. He pulled harder trying to wake up. His eyes fluttered a little. He could feel again.

Malious and the Council were speaking of what

happened. "It seems the group is known to bully the boy Kane. Or at least that's what Kane and his two cohorts say.

"Did you ever investigate it?" It was a woman's voice. Kane didn't know there was a woman on the Council.

"There was no evidence of if other than his word so we ignored it."

"Well this certainly proves that something was going on! Don't you think?!" Her voice bit at the air in a harsh way. This topic definitely struck a chord with her.

"Yes, Councilwoman Theana. It does."

"Theana! Ease your tone! This is about the use of the flow against another not what these children were doing to the other!" a male voice called to her. Kane thought he recognized it but the angry tone distorted it.

"Yes, of course, Grand Magistrate. I apologize." Theana replied.

"And we still don't know which child did it. Was it the boy or the girl?" Another male voice.

"That's Aerika and Kane! And they are my children!" Sinal's voice echoed into Kane's mind. They must have pulled him from his duties at The Academy. Maybe he could come up with a way to help them.

"You will watch your tongue when you address The Council!" the Grand Magistrate bellowed. Sinal didn't reply. Kane was disheartened by how quickly his father was put down.

"When will the girl wake up?" one man said. Another councilman. Kane didn't recognize his voice. This was good news to Kane. He had woken up before Aerika. That was all he needed to know. He opened his eyes slowly trying to pretend that he was just coming to.

"The boy wakes." came the voice of one of the councilman.

Standing before him were thirteen hooded figures. The Atrethian High Council, the governmental authority on

Atrethia. Between Kane and them was Instructor Malious. Sinal was sitting in the corner near the door. Kane was lifted from where he lie by the power of one of the council. He came to rest before them though not standing on his own.

"Kane … Do you know why you are here?" The Grand Magistrate spoke directly. His voice was oddly soothing. He recognized the voice now. It was Doe'n, his father's friend.

"Yes, Sir."

"Explain yourself than! What happened?!" Malious said angrily.

"You will be silent! The Council will handle this as you are obviously incapable of keeping peace in your own classroom!" Councilwoman Theana exclaimed.

"While out of line, your instructor has the right idea. Tell us what happened, young one." For the first time since hearing them speaking, Kane thought maybe everything might end up alright. With his father's friend as the Grand Magistrate, they might just get out of this.

"Well, Sir, I was waiting for instruction to begin when Janus and the others entered. They didn't stop in the door or anything, like they knew I was there alone. They came right for me. I didn't move to get away; because I knew what they intended and I could do nothing to stop it. They began insulting me and Janus pulled me up out of my chair. Aerika, my sister … she came into the classroom at this point."

"Did she do this?! She certainly has the power to!" one of the councilman said.

"NO!" Kane replied quickly. "She didn't. She pushed Janus off of me. He reacted violently as he did to any such attack. He raised his fist to strike her. I had to protect her and I knew that I couldn't do anything to stop him with physical strength. He's stronger than I am you see. I just reacted in the only way I could that would protect her. I hit him with as much wind as I could muster in that moment. It stunned him and knocked Aerika to the floor away from him and the rest of the kids. That's when I lost control. I don't remember what happened after that. I only recall seeing them where they were when the instructor came in with the damage done. Aerika was still on the ground near door where she had fallen when it all started."

"You're in the normal classes! How could you have done this?!" Malious had seen Kane's progress and still denied that he had the power to do such a thing.

"Silence or I will have you removed!" Grand Magistrate Doe'n screamed angrily, "Can't you see he has platinum eyes? He is no normal student! He never should have been in those classes! But that is a discussion for another time! Kane … are you certain that is what happened?"

"Yes, Sir." He continued the lie. He knew what was coming. It had worked. Or he at least just hoped it had worked.

"This is disturbing indeed. The only conclusion is that you were the one that did this." Doe'n explained, "This leaves us with a clear answer of what must be done. Kane Malacor! Your actions were in clear violation of Atrethian Law and caused the death of the boy Janus and seriously injured five others! The rightful punishment for this act is death!"

"NO!" Sinal cried half in anger and half in anguish. Kane couldn't begin to imagine how much this must be eating at his father.

"HOWEVER," Doe'n continued, "in light of the fact that you were defending yourself and your sister … no matter how excessive your reaction … you are to be sentenced for that act of violence against another not the death of the boy. So your crime here is the use of The Flow against a fellow Atrethian. You are hereby found guilty of this crime and sentenced to 25 years of exile to the Terrei Desert! In 25 years you will be retrieved if you still live. Before this sentence is carried out, do you have anything left to say?"

"I have a request, Sir." Kane replied. He hadn't thought anything like this would happen, but he was glad it turned out this way. He had saved Aerika. Now he had to talk to her. To tell her so that she didn't alter what had been done when she regained consciousness.

"Speak it and I shall consider it."

"I would like to say good-bye to my family, Sir. Including my sister."

"Of course. We shall grant you this request as it may be your last. You may spend one final day with your family, supervised by The Enforcers. They will ensure that you return for your punishment. Though I know that will not be necessary."

"Thank you, Sir." Kane spoke softly, bowing low in respect. He realized now that he was standing on his own.

"Thank you, Grand Magistrate! Thank you ever so much!" Sinal said. He knew it was Doe'n, but he was so overcome with all that had happened that he couldn't help but be formal.

8

Liana waited impatiently for the return of her husband and children. She had heard from The Academy some of what had happened and was worrying herself almost literally sick about the fate of her children. The person she had spoken to about the incident knew little of what had actually happened, only that one child had been killed and several others injured and Kane had allegedly taken responsibility for it. But no one knew for certain.

She had asked around and called on several people she knew at the school, but no one could tell her what happened. What they did know was that her children were taken to the Council to find out what had happened and pass judgment on whoever was to blame.

She couldn't bring herself to sit still. She busied herself with house work, cleaning dishes, making beds taking them down and remaking them. These, of course, were all things she could do through her connection to the Flow and achieve them perfectly on her first attempt but she found a sense of calm in doing them by hand.

She was wrist deep in thrice dirtied water when she couldn't contain herself any longer. She broke down into tears dropping her face down into her hands. Her muffled sobs, which barely broke free from her hands, were easily overpowered by the sound of the door squeaking open. Sinal walked through the door carrying the still unconscious Aerika. He walked straight to the couch to lay her down. Liana rushed to see him and their daughter. Once she was rested comfortably enough, he turned to embrace his hysterical wife.

"Hush, my dear. Calm yourself. You won't do the situation any good in this state." He whispered trying his hardest to remain calm himself.

"What … where … how ..." she sobbed. She couldn't complete a thought. So many questions unanswered and then seeing her daughter in this state. It didn't help her hysteria.

"Calm yourself, Liana." He whispered again while running his fingers through her hair to try to calm her while she cried into his shoulder, all the while looking at his son standing in the doorway.

Kane just stood silent watching the scene. His mother … Kane dropped his mouth open to speak but he couldn't decide where to start let alone find the words to tell what had happened. He swallowed the desire to scream at the top of his lungs and tell what had truly happened. It wouldn't do him or Aerika any good.

After several minutes, his mother finally calmed herself down. When she pulled her face from her husband's shoulder, she spotted Kane in the door. Their eyes met and he lost control of his own emotions. Kane ran to the comfort of his mother's arms. She hugged him strengthened now by his need for someone to calm him down. Kane buried his face in her dress and just cried. He had this secret that was literally tearing the family apart.

Though Kane had slept for a while following what happened, thanks to Malious, he cried himself to sleep. His mother carried him to his room and sat on his bed just running her fingers through his hair. Kane's even breathing seemed almost uncharacteristic considering what had happened. His father stood in the doorway smiling weakly. He wanted to cry too but someone had to remain strong through the whole ordeal.

"Are you ready to hear what happened?" he finally

asked. She didn't look up, just nodded.

"Kane was being bullied and Aerika tried to protect him. One of the bullies was going to hurt her and Kane …" his breath caught in his throat. It was almost as if the lie didn't want to come out again. "He used the Flow to protect her. He's …" Sinal swallowed hard fighting his own pain and sadness. "He's been exiled for his crime."

Tears came anew to her eyes. She had nothing to say. Her son had done the right thing in her eyes and he would never be wrong. Especially not for this. She had known the truth all along that Kane was telling the truth, but no one else had believed it. Now the truth was out and in the worst possible way.

Kane awoke sometime in the middle of the night. His father had pulled a chair into the doorway and fallen asleep. His mother was asleep cradling his head in her lap on his bed. He got up out of the bed and walked out into the living room where Aerika was.

She was awake and sitting on the couch. She turned her head slowly dragging her solid white eyes to him. He couldn't help but think of how calm she looked in spite of all that had occurred. Kane sat down next to her and put his arm around her shoulder.

"You protected me." He said it almost like he didn't believe it himself. Like the lie he had told to protect her had become the truth just by him saying it. *'And why not?'* He thought. He had told the truth about everything else and it had all been revealed. They had to believe him now.

"What happened? I remember seeing Janus about to hit you and then, nothing. It's all just black. I woke up here. Where are mom and dad?" Her voice was soft and held the weight of fear. She really didn't know what had happened.

"Listen, Aerika. I have to tell you something and it's not going to be easy for you to hear but I need you to be strong." Kane said turning to face his sister directly.

"Tomorrow I'll be going away … for a very long time. I'm going to the Terrei Desert."

Tears brimmed in her eyes. She shook her head just the slightest little bit like the words wouldn't be true if she did it.

"I've been exiled for using the flow to protect you."

"But … you said I protected you. I … should … be …" sobs broke up her words and then cut them short altogether. Kane moved closer and pulled her head down to his shoulder.

"You protected me, Aerika. Now, I'm protecting you. That's how it works. That's what brothers do for their sisters. They protect them. I won't let you go to your death"

"You'd rather go yourself?!" She pushed away smoke rising from her eyes.

She was suddenly furious. Kane had no response. It was true. He would rather go off to his own death than deal with watching his sister do the same. But he could try to make this transition easier for her.

Kane placed his hand down on the stone tile floor, pushed down hard and jerked his hand cutting it open. With his other hand he wiped a tear from her cheek as she watched him furious and scared and any number of other emotions that his actions were causing.

He put his hands together cupped them open just a little towards himself and blew into them. When he opened his hands, a tear-shaped, blood-red jewel lay in his now healed hands. A small loop adorned the end of the jewel.

A light gust of wind swept through the room catching dirt and small rocks lifting them into the air and flitting them about as it gathered more. When enough had collected they floated as a mass over near the twins.

She looked at the jewel in his hand and then at the mass of dirt and rock. The mass burst into flames and when the sudden conflagration ended, the dirt and rocks had been replaced by a thin, silver-colored chain. She smiled for the first time since she had woken up. Kane slipped the chain through a small hole in the jewels neck and hung it around Aerika's neck.

"This is my promise to you. I will come back. We will see each other again." Kane said to his sister. He had to choke back his own emotions. He wanted to cry but he needed to be strong for her.

She smiled at the small jewel hanging around her neck. "I know we will." she said almost inaudibly.

A knock came at the door. Their mother and father stepped sleepily out of Kane's room and just stared at the door. They let their eyes slip over to Kane and Aerika who were both looking at the door. The soft beat of a gentle rain was the only thing stemming complete silence in the home. The knock came again.

"Yes?" Sinal finally gaining control of his voice.

The door opened. Though it was night and raining, the plate armor the two men standing in the door were wearing from head to toe shined as if the sun were beating down upon them. Kane and the rest of his family knew who they were.

"It's time," one of them said in a deep, authoritative voice. Though his face was hidden, everyone in the room somehow knew he was looking straight at Kane.

Kane stood slowly. Aerika dropped her hand into his as he stood up. She couldn't pull her eyes away from the men in the doorway. Though the rain was still falling, it didn't make a sound in the home. It was as though time stood still for this family about to fall apart.

"I'm ready." Kane's voice broke the silence and the steady drum of the rain continued upon hearing his voice. Almost as if it had been waiting to see what happened.

His family broke into fits of sobs. Even his father who had maintained his composure through it all had broken into tears. Kane stood maintaining his strength in the situation and proud of the decision he had made to protect his sister. Deep down, he was terrified and wanted so badly to tell the truth.

He wanted to cry with them and let them know the truth of it all, but what good would that do. He just hugged his family and looked one more time into his sister's eyes. He opened his mouth just the slightest and mouthed the words 'I promise.' Aerika nodded the softest little bit.

With that Kane turned and joined the Enforcers outside his home. One of them placed his hand reassuringly upon Kane's shoulder. It was like they understood and weren't judging the boy. Kane didn't think he knew any Enforcer's, but this one seemed familiar somehow. Though with the armor covering every inch of him there was no way to tell.

They stepped off towards the center of town and the Mythril Hall where the Grand Magistrate awaited his return. It seemed a much shorter walk than Kane had thought it would be. Kane and the Enforcers stood before the entrance to the Mythril Hall. He looked up at the imposing building that had obviously been built to instill fear into any that came upon it under these circumstances. It's huge, black doors reflecting the light of the moon that barely peeked through the clouds which had finally let up raining. The intricate carvings on the door depicted the most severe laws of Atrethia, one of which he was being exiled for.

He stood for a moment in awe. Despite having been inside the building and exiting these very doors just this morning, he hadn't actually seen them before. It was incredible. Each scene depicted seemed to come alive when you looked at the door as a whole but when you looked directly at it froze as if to pretend it weren't living.

The door, imbued with the Flow as most things were, opened when they finally stepped towards it. Kane walked as tall as he could trying very hard not to show the fear he felt, trying not to show the sadness of leaving his family behind. But he would be strong so that he could survive the exile. He had promised Aerika and it wasn't a promise he was about to break.

Upon entering the council chamber he saw only Grand Magistrate Doe'n. He stood in the back of the chamber with his hood drawn low over his face. The violet robes that depicted his station in the High Council flowing down around his feet.

"Kane ... It is time to carry out your sentence."

Kane just nodded holding his head high. He was terrified, but more than that he was proud that he had successfully protected his sister from this fate. The Enforcers lifted him up by his arms and carried him to a ritual circle drawn on the floor in the center of the chamber. The symbol, drawn in four different colors of sand, filled the majority of the chamber.

The outer circle was drawn entirely in a dark brown. A square drawn in blue sand met at four points with the circle. A red line dissected the circle completely cutting through one corner of the blue square and exiting out of the other. Within the circle were several symbols drawn with white sand. Each symbol had a distinct deliberate shape. They fill the entire circle save a three foot area in the very center.

The Enforcers, stepping carefully as to not disturb the sand and set Kane down in the center of the symbol. The enforcers took their places at opposite ends of the red line facing in towards the center of the symbol.

"Before we begin, Kane. I want you to know that despite what our laws say, you did the right thing in protecting your sister and should you survive, you will be welcomed back into society with your honor intact."

"Thank you, Grand Magistrate."

Doe'n began speaking softly. His words were almost completely unintelligible. What Kane could make out was that the words were in Ancient Atrethian, the language of the Flow. His words grew louder though his lips didn't move any more than they were.

It was as though the words were taking on a life of their own in the chant. Growing more powerful as he repeated them over and over.

Mat ay noe't qu ai paltea! Mat ay noe't qu ai paltea!

The white symbols inside the circle began to glow brightly and they lifted completely from the floor. They floated to differing heights within the room though they seemed solid as if the sand had become stone. The symbols began to flip in place as if they were dancing to the sounds of the chant. Doe'n's words changed.

Tonhek lap'it tuul marat! Tonhek lap'it tuul marat!

The square began to glow as if showing the light of the sun itself. It too, now solidified, floated up over all of the symbols and began to spin in tune with the speed of the words. Again, the words changed.

Bahet moliu! Bahet moliu!

The red line split beneath Kane's feet to form a circle around him. It too was emanating a deep glow. It rose up, connecting the shafts on either side at chest height on the two Enforcers. The points of the lines extended suddenly seeming to stab into the violet eye upon their breastplates. They grunted with the impact though it wasn't a painful sound.

The Enforcers lifted from the ground with the newly solid piece of this puzzle to hang between the circle on the ground and the blue square overhead. Doe'n's words changed once again. Though they sounded more commanding this time.

Bhi nahck tu lisz Terrei! Bhi nahck tu lisz Terrei!

He continued the chant several times before the circle

began to solidify though it did not glow like the others. In fact it seemed to be absorbing the light from the other symbols. The walls of the room beyond the symbol began to disappear in the failing light of the symbols. The entirety of the rest of the world outside of the ritual began to fade as the light in the room retreated into the brown circle on the floor.

Doe'n even faded from Kane's sight; His words, however, sounding more powerful than they had before. The sound seemed to resonate as though they were in a chamber larger than they were.

Kane's stomach began to twist just the slightest but no matter how hard he tried he couldn't move his arms to put a hand on it to calm it. He looked down to see what was happening to the circle. His eyes locked open wide in shock at what he saw.

The brown circle hadn't been absorbing the light from the other artifacts. The light had been filling the empty area within the circle. The light carried a myriad of colors, though he couldn't pick any that stood out to him as more prominent. The light beneath his feet shifted as if it were a living organism.

Grand Magistrate Doe'n's chant came louder suddenly. When it did the light beneath his feet flashed white and seemed to show an image for just a moment. It didn't remain long enough for Kane to see what it was.

The chant came louder again. The light flashed once again, brighter this time. He saw what looked like a hill beneath his feet but he couldn't tell in the moment that it was there.

Doe'n's voice boomed deafeningly continuing the chant. The light beneath his feet faded save for the very edges of it. Beneath him was a very clear image now. His new home for the next twenty-five years. Kane raised his eyes to the Grand Magistrate who had stopped chanting once the image appeared. Kane could see him again through the darkness beyond.

"I am sorry for this Kane. Our laws are clear, however. But, I wish you the best of luck. May the Flow grant you safety. And if that is not the case, then a quick, painless death."

Qui'l vanie … TERREI!

Kane felt a power take hold of him. Fear gripped at him finally and his eyes filled with the tears he had been holding back. He shut his eyes tight and clenched his teeth trying to bite back the emotions that would not serve him where he was going. The power that held him ripped him down into the image on the floor of the chamber.

After a moment of suspension in the air, he felt earth beneath his feet. The power that held him suddenly released and he finally had control of his body again. His exile had begun.

9

Kane opened his eyes tentatively. He was afraid to see what was around him. Though it was night-time, the light of the moon cast upon the area rather brightly. He could see as though the sun were still out. All he could see, in every direction he looked, was sand. Dunes, as far as the eye could see. Though the light was enough for him to make out what was around him, he couldn't make out any colors.

He tried to take a deep breath but it came just a bit too shaky and ended up cut short. He decided it would be better to just find shelter for the night. He did his best to compose himself before setting out. He wiped the partially dried tears from his eyes. He took in another shaky breath, only a little bit deeper this time.

He shifted his weight to his right foot to step off with his left. When he did, the dune beneath his foot gave way and he slid down the steep slope. After sliding for a while his foot caught into some dirt and he turned just enough to the side to start rolling. It seemed as though he rolled forever.

When he finally came to a halt, he pushed himself up out of the loose dirt that surrounded him. He shook the sand from his hair and spit out some that had gotten into his mouth. He got to his feet and took in his new surroundings. He could see in the distance a tall cliff-face. If he could make it there maybe he could find a cave to take shelter in. He set out. He had to do everything he could to survive. He had to keep his promise.

The walked seemed to take hours but he finally made

it. Kane approached the cliff face. It rose up into the black of the sky and disappeared to his right and left as though it went on forever. His hopes were dashed that he would find a cave as soon as he got there. The rock was smooth in all directions. He had to choose a direction to start walking and hope he could find someplace to stay for the night.

He started walking along keeping his eyes peeled for anything that might be a shelter at least for the night. A shiver ran down his spine. It was too cold to be out in the open like this. He concentrated for a moment and created a flame to followed close by him to light his way and to keep him at least a little warm.

In the shadows, it followed on the edge of the light. Even without eyes, the creature knew where the light was. It could feel it. It knew exactly where its prey was and it knew that he hadn't seen it yet. It would follow and wait for the right time to strike and have its meal.

Its sensitive ears detected even the smallest change in its prey's breathing. It gripped the side of the cliff like it was walking normally on the ground. It could stay above its targets sight and not have to worry about being seen or heard, but only until it was ready to strike. It was curious about this newcomer. It would learn from it before feasting.

Kane continued along the cliff face. He was giving up hope of finding a shelter and now was thinking of a way to make a shelter. He stopped for a moment to think. There was no water to control so he couldn't use it to erode the rock. And he didn't think he could make fire hot enough to break away the cliff to make a cave. He thought that maybe he could use wind, but he couldn't think of how.

He paused and stared at the cliff face. He would come up with a way to cut into it. He had to.

This was its chance. All it had to do was get up high and pounce on him. It could take its prey now. Shame it wouldn't have more of a chance to learn from it. If it waited though, something else might get to it first and then it would be out of the meal. Or more likely, part of the meal.

It clawed its way up the cliff and turned down to face its target. Now it would have its meal.

Kane began to focus. He concentrated on the world around him. First very near sensing the cliff and then reaching out farther to the area around him. This place made him feel sad. Everything felt dead. It had little to no energy within it at all. It was almost like it was never alive to begin with.

He didn't know how much energy it would take to dig in to this rock so he began reaching out farther. But he sensed something alive as he did this. At least it was almost alive. It felt strange to him. It felt like it was dead but at the same time alive. Almost like it was something that was alive but shouldn't be. It seemed to him that death was more alive in this desolate land. But what was more alarming, it was coming towards him … quickly.

Kane slid through the dirt. He dove to the side just in time to avoid the sharp claws reaching out for him. The friction from sliding face-first through the sand hurt but it was better than what this thing obviously had in mind. He turned to face his attacker and was terrified by what he found before him.

Crouched where he had been is what appeared to be a walking suit of armor though it was obvious that next to nothing filled it now. The flame Kane had conjured lit it well enough for him to make out its hideous features.

It rose slowly from the crouched position though it still seemed poised to strike again. It turned towards Kane as it rose. The creatures face was covered by what looked like a plate helmet, though it was melted to the shape of the skull on which it now sat. Where the creature's eyes were was a smooth piece of metal. How it could see, Kane couldn't even begin to guess at though he was sure it knew exactly where he was.

The metal of the helm seemed to instinctively leak away from the creatures teeth which were in surprisingly good condition despite their apparent age. The lower jaw of the creature remained bleached white bone with a metal lining across the jawline.

The breastplate had melted leaving gaps showing the bones and organs beneath. The paint that adorned it had long ago been stripped away by the sands of this great desert. The metal of the gauntlets clung to the creatures hands forming a gnarled set of claws. The feet appeared in much the same fashion.

This creature was obviously Atrethian once but whatever dark energies were used to kill it had turned it into this. Though it seemed that the creature was alive despite itself. Like its unlife wasn't intentional. The armor adorning the creature led Kane to believe that it had once been an Enforcer, but the only Enforcer's he knew of that had died inside this place were the original group sent to bring The Malicious One to justice.

Kane pushed up to his feet slowly hoping to avoid provoking a premature attack from this beast. He would have to start naming these things so he could share what was in the desert with people when he got back. But if everything else was like this, he seriously doubted his ability to return alive. He had to make it through this first to even worry about survival later.

He had hardly gotten to his feet when the creature shifted to the balls of it 'feet' and leapt for him once again. Kane jumped to the side, away from the cliff-face, trying to keep on his feet this time. That was his mistake. The creature's claws reached out at his chest and raked across opening a vicious wound. Had he just dove he would have dodged this attack.

He screamed out in pain. Tears stung at his eyes. He

wanted so badly for his father to be here so he could show this creature who was boss, but, more than anything, Kane was sorry that he would be breaking his promise to Aerika. It didn't seem he would make it back. He wouldn't even survive this first night. The creature turned to attack again. Kane resolved himself to death.

The creature shifted its weight again and launched towards Kane. Moving purely on instinct, Kane threw his arm across himself to block the coming attack but instead of just blocking, a blade formed only of wind cut across the creature. The wind was so sharp it cut the creature asunder sending bits flying all over.

When Kane opened his eyes, the creature was gone and a large gash had been cut into the cliff-face. One just large enough for Kane to crawl into and go to sleep. Though he wasn't sure just how much sleep he would get after that. He hesitated to think of what else might be out there stalking him in the night as this had. It then dawned on him. He would call it a Stalker. He only hoped he would live to share this with others.

Aerika sat up with a start. She couldn't feel her brother anymore but she somehow knew he was hurt. She couldn't explain why she knew she just did. Tears came fresh to her eyes. Her brother was hurt, maybe worse, because of her. She feared that Kane wouldn't be able to keep his promise.

"FATHER!" she screamed through her sobs, "FATHER!"

Sinal ran into the room. "Aerika?! Are you alright?!" He had been woken by her screaming so he was obviously out-of-sorts.

She looked at him, pleading silently for him to fix all of this. Though she knew deep down that he couldn't. Sinal sat down next to his daughter and gathered her up into his arms. He let go of his initial shock and put his strength back on his face. She pressed her head against his chest and just cried. They all shared in the pain but Sinal thought maybe Aerika hurt worse than everyone else.

"He's been hurt." she managed through her choked sobs. Sinal didn't understand how she could possibly know that. He was so far away.

"How do you …" He cut himself off. He thought better of asking the question. "I'm sure he's perfectly fine. He's a strong boy. He's brave and he loves you. He'll come home in one piece when all this is over. You just wait."

Aerika looked up into her father's eyes. She knew he didn't believe a word he had said but it was the thought that mattered to her at the moment. Aerika and Sinal sat in silence for a moment before the soft whimpers of Liana echoed into the room through the rest of the house. They all felt the loss of Kane. They all felt like they were missing a piece of themselves.

Kane stirred. A breeze blew through the gash he had created the night before when he had done away with the Stalker. The sun glared in at him. It was very bright, almost like the sun was closer here than it was where he lived outside of Mi'Tiya.

He felt a grumble within his gut. He was hungry. He would have to find something to eat or he would starve to death. He looked around for any sign of anything he could eat. He thought for a moment and decided he would try something new. He concentrated for a few moments trying to draw on the energy around him.

He tried to bring the wind in to lift him up to the top of the cliff so he could see around the area. Maybe he could spot some food from up there. He called on the wind. Nothing happened. He tried again but again … nothing happened.

He thought again and came up with a new plan. He envisioned wind gathering around him. The element wrapping itself around him where he stood. He felt a sudden gust of wind and then it became constant. It was working. He envisioned the wind lifting him and it did. And up he went, ascending the cliff-face and seeing just how much damage he had done. The two-hundred foot tall cliff-face was almost cut all the way up by the force of wind he had used the night before. No wonder he hadn't seen any remains from the Stalker.

Once settled atop the cliff, Kane turned and looked out over his new home. He would be spending a great deal of time here. He had to learn the surroundings. It seemed this wasn't a cliff but one of many rocky rises in the area. There seemed to be an area very nearby that held many rocky protrusions less grand than this one but still substantial. But between here and there was a large open expanse of sand. It would take a few hours to walk the whole way. Though he saw something between him and that field of stone. It looked like it might be a watering hole. Maybe he would be alright.

Food was close-by and he now knew how he could create a shelter for himself. He glided back down from the top of the cliff on the wings of the wind and started out on his trek to the watering hole he had spotted.

The wounds on his chest ached horribly. He would have to heal them once he had some strength. He would need some sustenance first. Kane pulled himself up to the top of what seemed a particularly tall dune, though it didn't look any higher than the rest when he looked around. A small pond resided below him. It seemed rather oddly placed in the middle of the desert. But he wanted water so badly he put the thought from his mind.

It was peculiar. There seemed very little greenery around this body of water, no matter how small it was. There were only a few small bushes with tiny red berries growing on them. At least he had some food. That might help a little bit.

The water in the pond was very inviting. The sun glinted off of it and even shimmered a bit on the floor of the pond itself. He wanted very much to just dive in but he thought better of that. He would need clean water to drink and that would surely dirty it.

Kane made his way down the dune to the first of the bushes. He pulled some of the berries free and popped them into his mouth. They were quite bitter but he was still alive so he grabbed more, folded them in a leaf and shoved them into a pocket. He started to the water but something seemed wrong as he approached; like the water level was higher than the ground itself.

He stopped mid-stride. The ground trembled just the slightest little bit. Kane took a step back. When his foot hit the ground it made its move. The pond, water and all, rose up out of the ground. As the creature lifted itself up out of the sand, Kane realized what was going on. This creature was just waiting for something to come along for a drink to strike.

The beasts flesh was the same color and almost consistency of the sand that inhabited the desert. The saliva that Kane had thought water began to spill out of the "pond." The creature's neck was a meaty extension of the pond's mouth.

When the saliva had emptied completely from the creature's mouth, Kane saw the razor-sharp teeth beneath. The saliva showed an illusion of what he had wanted to see. A pond full of cool, clear water. The teeth seemed to be vibrating in anticipation of the meal it surely thought it was going to get.

The creature snaked its way further and further out of the hole, making its way towards Kane. It's stiff, awkward movements told him it hadn't moved in quite some time.

As it drew closer, Kane realized he would have to act.

So he darted to the side and made his way quickly away from the hole. Kane didn't look back. He was sure the creature was following him but he didn't hear it moving through the sand after him.

After running for a short while he looked back and noticed it was not in fact chasing him. It had returned to its hole and retaken the illusion it had before. It would lurk there until it found more prey. That's what Kane decided to call it; A Lurker. He had dodged death yet again and he found himself oddly revitalized by the sudden action so he took to focusing on mending his wounds.

An Enforcer stood silently at his post, observing as the Atrethian High Council conducted their business. He was there to protect them and to assist them with anything they might need.

He was loyal to the codes to which he was sworn. Above all else, his order held the livelihood and care of the Atrethian people. The High Council was on the list as well, but the people were much more important. And preserving peace was part of that. Therefore, his job was also to watch the council and ensure that they were doing what they were supposed to do which was also to serve the Atrethian people.

He felt a pang of guilt deep within his heart. He had watched as a boy that he knew to be innocent had been sent into exile. He said nothing and did nothing to stop it. He even allowed himself to be used as part of the ritual to send him there.

He remembered the first day he had seen the boy. It was in the classroom just over seven years back. The class was preparing for their tests. The majority of the class had already gone to be tested and five students still remain.

That's when he had been taken. That Enforcer which was now his superior had come in and taken him. Before he had left the room he had made eye contact with the boy, Kane. After years and years of training in their special complex he emerged. They had warned him he would be an adult but the kids he may have once called friends would still be children but nothing prepared him for that.

Nothing had prepared him for having to send Kane into exile. He made a promise to himself. To ease his guilty conscience, he, Raven Mataius, vowed that, if Kane were to survive his exile, he would be there on the day he returned. And he would ensure that never again would an innocent be sent into exile on his watch.

Kane had healed his chest though scars remained in place there. A testament to the trials he was going through. He had tried to heal them but the wounds seemed unwilling to heal completely. The dark energies of the desert prevented anything further.

He sat silently next to the stream he had found in the rocky area he had seen before. This seemed a good place to relax for now. At least for the moment while he rested and regained his strength. He would need to cross back to his new home and dig it out to make it more defensible after he was rested. For the moment, he just sat and ate his berries.

He sat for what seemed like minutes. Time always felt short when you want it to last longer. He rose to his feet knowing he needed to prepare his new home. He started back the way he had come.

He crossed out of the rocks and started up the first dune, but he wasn't alone. He heard what sounded like metal banging against stone in quick succession. Kane turned to see what it was. The sound grew louder before a creature the likes of which Kane could never imagine in his wildest nightmares emerged from the rocks.

Its body appeared to be a malnourished person. The ribcage pulling at the flesh almost to the point of transparency. Sticking up out of the torso wasn't a head but a flat surface that looked as if it were made for smashing things to dust. No mouth or eyes. Nothing that would be used to ingest for sustaining life.

The creature's arms were flesh and bone like his torso except that the hands were scythes formed of bone. Extending out behind the creature as it charged at him. Its legs extended down but instead of a shin and feet it had twin blades that dug into the dirt and cut back out as it ran. This creature was obviously created for one purpose; to kill.

Before Kane could even think to focus his energy the creature was in the air with one of its scythes raised ready to cut him down where he stood. Without missing a beat, Kane leapt back barely dodging the first strike. His survival instinct had taken over once again. He felt like he had just moved like he had seen his father do on the few occasions he had gotten the opportunity to watch him fight.

The creature followed with its other scythe cutting horizontally across at Kane's chest. Kane bent back allowing the scythe to cut through the air just over his face. As it passed he grabbed hold of the beasts arm at the elbow and spun in towards its chest. He jerked hard at the elbow as it went to kick its feet up at him to stop him.

The arm snapped off at the joint. The creature didn't pause. It spun away and swung its remaining scythe down at Kane. With a deft move, Kane sidestepped and severed the remaining arm from the creature using its own blade. He caught the arm before it hit the ground to use as his second weapon and leapt back away.

He still hadn't taken a moment to think. He couldn't. If he did, he would surely be killed. The creature darted forward. Kane mirrored the movement but he flipped through the air the wind carrying him in the movements that came easily to him for reasons beyond him. He rolled over the creature as it tried to cut him with its feet.

Kane brought the scythes to bear as the beast became upright again. He ripped one through cutting the creature off at the hips and the other tearing it off at the neck. The creature made of blades split to the ground in pieces.

Finally, thoughts came to Kane's mind. His instinct had given up control and he was terrified of what he was apparently capable of. He had never been trained to fight. He couldn't think of where he might have learned what he had just done. He tossed the two arms away as if they were disgusting, diseased bits of food. He stared, terrified, at his hands. He had no idea where he had learned these things. His father had never had the chance to teach him.

He may never know. But it would come in handy. Maybe he could train himself to use these instincts. It might help him to get home to Aerika.

AERIKA! He hadn't even thought about how she must be taking all of this. But, he admonished himself for such thoughts. He put her out of his mind and started back towards the cliff he now called home. He would have to focus on himself to survive these next twenty-five years. If he ever wanted to see Aerika again, he couldn't let his mind wander from survival.

10

Sinal fought back tears of his own. He watched now as his daughter cried herself to sleep, as he had every night since Kane's exile. And what's worse, Liana had grown more and more depressed over the days since their family was broken apart. Sinal had been given a leave of absence to take care of matters with his family.

He walked quietly from his daughter's room and sighed as he shut the door. It used to be the room both his children shared. He knew now why Aerika cried herself to sleep every night. She had never slept a single night alone in that room until now. He couldn't imagine how hard it must be for her.

He strode silently to the living room where his wife sat. She hadn't moved all day. He stopped in-front of her and dropped slowly to a knee. "My love," he said, "we should get some sleep. It has been a long week for all of us."

She didn't even blink. She just sat in mute shock. She had been living under this haze for days now and it only seemed to be getting worse. Tears brimmed in Sinal's eyes. It pained him to see her like this.

"Liana ... please come to bed."

Her eyes shifted to look at him but she made no other move. Sinal stood up and pushed Liana to lay down where she was. After he got her settled there he went to get her a blanket. He stepped from his room with a blanket in his hands and laid it over his wife. He leaned down and kissed her forehead.

His family was falling apart before his eyes and, it seemed, there was nothing he could do about it. He just hoped beyond hope that Kane was doing better than they were.

On the other side of Mi'Tiya, Jerek Kis'tohl sat silently on the edge of his bed. He had planned on bringing his existence to an end, but he felt he still had something to do. He could not, however, imagine what it might be.

He still hadn't figured out which punishment he had issued that would cause the peace they had worked so hard to maintain to end. He couldn't even imagine how any one man could end something like that.

His wife placed a hand on his shoulder. Through the years she had been faithful. A rock outside of the Mythril Hall for him to rely on. She had never once asked him to give up his service to the people, but it obviously pained her to know how it had ended.

"Jerek … you mustn't let this change you. You have always been strong. Whatever happens, you can't let that stop you from continuing to do what you think is right."

He placed his hand atop hers and smiled back at her. He nodded silently and lay down with her. He would think of a way to put this right. If it was the last thing he did, he would fix this. Perhaps he could keep the peace in some way. Perhaps there was a way to sustain what they had worked so hard for.

Doe'n lay out his deep violet robes. He still couldn't believe he was the Grand Magistrate. It was an easier job than he thought though. There never were many decisions for him to make and in all his time on the council he hadn't seen Kis'tohl make many either. They were few and far between.

It seemed to him the job mostly meant maintaining the peace in the Council and being a tie breaker on votes. He folded the robes end over end and laid them inside his wardrobe. His eyes caught on a black cloth belt before he closed the door. He leaned down to pick up the belt.

Sinal had given it to him as a gift when he had joined the council. He and Sinal had gone through training together at the Academy. They had been the closest of friends almost their whole lives. When Doe'n had joined the council, it marked their parting. They wouldn't see each other for a very long time. Sinal gave him the belt as a reminder of their friendship. It was the belt Doe'n wore when he fought.

He had a sudden pang of guilt at what had happened. What he had been forced to do to Kane and to the rest of the family. He somehow knew that the Malacor family was suffering for what had happened. He only wished that he had been able to stop it all from happening in the first place. But it had all begun a long time ago.

Far outside of Mi'Tiya on the opposite end of the continent, the one that many thought of was staking his claim. Kane stared at his makeshift home. The one he had inadvertently made for himself that first night in the desert. He then thought that maybe it would be a good idea to make it bigger and more comfortable. So he focused on the energy around him. He called in the wind to aid him.

He thrust his hands forward, palms open parallel to one another guiding the wind in what he wanted it to do. The wind did as it was told, cutting deep into the cliff. Kane rotated one hand up and one down to make another cut. He thrust his hands forward again guiding the wind. And again the cuts were made.

He extended his hands out towards the rock he had just cut as if he was taking hold of it from behind. He gritted his teeth and strained his muscles for a moment before jerking his hands in towards his chest in a pulling motion. The rock he had just cut from the cliff flew from the newly created cave.

Kane set the rock to the side and stepped into his new

home. He would be much safer with this deeper home. Hopefully this would make life easier for him in this place of so much death.

The days came and went. Time past and life for Kane came to a state of normalcy. Kane sat in silent meditation. He hovered only a few inches over the top of a dune. He had to continue to grow. He had to continue to practice and discover his power otherwise he would never be able to survive. He wasn't sure exactly how he would do that without a trainer to show him the way but he would have to figure it out somehow. That much he knew.

Later he would go to find a source of food. There had to be something. Otherwise he would have to continue to kill and eat these creatures every day for the rest of his time here. But for now, he had to try to grow further.

He focused inward drawing himself into his sanctuary. The walls of his and Aerika's rooms came into being. He could scarcely remember what they looked like. If it had been that long, he didn't know. Time seemed to almost stand still in the desert. He wasn't even sure just how long he had been in exile. He knew it was more than a couple of months but it couldn't have been a year yet.

He sighed and pushed the thought from his mind. He focused on drawing the room together but it just didn't work the way it had before. The color seemed wrong. It didn't bring him the same peace that it had brought before.

He sighed in frustration. He cleared the room as it was from his mind and tried again to rebuild it. But it just didn't seem to work again. No matter how many times he tried he just couldn't rebuild the sanctuary in the same way as it used to feel.

Just then the words of Councilman Doe'n came to his mind. "Think of a place where you are most comfortable. Where you feel the safest." He remembered when he had first heard these words. When he had first felt that solace of his sanctuary.

He focused again. Thinking of the place he now felt safest. Grays and browns came together around him. The natural shadows created by the rocks crawled across the stone floor. The smell of the stone crept into his nostrils. The comfortable solitude fell around him. He recognized where his sanctuary was. It was his new home. His cave in the rock face amongst the dead lands of the Terrei Desert.

The rock walls of the cave came together forming his sanctuary. He stepped over to where the entrance should be, but there was a rock wall there. He thought for a moment of how to open it. He pushed against it, but it wouldn't give.

Then, the thought came to his mind. He called upon the winds to cut a door into the wall. Just then the walls exploded around him allowing the world in. He had found his new sanctuary and he had found his way out.

He opened his eyes to see the world around him. But it was not as it was before. The world was black as death. He saw the physical sand and the unclean energies that kept the creatures alive, if you could even call it that.

They flowed together as one. The physical world and The Flow inhabited the same space at the same time. He had felt it before but seeing it was a completely different sensation. He blinked and it remained. He planted his feet and stood up. The world remained as it was.

He had never seen it come together in such a way. He had always seen them both separately, but he knew for the first time, that everything truly did act as one. He looked at himself. The black energies of the desert were mixing with him and his own were mixing with it.

He walked silently looking around as if he were observing the world for the very first time. He watched as his energy seemed to cleanse the desert with each step but at the same time the desert seemed to corrupt more of his energy with each step. It was a terrifying and interesting process. The coexistence was an amazing and beautiful fight for survival.

He spotted an oddity. A white spot amidst all the black off in the distance. Maybe this was food. Maybe he had found a source of life in the desert. He would have to find out.

Aerika sat silently in her dark room. HER room. That thought still weighed on her. She stilled cried herself to sleep every night and then would awaken, every night, from nightmares of what she could only assume were the creatures that Kane must be facing in the desert. Her heart sunk. This was all her fault.

'NO!' she admonished herself. He had made the choice to protect her! And she had a choice to make now! She would ensure that nothing like this every happened again! She would work her way up to become the first female Grand Magistrate and there would never be a punishment like this again. That was her goal. She would grow and move forward for that singular purpose. She would be the one to welcome Kane back when his exile was over. She would be the one to make the choice so that it never happened to another child … to another family. And suddenly, in that moment of clarity, she felt him again. Her brother, so far away in exile, was with her once more.

Sinal lay silent in his bed. His wife had finally made her way back into the bedroom but her mood hadn't improved. And it seemed her depression was giving way to an illness of some kind. He worried for his beloved wife. He wanted nothing more than to go to the desert to bring their son back for her. To bring the light of hope back into her life of darkness. He couldn't imagine how it must feel for her. To have lost part of herself in such a way.

And he felt responsible. If only he had been there … if only he had believed his son … if only …

The Twelve sat silently in a circle. Their entire

bodies shrouded beneath the black robes that marked their status. Twelve prophets … each one with a different color and depth to their eyes yet all seeming to mix and flow together at the same time.

The flames upon the torches flickered lighting the expansive Vi'jal Rotunda dimly. The very center of the room blackened from the mixture of the shadows of each prophet coming together. This blackness at the center was symbolic of the unknown that lay before in the future.

The flames upon the torches flickered wildly for a moment before sizzling to nothingness. The center of the room filled with an eerie light. The energy of the world came together only so often for an event such as this. The prophet's eyes had all gone dark. Such was the way of viewing a prophecy.

Atrethia appeared in the light in the center of the room. The world itself in all its glory and splendor. The flow of energy shown deep within and around it. For a moment it hovered, as if flaunting its beauty for all to see.

After that moment, a creeping blackness began to wash across the energies of the world. It corrupted everything as it went … all of the people, every animal and even the planet itself. The corruption spread from a single source across the entire planet. Once the blackness had engulfed the world … Atrethia, its former glory gone, shattered into dust.

The image disappeared and the flames returned to the torches upon the walls. The light returned to the eyes of the prophets. They all knew what this was and what this meant. The unknown that lay before them was now known. The end of their world had been seen.

//

Kane made his way along the barren landscape of the desert with only the hope that this glimmer was what he wanted it to be. He crested the top of the last dune before reaching the one sign of life besides himself in this desolate place.

He was struck in awe of what he saw. An oasis amongst all this death. There was water and fruit baring trees and bushes and even vegetables. He wanted to take everything back with him but he knew if he did it would all die and he would be left with nothing. So he approached slowly, trying to calculate exactly what he could take to survive and only what he needed.

He was still in awe. The myriad of colors that were held within this single place stood out in stark contrast to the dull tan around it all. But even more beautiful than the contrast of what he was seeing here was the brilliant life hiding and surviving amongst all this death.

The fact that this place, this amazing and glorious, source of life could survive in spite of its surroundings gave Kane hope that he could make it. He knew now, beyond a shadow of a doubt, that he could make it through this. He would not lose hope. Not anymore.

Kane gathered only a few days' worth. Anymore would spoil before he would get to it. He stuffed it all into a large leaf from one of the trees and folded it over into a pouch. He then used a vine to tie the pouch around his waist.

He took a drink of water from the small pond before

beginning his trek back home. He thought that maybe things might not be so bleak.

Aerika went back to her training with more determination and drive than ever. She was renewed. She had that purpose to push her through any hardship that may come upon her. Her instructor was very impressed, even if somewhat unsettled by how powerful she was becoming so quickly. She could control her energies without so much as the slightest hint of meditation or concentration.

None that witnessed Aerika at work had ever seen the like. The instructor had called her father to witness her control. He had pleaded with the headmaster to allow Liana to see this. He hoped maybe their daughter's strength would bring her out of this depression. Give her hope. It had been allowed. Liana sat silently watching and yet seemed she was not seeing. Her blank stare did not change at all.

Liana's mind worked over just how hard her life had become. When her son was sent into exile, she had been so wracked with grief that it had made her physically ill. It became impossible for her to find joy even in things that had always made her happy, like seeing her husband and watching her daughter play. In this moment, seeing her daughter as strong as she was, she realized that even she didn't need her.

Aerika used her energy with such grace, as if she were dancing with the elements themselves. She was doing nothing more than exerting her control. She had no purpose for what she did. She just did it because she could. Exerted her control of the energies around her because she could. And it was beautiful.

Sinal watched in wonder for a few moments before dragging his gaze upon his wife. His hopes seemed dashed. Her blank expression had not changed. He dropped his eyes to the floor. Then, the softest sound made its way to Sinal's ears. He looked back up at Liana. "Liana …? Did you say something?"

A single tear crept from beneath Liana's eye and crawled down her cheek. "It's … so beautiful." Her voice was so soft Sinal almost didn't hear it. This brought tears to Sinal's eyes. She had spoken. For the first time since Kane was sent away, she had spoken.

"Yes, Liana. Our daughter has grown and gotten stronger. We can too. We can get past this … together."

Liana drew her gaze slowly from Aerika to Sinal. She parted her lips just the smallest amount to draw in a shaky breath. "Sinal … I love you. You and Aerika both. I'm so sorry." Sinal was confused.

Then, her eyes darkened without warning. The baby blue color drained into blackness before her eyelids closed. Tears came anew to Sinal's eyes. He dropped down beside Liana and pulled her head against his chest. "No, Liana! No! Please don't leave me! Don't leave us!"

Aerika stopped what she was doing when her father started screaming. She hadn't even known that he was there, let alone that her mother had been there. She saw what was happening now. "Father?"

Sinal kissed the top of Liana's head before resting his cheek against it. "I'm so sorry, Liana. I'm sorry I couldn't save our family. Aerika … your mother … she ..." He couldn't seem to find the words. He laid Liana back and opened his arms for Aerika. Tears streaming down her face, she ran into the arms of her father and cried into his shoulder.

Kane had placed the food within his home and was now out among the dunes. Founts of sand swirled around him blocking him from view and blocking his view of the world around him. Something felt wrong to him in that instant. It was almost as though something were near him. He released his power allowing the sand to fall back to where it belonged.

Only a few feet from him, standing over two men tall, was the most massive creature he had ever seen. Hair covered the behemoth from head to toe. The maw upon its face held hundreds of razor sharp fangs. Its red eyes seemed to stare into Kane's very core.

A deep growl groaned out from within the brute. It flexed its four massive arms and clenched its claws into balled fists. The intent was clear at that point. Kane dove to the side as the first fist came down where he once stood and the next followed where he was now. Kane moved again in the same direction to use his momentum to avoid being pounded into dust.

Kane created a stream of water beneath his own feet and cooled it into a sheet of ice to slide away from the barrage of fists slamming down where he stood. But this creature was intelligent. The fists stopped falling and instead arced around to catch him in his midsection.

He ducked the first and jumped hard using the wind to carry him over the behemoths head as the second swung low at him. Kane took off in a dead sprint for the rocky fields near his home. He would try to lose the creature there and hide for a while before returning home. The creature, again proving its capacity to learn, followed with surprising haste.

He made his way into the fields bolting between boulders. Darting this way and that. As he turned yet another corner, he found himself in a dead end. He turned to go back, but it was already too late. The behemoth was there and stalking slowly towards him. Kane looked into its eyes as it approached. It bared its teeth at him before opening its mouth and releasing a deep guttural roar from deep within its foul-smelling throat.

It pushed in close. The behemoth opened its mouth baring its fangs drawing closer and closer to Kane. He pressed his body against the stones behind him. This was it. It seemed his journey would end here. One single thought came to his mind … 'I'm sorry Aerika.'

Raven sat silently upon his bunk. He drew the rag slowly across his chest plate again. His long, black hair resting on his bare shoulders. There were few things in which he took pride. One of them was what this armor stood for. What he stood for. The defense of the people above all else.

He made another pass with the rag. He polished his armor every night. He kept his appearance professional at all times. He smirked just the slightest bit at his own clear reflection in the armor. This was just one of the many pieces that made up the armor he wore daily.

"You know you really should find something else to do. You're going to polish a hole right into that armor of yours." It was a female voice and one that he knew well.

"Nih'al … you should know me better than that." he said as he put his chest plate down. He got to his feet and wrapped his arms around her waist. She laughed and pressed her lips against his. Her deep brown locks mixed with his in their embrace. Enforcer Nih'al Trena had grown close with Raven since being stationed in the same barracks as him.

They pushed away reluctantly and stared into each other's eyes. Her dark red eyes seemed to peer deep into the gold of his. She sighed before speaking, "As much as I want to stay like this, we've been summoned." She pushed away from him and smiled her sly smile. "I'll go change into my armor and meet you back here."

"Aw … can't I come?" he said, smirking at her.

"No," she replied, "You have to get ready too."

She grinned at him as she slid out of his chambers. He watched her athletic form with rapt attention as she glided out of view. It took him a few moments to regain his composure. He shook the sense back into his head and got to the task of donning his armor. He wondered to himself what he could have possibly been summoned for. It wasn't long before he found out the answer to that question.

Grand Magistrate Doe'n stood with two Enforcers flanking him. Sinal and Aerika stood nearby. Tears were streaming down Aerika's face and Sinal was barely maintaining his facade of strength. The memorial for Liana hadn't even started yet. They would hold a short ceremony to bid her farewell and then they would hold a party in her honor. Such were their customs. Though Doe'n imagined that Sinal and Aerika would rather have just been left to their grief.

The healers all said that Liana had just given up hope and went. The loss of her son must have been too great for her. Doe'n felt responsible for this. It was his fault that Kane was where he was. He had made that decision even though he really had no choice in the matter.

Sinal had made eye contact once when Doe'n had entered the room but hadn't even looked in his direction since. Doe'n knew that Sinal blamed him too. He didn't blame him for that either. He would stay for the memorial and then leave. After all, he had been friends with them for most of their lives. He owed them at least that much.

He couldn't even begin to imagine the pain that Sinal must be feeling because of all of this. It seemed a bit too much to put on one family. But from what he had been told, Aerika was doing well enough.

Tieg and Magus were here as well. They didn't know Liana but they knew Aerika and they knew that it couldn't be easy to deal with this on top of being without Kane. They both thought it might do her good to have some friends there. Or at least people that thought of her as a friend. Even Magus missed Kane. At least he missed the competition with Kane. They would go speak with her once the party had started. They thought it better to hide in the back until then.

Raven couldn't take his eyes from Aerika. He hadn't noticed Magus and Tieg in the back but Aerika he couldn't miss. This was horrible. He hadn't known that it was her mother's memorial they were going to. He could hardly believe the amount of misfortune that had befallen this family. He thought of one thing he could do for her. Maybe it would make it all a little easier.

Raven looked to the Grand Magistrate. "Grand Magistrate? May I go speak with Aerika? I ..." he stumbled a bit on the question. It was difficult for him to handle even with all his training. "I was there when her brother was exiled and would like to share his thoughts with her."

Doe'n had known that Raven was there. He had thought it appropriate to bring at least him along to be there for this. Though he had not foreseen this. He thought it over for a moment and simply nodded.

Raven stepped away and approached Sinal and Aerika rather sheepishly for an Enforcer. He dropped to a knee and locked eyes with Aerika. He could somehow feel her eyes peering through the helmet he wore into his eyes.

"Aerika," he paused for a moment to try to find the words. Sinal just stood silent. He was amazed that any Enforcer could sound as compassionate as this one did at that moment.

Raven continued, "I was there when your brother was exiled. You never left his thoughts. Not even for a moment. You gave him the strength to be brave through the whole thing. I just wanted to tell you that."

Aerika smiled a little. She already knew all of that, but to hear it confirmed by someone else was comforting. She left her father's side and pressed herself against the armor of the Enforcer. She wrapped her arms around Raven's neck. He placed a hand upon her back and smiled beneath his helm.

Sinal smiled softly at this scene. He had seen many

Enforcers in his time, but never one that had ever shown compassion in such a public way before. This one was special indeed.

Aerika stepped back from Raven, the smile still on her face. "Thank you, Raven."

Raven was struck dumb. "How …"

"I felt it. Ever since you came in the room." She cut him off with her explanation. "I knew it was you at the door the night he was exiled just like I knew it was you tonight."

Raven shook his head. He probably shouldn't be shocked by this but he was. Everyone else in the room was shocked as well. No one had ever been able to tell who an Enforcer was beneath the armor before. At least none but other Enforcers.

Aerika went back to her father's side. She wasn't crying anymore. Raven returned to his post flanking the Grand Magistrate. Nih'al hadn't taken her eyes off of Raven since he made the request to speak with Aerika. The exile had happened before she had met him and he never told her about it. She had no idea that he was connected to anything like that.

12

The rancid breath of the behemoth slithered into Kane's nose. He couldn't believe it was going to end like this. Rotting in the stomach of this foul creature. And just as he had given up hope of getting out of this, something caught Kane's attention. A scratching noise. It sounded almost like rock against rock but there was something off about it. Though he couldn't quite place it behind the growling of the behemoth.

It rose up the slightest bit as it prepared to finish Kane. Then, it suddenly jerked up began flailing around trying to get at something on its back. Kane wasn't about to waste this chance. He ran straight at the behemoth and dropped to his back just before running into it. He slid between the beasts legs only to catch a glimpse of the stalkers attacking the behemoth.

Several more stalkers had joined in and were all clawing and biting at the behemoth but they didn't seem to be doing any damage. Kane didn't wait to see how it turned out. He ran as hard and as fast as he could back out of the rock fields and turned for his home. He would hide out for a while. Hopefully the behemoth would move on to another part of the desert.

Kane's legs ached and his lungs burned from the exhaustion of that escape. He crossed the final dune to his cave. He pushed his legs as hard as he could to finish that last small distance to his home. He would be there soon. As he crossed the threshold his left foot caught the heel of his right. He fell forward in skidded to a halt.

"Ow …" Kane said it aloud although he knew that no one would hear it. He pushed himself up from the floor of his cave. He had made it. His whole body ached with the physical exertion but he had made it. That's when he realized that he would need more than The Flow to survive in this place. He would need to get stronger.

Aerika stood in the center of a large chamber within the Academy. This room was designed specifically for training in control. The walls were bare as were the floor and ceiling. The door was the only part of the room that stood apart.

Aerika took a deep breath and concentrated for just a moment before white smoke began to rise from her eyes. Her power began to flow out from her. Founts of water and flame began to dance around her. Aerika's robes danced as wind flowed around her. The dust and stray stone in the room came together and gathered around her floating completely under her control. All of the elements came together to work for her simply at her call.

Her determination was guiding her control of the elements. She would continue to grow stronger. She would be better than everyone else so none could contend with her for the position of Grand Magistrate. She would be there when Kane returned from his exile.

The house was silent. It was the first time that Sinal had ever been in the house alone. He had resigned from the Academy. He didn't see a point at doing anything anymore. His wife was gone. His son was in exile. And his daughter was only home for a few weeks at a time. He didn't need to provide very much of anything anymore.

The house felt so cold and empty without Liana and the kids. Things just weren't the same. He imagined they never would be again. Sinal didn't know what to do with himself. He was so lost without Liana. They had been together for hundreds of years. He just didn't know what to do.

Kane extended his arms pushing himself up from ground. They struggled with the exertion. He had lost track of how long he'd been at this, but he had to continue. He had to get stronger. He lowered himself once again. It burned but it felt good. It was strange to him, though none of that mattered.

He pushed again trying to get back up but he didn't have enough strength. His arms shook with the effort. He gritted his teeth and pushed with all his might. He even opened his mouth to growl a little with the effort. His left arm caved first. He fell flat onto his chest.

He took in a deep breath and rolled over onto his back. He just let his arms rest at his sides. He would need to keep at it. He was just too tired at the moment to keep going. At least he had gotten started. Life would only get easier from here as he got stronger. Maybe one day he could fight the behemoth. Or maybe he just won't ever need to. What he did know, he would need to get much stronger before that day came.

Kis'tohl had figured it out. He knew which decision he had made that had made the end of their peace come. He knew who the warrior was. He would be prepared. He could still do something to keep the peace that they worked so hard to maintain intact. He would have this warrior killed before he could break the peace.

He just couldn't do it himself. He would never be able to bring himself to harm another with his own hands or even use The Flow against another. But he knew of others that could. He would just see to it that they would be in the right place at the right time.

He stepped out onto Molara's Crossing in Mi'Tiya and scanned around for a moment to see if anyone noticed him. They didn't. People were milling about taking care of what business they had in the crossing and moving on. Some

116

children were running and playing in the crossing. One child was sitting by himself. Kis'tohl had found another candidate. He had already set three on this path. He would need to set more.

Magus watched as Tieg and his friends ran around. He thought to himself how silly they all looked, running and laughing and pretending. It all seemed so juvenile and pathetic to him. A small smile crept across his lips before fading as quickly as it came. A man in very plain clothing approached. He had a white shirt and brown slacks. His whole outfit was plain but it seemed out of place on him; like he was above wearing such things. Magus didn't recognize him.

"Hello little boy," Kis'tohl spoke in a friendly manner as to not scare the child.

"Who are you?" Magus practically snorted the words.

"Who I am is not important. The better question here is what do I want. And what I want is to ask you a question."

"Fine. Ask it and leave."

Kis'tohl thought this boy would do nicely. He fit exactly what he needed. "What would you say if I told you that you could be a hero?"

"I'd say you were an old cook."

"Well you can. And I'll tell you how if you'll listen. And you can choose to believe me or not."

Magus got too his feet and looked into Kis'tohl's eyes. He glared at Kis'tohl for a moment and shifted his weight. "I'm listening."

"There is a man. A man that wants to end the peace that we work hard for. But you can stop this man before he does it."

"And how am I supposed to do that? I'm only a boy."

"And so is he … for the moment. You are the same

117

age, if I'm not mistaken."

"Fine so where do I find him? I'll put a stop to it today."

"He's not here right now. But he will be. Many years from now he will return to this city. I need you to simply make sure he leaves Mi'Tiya when he comes back and then make sure he stays away. And if he even looks like he might be coming back ... you must stop him. By any means necessary."

"And I'll be a hero?" Magus was intrigued. This man apparently knew quite a bit of what would happen in the future.

"Yes. You will be the man that saved our peaceful society."

Magus liked the sound of that. That self-absorbed smile crawled across his lips again. He would be a hero. People would cheer his name. He would be revered and loved by all. They might even make him Grand Magistrate for it. Grand Magistrate Magus. He really liked the sound of that.

"Alright. If I find this man when you say I will. I'll do it. No problem."

"Good ... Very good." Kis'tohl turned around and started away.

"Who are you that you know all of this?" Magus' words stopped Kis'tohl in his tracks.

"Just ... a concerned citizen is all. One that knows you are the only person that can stop this man."

Kis'tohl disappeared into a dark alley leaving Magus to ponder what he had just been told. Magus sat back down but didn't lose that smile. He was imagining himself wearing the Grand Magistrate's robes. He was very pleased with himself suddenly.

Doe'n had not left the Chamber of Visions since he and the other Council Members had been told of the end of their world. He wanted to find out if there was a way to stop it. Or maybe find out what is going to cause it so he can figure out a way to prevent it. The door to the Prophet's Hovel clicked and creaked. One of the black hooded prophets made his way towards Doe'n.

"Grand Magistrate … It is unusual for one of your station to come to hear a prophecy."

"I was already here. Tell me what it is that you saw, prophet."

The glow from beneath the prophet's hood shifted its hue. The color began to mix as though his eyes were changing color. The glow now held a myriad of colors ranging from yellow and red to blue and green. Every color eye that Doe'n had seen mixed with the color of this man's eyes. When the prophet spoke his words sounded as though a dozen people were speaking all at once. Doe'n had seen this all many times before so none of it surprised him.

"The Warriors path is set. He will meet The Betrayer on the crossroads as set by another. The Warrior will become more with this crossing. The man formerly of station and now a shadow of his former self has set this path. War will rage because of him."

The many voices fell quiet. The glow from beneath his hood returned to its blood red shade.

"Who is this 'man formerly of station'? The man that caused all of this?" Doe'n would stop this. He didn't know how but he would stop it.

"You know this man. We recognize his face. He is the former Grand Magistrate … Jerek Kis'tohl."

The prophet's words burned in Doe'n's ears. He felt a deep pang of regret and then it was replaced with anger. Jerek had betrayed them all. He would pay for his transgressions this time. Doe'n wouldn't let him by. He had a lot to do to make this right. He left the Vi'jal Temple with haste and headed straight for the Mythril Hall. The Council must be convened.

13

Nih'al stepped out into the night air. It was a little cold but she wouldn't be outside long. She looked down the empty streets. Fog was settling in and it seemed particularly thick. Although that could just be the darkness as well.

It felt very lonely at night. These streets would be filled with people in just a few hours, but Enforcers weren't to be seen out of their armor so she had to hurry back to the barracks before anyone woke. It had become more difficult for her and Raven to be together since he had been moved into his new home. They made it work though.

She stepped off. Her swift movements cut through the fog. She had plenty of time, but she wouldn't take any chances. Risks got people hurt or worse. Nih'al knew that better than most. She would hurry even if she had more than enough time. It was just how she was taught while growing up. Move with a purpose and never against it.

Nih'al passed empty street after empty street. She was only two more streets over from the barracks. She had made even better time than she had hoped. Just one more turn and … Nih'al stopped dead in her tracks. She hadn't expected this.

Kane lifted himself from the ground. He grunted with the effort but he was getting stronger. He was getting faster too. He was hungry though and that didn't help with his strength. He grew tired too quickly. He needed to get more food, but he feared he wouldn't survive an encounter with the Behemoth again. Without sustenance though, he would not get any stronger and would surely die later. He had to take the chance.

Kane climbed to his feet and made his way to the cave entrance. He pressed himself tightly against the wall and peeked his head out slowly scanning every inch for anything that moved. There was nothing ... or at least nothing in the open. But there was only one way he would know for sure. He had to hunt down and confront the Behemoth.

He slunk out from the cave moving quickly to the rocks. He would need to get the jump on the creature to have a shot at beating it, but he knew he needed to try. Something seemed off to him. It felt like the world beneath his feet was more alive and less alive at the same exact time. He would have to meditate on this feeling later. For now he had to focus. One problem at a time.

He pushed himself forward through the rocky field. There was no movement at all. No skittering from the Stalkers. No raging beast he hadn't encountered yet making a racket because it couldn't find the thing making noise. No nothing. He moved ever forward despite his fear of what this might mean. He had a purpose and he would see it fulfilled this day.

He stopped a moment. Had he heard that or was it a figment of his imagination. His mind playing tricks on him because of the unusual quiet in the fields. He stood completely still, listening for the familiar skittering of a Stalker or the clicking of metal on stone of a Marauder. He heard a heavy grunt. It was exactly what he had hoped. The Behemoth was close. He would get the drop on it.

He crouched low and leaped up hard using the wind to carry him to the top of the rocks and soften his landing upon them so as to avoid making a sound. He scanned around for it and finally saw the beast. At least the top of the beast. It was on the other side of a row of boulders. Kane slid deftly from rock to rock, ensuring his movements didn't betray his location.

He was resolute in his purpose. He crouched upon the rock just behind the Behemoth. It hadn't noticed him yet. It was standing still. Breathing heavy breaths as it surveyed several freshly smashed … somethings. Kane wasn't entirely sure what they used to be but they weren't much anymore. If nothing else the Behemoth's strength was a thing of beauty.

Kane was ready. He had prepared himself for this moment. His legs flexed as he pushed off of the rock to jump at the beast. Just as Kane was about to leave the rocks surface, the Behemoth turned as fast as it was strong and swung it's heavy arms at Kane. It had been waiting for him.

A man was standing in the road before Nih'al. He looked as if he had been waiting for someone but how could that be at this time of night. That's when she felt the two men stepping up behind her.

The man before her smiled. It felt very sinister to Nih'al. This man wanted to hurt her that much was clear to her. "Well, well, well. What have we here? What's a pretty little thing like you doing out at such a late hour without an escort? Someone might try to hurt you."

His voice was just as sinister as that smile of his. He didn't know who she was and that was bad for her and for him. He wouldn't dare try this if he knew she was an Enforcer. His friends were getting closer.

"No one will get hurt if you boys just leave now. This doesn't have to happen." She really didn't want to have to hurt them; it would draw attention to her being out and not in her armor.

"And why would we want anyone hurt?" His voice slithered out from between his lips. She imagined this man could get anything he wanted just by talking to someone. But she wasn't just any someone.

He stepped up closer to her … close enough for her to

put some serious pain into him before his friends had a chance to move. He brought his fingers up to brush the hair out of her face and back behind her ear. "We just want to protect you, beautiful. That's all. I sw-"

He hadn't had a chance to finish his words before she had snapped his arm in two and smashed his nasal bone into his brain. And he was down and out before a cry of agony could escape his lips. She turned to face her two other opponents. They were closing fast, but they weren't fast enough.

Kane was in the air and the Behemoth's fist was flying straight for him. He didn't have time enough to think and no physical contact to anything to move himself. He had to rely on his energy. He called a gust of wind to push him out of the path of the beasts flying fist. It only half worked.

The glancing blow still threw him a good ways and hitting the rock wall and then rock floor didn't help. He recovered quickly though and got to his feet. He couldn't afford to feel the pain right now. He would die if he did that. The Behemoth was on the move heading his way and it wanted blood. Any blood would probably do but it wanted his.

Kane crouched low and leapt up clear over the beasts head as its claws crashed down where he once was. Kane landed behind it and kicked hard at the back of its knee using the wind to help give it a little more force. It worked a little. The beast merely wobbled. He wasn't strong enough. He knew that now. Something was missing.

He stalked his way to his own death. Kane tried to think of an escape but he took too long. The beast swung back and low smacking him hard. The hit sent him flying clear out of the rock fields to the open area near his own home. And Kane's luck had him land on one of the few rocky spots instead of the softer sand.

He hurt everywhere. He had several broken bones. He could tell mostly because of the way his limbs twisted in the wrong directions. He was bleeding from lacerations all over his body. The one smack from that beast had caused more damage to Kane than anything else that had happened to him. He tried to get up … to get away before it was on him again, but he couldn't move his legs. His muscles didn't have the strength or maybe they were just facing the wrong direction. He couldn't tell.

Nih'al stood over the three men. All dead. They had brought this on themselves, but there would be trouble. Three men dead and she was covered in their blood. They would take her word that she had defended herself, of course. But being out without her armor … that would not be excused. It was a law within the Order of the Enforcer's that none be seen by outsiders without their armor.

She surveyed the bodies of the three men. Broken arms. Broken noses. Cracked and broken ribs. Smashed in faces. One of them even had the contents of his head spilling out onto the street. This had been a bad situation made worse by the fact that she was someone they never should have encountered out there. She knew what this would lead to, and it tore her up inside.

The Behemoth came barreling out of the rock fields and leapt as hard as it could to get to Kane. Kane pushed himself back away from the beasts landing spot by force of will alone. The impact was heavy and almost drove the wind from Kane's lungs, but he held it in. It raised its arms quickly, ready to bring them down for the killing blow.

'So this is it?' he thought. He would die here because he thought to test himself instead of just trying to survive for Aerika. Aerika. 'No!' he thought. He would keep trying! For her!

It brought its fists down together. It wanted to crush him. Kane threw his hands out at the beast, more out of instinct than anything else. A gust of wind pushed forth from his palms launching the beast back only a few feet. It landed on the sand and almost lost its footing but it quickly regained its balance.

The momentary lack of balance was all that was needed though. The ground shook and a moment later the sand beneath its feet erupted around the Behemoth. Kane put his arms up to guard his face from the dirt raining down. A fleshy-funnel extended up and up and up into the sky. Kane lost its top in the sun.

The tan exterior of this massive new creature was divided into sections. The funnel began retracting back into the hole it had seemingly grown from. As its top came closer Kane saw it had no eyes. Its mouth was a gaping maw in the center of its face, if you could call it a face, filled with thousands upon thousands of teeth. The Behemoth was nowhere to be seen. It had been torn apart and devoured already.

The creature's stench was unmistakable. Death. It smelled of death. Kane laid his head back as the worm fell out of sight and the hole filled in again. He breathed a painful sigh of relief and then let the pain take him into unconsciousness. Nothing would come for him here. Not with that worm out there. He was safe for the time being. He could sleep.

Raven stood at Nih'al's side. They were both wearing their armor as now there were people milling about, some stopping to view the scene of the three dead men. Raven wanted so badly just to hold Nih'al but they couldn't. Not in public. Another law within their order.

Nih'al was just happy that she wasn't alone anymore. Raven had brought her armor as soon as word got to him what had happened. She was able to get it on before anyone came out into the streets. She had told him she would tell the truth though. That was part of being an Enforcer. Lying was never an option. There was only the truth. It was what they were trained for.

Councilwoman Theana was there to investigate what had happened. Nih'al stood silent waiting for the Councilwoman's approach. Theana spoke silently with several other Enforcers and she commanded them to clean up the mess. They conjured founts of water to wash away the blood, then gathered the bodies and took them away. It was all very quick and clean. The Enforcers were good at everything they did.

The Councilwoman strode with a very deliberate edge over to Nih'al and Raven. They both snapped a salute to the violet eye in the center of their breastplates. Theana looked straight to Nih'al. "Well, it was obviously self-defense so you won't be in trouble for that. What I need to know now is why these men would dare attack an Enforcer."

Nih'al grimaced beneath her helm. This is what was going to get her in trouble. That was the question that would do her in. She grit her teeth and sighed before answering, "They didn't know I was an Enforcer. I wasn't wearing my armor."

Theana took a shocked step back. The law about Enforcers always wearing the armor outside was in place so that no one could gain leverage against an Enforcer nor think any one Enforcer was giving special treatment. Nih'al was an exemplary Enforcer and had been for many years. This development settled the matter though.

"You know the punishment for such a transgression, don't you?"

"Yes, Councilwoman Theana. I do." Her words carried the pride of her service and, at the same time, the shame of what had occurred.

"Would you tell me why you weren't wearing your armor?" This was an unnecessary question but if the reason was good enough maybe some other punishment could be recommended.

"I …" Nih'al tripped on her own words. She couldn't bring herself to say the reason.

Raven chimed in, "She was meeting with me Councilwoman. Nih'al and I have been seeing each other for some time."

This took Theana by surprise as well. She had heard rumors that Enforcers still sought emotional connections but she had never seen or even heard evidence of it. They were that good at hiding their actions to any they thought needed not see.

"I've recently moved from the barracks into new housing and Nih'al was coming from my home."

Nih'al found her words again. Her pride wouldn't let Raven explain alone. Neither would her love for him. "I thought it would be easier to hide our relationship if I didn't go in my armor. That was why I wasn't wearing it."

Theana thought for a moment. This did indeed bring new light to what had happened, but it didn't change what had happened because of it. A punishment was unavoidable.

"Enforcer Nih'al …" Councilwoman Theana's voice took on a very official tone, "You will confine yourself to your barracks while the High Council deliberates on your actions. You will be sent for once a decision has been made."

"Of course, Councilwoman." Nih'al dropped her head in shame at all that had happened.

Raven took a small step forward, "Councilwoman. Could I be permitted to stay with her until the decision is made? … Given the situation, I fear this may be our last chance to see one another."

The Councilwoman thought for a moment and nodded a small smile crawled across her lips. "I see no reason that you can't be assigned to ensure she doesn't leave her quarters."

Raven smiled under his helm. "Thank you Councilwoman." He and Nih'al clapped a salute before the Councilwoman disappeared. Raven turned to look at Nih'al. Despite the situation, they were both smiling. At least they would be together through this difficult situation.

Kane felt the pain come back as strong as if it had never gone. He grit his teeth and forced his eyes to open though he couldn't see for a moment. His vision blurred by the biting agony. He took in a few shaky breaths to try to compose himself. It worked a little. He could see only a small portion of the world around him. He was still atop the rock he had landed on.

The dark of the night seemed more encompassing than it had before. It felt much more lonely. He had to get back to his home. He didn't know how long the worm would be there to protect him. He tried to move his legs again. Still nothing. Just the pain. It always seemed to be there, like an old acquaintance that just wouldn't go away.

He pushed with his arms. Kane forced the adrenaline back into his body to get himself moving. He slid back until a thought struck his mind. The worm would probably eat him too. He couldn't touch the sand. He thought for a moment and came up with an idea.

A chunk of the rock beneath him broke free from the rest and lifted Kane into the air. It wasn't a large chunk; just big enough to lift him from the ground. He rose from the ground a few feet just to be sure he wouldn't accidentally touch the sand and began focusing to move towards his cave.

As he approached the opening to his home … his sanctuary … the rock beneath him broke and he fell to the sand. The impact hurt more than it would have had he not been injured already. The ground rumbled and shock slipped into his mind. He had to move. And he did.

Suddenly his legs worked. He scrambled to his feet, which hurt more than anything he could imagine but at least he would be alive, and dove to the side just in time to miss being devoured as the worm exploded from hiding. Kane didn't wait to see what happened next though; he pushed off and ran straight for his cave. Each step was agony. He knew, though, that he didn't have time to wait for his body not to hurt. The worm didn't go back into the dirt like it had before though. It anticipated his move and dove for the sand before the mouth of his home.

It could probably feel where the sand ended. Kane leapt towards the opening that was his home and called the wind to help him get past the worm. He just narrowly avoided the worm's mouth. The edge of the beasts head knocked the wind from his lungs and threw him hard into the wall of his cave. The sudden pain of the collision with the wall coupled with the pain he was already experiencing drove consciousness from his grasp once again. The world went dark, but the pain remained and it was worse than before.

"This incident with Enforcer Nih'al comes at a very inopportune moment. We must begin the search for Jerek Kis'tohl. He is not at his residence and we need him to find the rest of the conspirators. The prophecy named two at least. 'The Betrayer' and Jerek as 'a man formerly of station.'"

Grand Magistrate Doe'n was very focused. He would have a hard time deliberating on anything. His words were notably irritated at having to even notice something else.

"Councilwoman Theana, what would you recommend be done with Nih'al?

"Well Grand Magistrate … Given her record, I recommend the minimum punishment. Expulsion from the Order."

"That sounds sufficient to me. Does anyone object?" Doe'n surveyed the room. He very obviously wanted this off their plate. They needed to focus on finding Kis'tohl.

There were agreements all around that it was enough. It seemed everyone else wanted it out of the way as well. Doe'n wasn't the only one. That was a good thing. They would form a united front against the former Grand Magistrate and that would drive the search.

14

Raven and Nih'al stood side-by-side before the members of the Atrethian High Council. Both stood proudly wearing their Enforcer armor, though they knew already what would happen to one of them. They would show no emotion though, at least not to those outside the order. That was their way.

Grand Magistrate Doe'n shifted his weight. He was uneasy. With all he had on his mind, it was all he could do to focus on what was before him and it was not something he could hide. Doe'n looked from Raven to Nih'al and back.

"Enforcer Nih'al Trena," he said finally, "You understand the charge before you?"

"I do, Grand Magistrate." she replied. It was simple enough. She had violated one of the most sacred tenants of the order and in so doing, got three men killed. Of course she could hardly be blamed for that.

"Due to your exemplary record as an Enforcer, we have decided that you shall receive the minimum punishment for your actions. You are hereby stripped of your status as an Enforcer and expelled from the order."

His voice hadn't actually gotten any louder but the words sounded much more harsh than anything Nih'al had ever heard. She, like all other Enforcers, had been in the order since she was five years old. That's when they took you from your family. You were integrated into the order and trained for twenty years until you stopped growing.

Her heart sank. She had almost wished for a death sentence for killing the men. She had no purpose outside of the order. She knew nothing else. The only other thing she had in life was Raven. At least she had that.

"I understand, Grand Magistrate. Thank you for your leniency." Her words were hollow. She didn't truly mean it. It was just a formality; A show of respect.

"Raven … as I understand it," Doe'n continued, "You've been escorting Nih'al since the incident."

"That is correct, Grand Magistrate." He wasn't about to correct him. Escorting wasn't exactly what he would call it.

"In that case, you shall continue to escort her. You will take her back to her quarters and confiscate all of her issued armor. Once you have done that, you will escort her to a temporary home until she can find a dwelling of her own. Is that understood?"

"I understand, Grand Magistrate."

"And after you have done that, you will return here. You have further orders that are not for ears outside of the Enforcers and the High Council."

"Yes, Grand Magistrate." Those words stung even him so he knew Nih'al was in bad shape. He wished he could comfort her right now, but this was not the right place to do it.

"You're dismissed."

Raven and Nih'al spun on their heels and marched out of the room. They were both silent all the way back to her quarters. There was so much Raven wanted to say to Nih'al, but he couldn't come up with the right words. He would need to. She would have to know what this meant, though it was far better to talk about it.

Nih'al sighed as she flicked the lock on her helm. She rested her hands on either side and lifted it clear of her head for the last time. Raven clenched his fists as he watched her hair fall around her shoulders. The light brown of her long hair seemed almost golden in the light. It seemed fitting to him that she be adorned in gold. She was his idea of perfection. He hated what he had to tell her.

She unbuckled her pauldrons and placed them neatly upon her bunk. She still showed the utmost respect for the armor despite not being in the order anymore. She did the same with her greaves, sabatons and breastplate. When she bent to remove her leggings, Raven gulped and turned away. Her feminine form wasn't helping the situation. He wanted nothing more than to hold her.

He needed to focus. "Nih'al …" he said. His tone was pained and it was very obvious to Nih'al when she heard it. "We … we have to talk."

She paused. "Of course. You know you can always talk to me, Raven." She was puzzled by the pain in his voice; even a little scared by it. She had never heard him like that.

"Nih'al …" he continued, "You know how much I love you, right?"

"Of course I know. What's this all about?"

"Nih'al … we can't see each other anymore."

Nih'al swallowed hard and fell back onto her bunk almost knocking the armor to the floor. The color drained from her skin. She hadn't expected this.

"B-but Raven? Why not?" She choked back tears. Even now she didn't want to show weakness … especially not now.

"Nih'al … those outside of the order are not allowed to see us out of our armor. We can no longer be together. If we were, I would be expelled as well." His words hurt him as well. His heart felt like it was in his throat. "I'm sorry, Nih'al"

"I ..." She couldn't process this. This couldn't be happening. Her entire life was ending. Everything she had was gone. Her position within the order. Her relationship with Raven. Tears began flowing freely down her cheeks. She could hold them back no longer.

"Nih'al …" He wanted so badly to take back his words; to make it all not true, to protect her. But he couldn't make it go away. This was the truth and they both knew it had to be this way. He swallowed loud enough for her to hear him. He was hurting too.

"Raven … I …" She still couldn't find any words. The pain of this situation was just too much.

"No …" Raven said resolutely. "I'll leave the order too. I won't give up on our love. I love you too much not to do that for you."

"NO!" She was staring into his eyes like she always did; even through the helmet. "No I won't do that to you!" She stood up and walked to stand before him. She wasn't crying anymore, but her face was red and puffed from the tears that were already shed. "I won't take the order from you. When you are ready to leave the order on your own. We can be together. Until then, we will survive." She placed a hand upon his shoulder, "Swear it."

He looked away. He couldn't do it. He loved her and the order both. He couldn't stand to leave either. "Nih'al … I …"

"Swear it, Raven or damn you I'll leave and never come back!" She had an angry and determined look upon her face. She meant every word, even the threat. She would do it if she had to. He stared back into her eyes. "I swear. I will stay with the order and survive to be with you again." She smiled.

"I know you will. Because you wouldn't dare break a promise to me." She laughed a bit at her own words; it was a painful laugh, but it was still a laugh. She finished gathering up her armor and left it on display on her old bunk. She gathered up her personal things, however few they were, and stepped out of these quarters for the last time.

The pain never stopped. Kane could feel every single part of his body, but only because it hurt. He eased his eyes open, but the pain was blinding. He saw swirls of color, but he couldn't pick out anything solid. His whole world was a blur. He tried to remember how it happened. He couldn't remember where he even was. All he knew is that the pain was so intense he wanted for nothing but to die so it would stop.

Tieg sat silently at Aerika's bedside. He hadn't moved an inch since he brought her to the healers. She was mid-sentence talking with him at lunch about her training when she screamed out in pain and collapsed.

The look of worry on Tieg's face was hard not to notice. His brow was drawn tight in the frown and his lips were pursed tightly with a curl under his bottom lip. The bags under his eyes from his lack of sleep didn't help with his pitiful appearance. He couldn't let himself fall asleep though. He had to be up if she woke up and needed something.

Raven walked into the temporary home and held the door open with his foot while lifting Nih'al's bag into the door. Nih'al smiled at Raven. "You know, I could have carried that."

Raven ignored her and closed the door behind her. He set her bag on the bunk and turned to Nih'al. She smiled and then looked down at the ground. Raven smiled under his helm. Both of them were having a hard time with what was happening.

Nih'al sighed and looked back up at him, "Thank you … for everything. I ..."

"Damn them!" Raven cut in. He was looking straight down and clenching his fists tight. "Damn the rule! I will look at you one last time … with my eyes and without this helm."

He flicked the locks on the helm and tossed it back onto the bed as he stepped forward. She locked eyes with him. Before she had time to think, he had her in his arms and her lips were locked with his. Her eyes opened with the shock of what he did, but she quickly relaxed and let her eyes close.

She pressed her body against him. She wanted that armor to be gone. She wanted to feel the heat of his body against hers. His hands in the gloves pressed against her back made her want his touch even more.

Raven reluctantly pulled away from the kiss. "Oh, I needed that … I'm so sorry for all of this Nih'al. I wish there was something I could do to fix it."

She shook her head and looked into his eyes again, "Raven, this was my fault. Being with you was no excuse for not wearing my armor. There's nothing anyone can do about it. What's happened has happened and that's all there is to it."

Raven smiled. "You always were strong … That's one of the things I love about you."

Nih'al leaned up and kissed him one more time. "Now, put your helmet back on and get back to your duty, because your dedication is one of the things I love about you." She smiled and kissed him one more time before stepping back from him.

Raven picked up his helmet and looked at it for a moment. He ran his thumb across the face of the helm and looked back up at her. "Nih'al … I don't know that I can do this …"

She sighed and smiled, "You must be joking … Raven, you are the one that has the easy part! You have the job as an Enforcer to keep you busy while you wait for the moment that we can be together again. I have to figure out what I'm going to do."

He hesitated only a moment more and nodded. He slid the helm down and locked it into place. He brought his hand up and caressed her cheek with his thumb. She pushed her face against his gloved hand and closed her eyes, relishing this moment. It would be their last for a long while.

Raven dropped his hand away from her and strode out the door. He didn't want to prolong the good-bye any longer than he already had.

A smile crawled across Kane's lips. He closed his eyes enjoying the feel of grass on his hand. A slight breeze blew past him. The tall grass and the Barean Halos around him swayed in the wind. The purity of nature on these cliffs made everything fade away. Made everything all better.

Kane had nearly forgotten the pain; nearly forgotten where he really was. He opened his eyes and his hopes were dashed. The tan walls of his cave came into focus. The pain lingered a bit, but his wounds were healed, at least for the most part. His clothing was in tatters and scars marred his body.

He hadn't been in the Terrei Desert a year and he already bore marks that would never go away. He could hardly see himself surviving his exile if it was this bad already. He could hardly even remember his home, let alone imagine being there again. His mind went back to that cliff. He wanted to imagine it at least one more time.

Kane imagined Aerika as he had last seen her. He watched her run happily through the field of Halos. Her laughter floating on the wind. The sweet fragrance of the flowers and grass wet with morning dew crept into his nostrils. Aerika looked his way. She was happy. She was always happy with him.

He opened his eyes and let go of the image. Tears crawled out from within and he gave into the rising sadness. He hoped she had found some way to be happy without him there. She had their parents, at least. He hadn't even thought of how they must feel about all of this. He lay down on the hard floor of the cave. The hopelessness of his situation overtook him as he cried himself to sleep.

Raven stood outside the Mythril Hall. He waited for the summons that he knew would come. They had been informed of his arrival, but he had waited hours already. His mind ran over all that had happened. He couldn't focus on anything when his love needed him, though he had to try.

"Raven!" The call brought him out of his thoughts. Another Enforcer stood in the door of the Mythril Hall. This man's armor looked exactly the same as everyone else. The pride in uniformity that was instilled in them through their training made it so. He motioned towards the open door. "The Council summons you."

Raven nodded and strode in to see what was commanded of him. Maybe this task would set his mind at ease, whatever it may be. The entire Atrethian High Council was in attendance. The two Council Members closest the door wore brown robes. The next two wore green robes. The next wore blue and, after them, red. The final four were silver, then gold. At their center stood Grand Magistrate Doe'n. His violet robes set him above all the rest.

"Enforcer Raven," Doe'n spoke with authority, the chamber amplifying his voice as it did. "We charge you with a very important task, but before we explain the task, you must hear the reason for this task. What follows must never be spoken of to anyone outside of this chamber. Do I make myself clear?"

Raven thought this rather unusual but if it was really that important … "Perfectly, Grand Magistrate."

Doe'n continued, his words carrying the severity of the situation, "A disturbing prophecy has been seen. The prophets witnessed the end of life on Atrethian. The destruction of our world."

Raven took a step back as if he were physically struck by the words.

"We understand your unease at this news," the Grand Magistrate continued, "But you must stay focused. The man responsible for the events that will lead to this is still out there. We need you to find him."

Raven found his resolve, "Of course, Grand Magistrate. Tell me his name and I will find him at once. I swear he will be ..."

Doe'n raised a hand to silence him. "We have been searching for him ourselves. He is hiding his whereabouts from us. You are to retrace his steps from the last time anyone had seen him and figure out where he is. When you find him you will bring him to us ... alive, if possible."

Raven clapped a salute to his chest, "Your will be done, Grand Magistrate."

"I don't think I need to tell you that this situation requires haste. You have leave to do whatever is necessary without consequence to bring this man to justice."

"Who is it that I am looking for? Once I have his name, I will do everything I can to bring him in."

"His name, Enforcer, is Jerek Kis'tohl, the former Grand Magistrate."

Kane stepped out into the light of the new day. He wasn't sure how long he had been in the cave. He was in and out of consciousness. He knew only that it had taken him an exceedingly long time to heal those many wounds and broken bones.

The area was quiet. He really had no way of knowing if the worm was still around. He couldn't sense it. It felt like everything else around him. It felt dead.

He leapt into the air and called wind to carry him to the top of the rocks nearby. He thought it better not to take the chance. Once again he moved to the next grouping of rocks. There were still no sounds. It must still be around.

Kane scanned the horizon. He needed to find something that he could use to make new clothes. Just then he heard a familiar sound. A subtle scratching sound on the rocks. He listened a bit more intently, waiting for his chance to catch it.

A loud shriek pierced the air as the Stalker leapt towards him from atop another nearby rock. Kane reacted quickly calling a gust of wind to catch and wrap up the beast. It struggled to no avail. Kane surveyed the beast now at his mercy. Maybe he could find some way to use this beast's armor to fashion a garment of some kind.

As he looked at the beast, he saw what he needed. The armor upon the creature was melted onto its flesh but beneath and between the armor was a black fabric. It would suit his needs fine if he could just get at it.

Kane called on yet more wind to carry him and his captive to his cave. When he arrived he thought of how he would get at this fabric. He had to get through the armor somehow.

He thought for a moment that maybe he could melt it off but he pushed that idea away. Heat is what put it there in the first place. The metallic snapping of the Stalkers jaws brought him out of his thoughts.

Whatever he came up with the creature had to die first. Kane waved his hand calling a sharp gust of wind to decapitate the beast. Its head rolled over against the wall of the cave. He let the now limp body fall to the ground. The crack of the armor against the ground gave Kane an idea.

He summoned up some water and sprayed it against the armor chilling it at the same time. He did this until he thought it ready and he called some wind to lift up the body and slam it against the wall of the cave. The armor shattered and fell away. It worked. Now all he had to do was get at the rest of the fabric and he could fashion some clothing.

Aerika had returned to her training. She had been in the infirmary for just under two weeks, but she wasn't fully focused yet. She was worried about Kane. She knew the pain had come from something inflicted on him, but it was the first pain she had felt from him in some time, so it must have been very intense to have made its way to her.

She couldn't know for sure, but she just felt confident that he was still alive. She wondered what he might do on a day to day basis. She wondered what he had to eat and where he slept, but most of all she wondered what sort of horrors he was facing that could cause him such pain.

15

Raven sat in the corner of the tavern. His face shrouded in shadow though even if anyone saw him they wouldn't know him. He watched the inhabitants silently. He had heard rumor that a man by the name of Jerek had been in this particular town for some time, but he had gotten used to not finding him staying there. His search had led him from town to town to town.

He hoped that maybe it would turn out true this time. That he wouldn't yet again be one step behind Jerek Kis'tohl, though he was prepared for disappointment. He had been searching for nearly two years to find him. It was beyond Raven how he had evaded him this long, but such was the case. He would be very happy to have his search brought to a close on this night, but he wouldn't get his hopes up.

Several more people entered, but none of them matched the description he had been given. He sighed and reached down. He had been nursing a cup all night so as not to appear suspicious, but he would need to get a refill soon otherwise he would draw some attention.

Raven lifted his hand in the air until the waitress noticed and he motioned with two fingers for her to come over. When she got to his table, he pushed his cup towards her. "One more, please."

She took the cup and smiled.

"Thank you." He returned the smile as a courtesy.

She disappeared back into the taverns kitchen. She came back out shortly after with his cup again and set it back down in front of him. She went back to serving the rest of the very busy bar.

The drone of the crowd carried through the cramped surroundings of the tavern. Raven's eyes were drawn to the window near the entrance. It was starting to rain. Just a little at first, but slowly, the sound of the rain grew to a dull roar. The people inside the bar lifted their voices a bit more to compensate.

The front door creaked open, but, between the people and the rain, Raven almost didn't hear it. He drew his eyes across the rest of the room and to the door. A man shrouded in a heavy cloak stepped in. No one paid him any mind, which didn't surprise Raven too much.

The new man in the tavern stomped the mud from his feet and shook the rain from his shoulders and head. The man moved away from the door, but didn't lower his hood so Raven couldn't see his face. He kept his eyes on him hoping to catch a glimpse.

The cloaked man stopped the waitress for just a moment to place an order. She nodded and he walked to the bar and sat down. His back was to Raven. It seemed he would need to wait. Someone walked over to the man, but Raven couldn't see him through the crowd of people. He leaned a little to the side to try to catch a glimpse of who it was.

The crowd cleared for a moment, just long enough for him to see. It was one of the men that he had asked about Jerek. He spoke to the cloaked man for a moment and then pointed over at Raven. That's when he knew. The cloaked man was Jerek Kis'tohl.

Raven slid out of his chair and started through the crowd towards the bar. Jerek turned and saw Raven moving towards him and he didn't wait to find out who he was. He shot to his feet and started pushing towards the door. He knocked several people over in the process which slowed Raven down. He had to climb over them trying to get to his target.

He wasn't fast enough. Jerek made the door before Raven could catch him, but Raven was on his heels and, if he had his way, this chase would end his hunt this night. Jerek ran full sprint through the night rain. Raven got out of the tavern himself and took after him as hard and fast as he could. He would not let him get away. Not after this much time.

Jerek turned in between two farm houses and hurdled a fence into some grazing fields. Raven pushed over the fence and ran as hard as he could, trying to catch him. Jerek came up to the crest of a hill with a large tree. He slowed a bit and raised his arm in the air. He drew his hand down towards the tree.

A bolt of lightning shot down as if it were following his fingers and blew the tree right into Raven's path. Raven jumped as the tree bounced down the hill towards him. He noticed he wouldn't clear the tree as he was, so he called some wind for extra lift and he shifted himself horizontal to avoid the tree. He hit the ground and rolled back up to his feet to continue the chase.

Raven got to the top of the hill and scanned around. He couldn't see through the rain and darkness. Jerek had disappeared into the night. Just when Raven was about to give up the chase for the night, a bolt of lightning flashed across the sky and he saw him. Jerek was trudging through a pit of mud trying to get away.

Raven took off down the hill after Jerek. When he got to the edge of the mud pit, he flexed his legs and jumped as hard as he could into the air. It wasn't enough to get to Jerek, but it suited his needs. He cocked his arm back then whipped it forward as hard as he could. A ball of fire rolled forward off of his fingertip in Jerek's direction.

Jerek turned when he saw the new light and ducked down to dodge the flames. The ball of fire hit the mud, but didn't explode. Instead, it super-heated the mud around Jerek causing it to harden and lock him in place.

Raven came down on the hardened mud and rolled up next to Jerek. "Jerek Kis'tohl?" he asked as he pulled the hood back from his head, though he already knew the answer.

"Who's asking?" He shouted over the rain. The irritation in his voice was probably more at getting caught, then the fact he was being bothered by some stranger.

"My name is Raven Mataius. You will refer to me as Enforcer Raven. The High Council wants you brought in for crimes against Atrethia. I'm here to bring you back. Now, they would prefer you alive, but I've been given leave just to make sure we bring you in. I recommend you come quietly." The sky flashed once again as a bolt of lightning arced across it marking an end to Raven's long chase.

Aerika sat on the hill just before reaching the Barean Cliffs. The Halos on the hill across from her swayed in the wind. She let a frown crease her lips as it did every time she saw the flowers. She wished Kane could be with her here. He had always loved the Halos and she was sure this must be more beautiful than what he was seeing. Though, she really just wished that Kane could be back from exile.

Sinal stepped up beside her and sat down himself. He hadn't smiled in a few years; not since Liana had gone. His life was a mere shadow of what it once was. With Liana gone, the need for him to work at The Academy had disappeared altogether.

Sinal looked from the Halos over to Aerika. She was staring at him. She smiled at him. She wanted things to be normal between them, but it just wasn't. He had lost himself in his sorrow and given up on this world. He returned the smile. It was obvious to her it was forced. He hadn't been happy in a very long time, but she could hardly blame him for that.

She looked back over to the Halos. It was all too much. It was her fifteenth birthday and she just wanted to be back in training. She couldn't stand seeing her father in as much pain as he was. Sometimes she wished that it had been her sent into exile; though she doubted things would have turned out any differently.

Kane stretched his arms up high as he yawned. He had grown a lot since coming here. As far as he could tell, he had been out here in the Terrei Desert for around three years, but time didn't feel the same out here. He wasn't sure how long other people had survived during their exile. He was certain he had seen almost everything, if not everything, this place had to throw at him.

It was just a matter of biding his time. He knew what was 'living' out there. He knew how to survive encounters with each of them. He knew how to find food and water in this environment. He knew how to make clothing. Things were looking up for surviving this portion of his life.

He stepped out of his home. He had shifted the rock around to make it harder to get down into. Instead of going straight in now there were several turns before he got to where he slept. And there were other paths inside that led around to other caverns so he could lose or contain anything that followed him in.

He was nearly out of food and needed to go out to get more. So he stepped out into the light of the day and started moving towards the one oasis among all of this death. It had been his source of food for the time since he'd arrived. He could make water enough to survive so that was never an issue.

Kane slid between the boulders that littered the rock fields nearby. He had come to know the ins and outs of the field like he knew his own home. He could find any location in the field and knew every way out of every location in the field.

Kane quickly made his way to the far side of the rock fields and began crossing the dunes to get to the oasis. It wasn't a far hike, but climbing the dunes was tiring enough. If you lost your footing even one time you would lose even more time. But he had grown rather adept at climbing these dunes. So he made it well enough.

Things were getting rather routine. Kane made his way down into the oasis. There were bushes with berries and low hanging fruit trees. He gathered what he needed for the next few weeks. He created a cool pool of water to keep the food fresh until he needed it.

Once he had what he needed, he began moving back towards his home. The trek back was a little easier. There were far fewer dunes to climb up. More to climb down though. It took him just a little over two hours to get back from the Oasis.

Kane took the food back into his home. He put the food in a shallow hole he cut in the corner. He filled the hole with water and cooled it to preserve the food. Once he was satisfied with the temperature of the water, he went back out to climb the cliffs outside.

Climbing helped him maintain his strength and flexibility which, he had found, was important to his survival. Once he got to the top of the cliff, he took off running to make his way back around and down to his cave.

Kane stopped atop a hill not far from his cave. Something seemed strange to him. The color of the sand and skies were changing like it was changing to night, but the sun was still high in the sky. The sands of the desert became almost black as the shadows fell upon them like a shroud.

The skies became crimson and then darkened further. Kane looked for the sun to see what was happening. He had never heard of anything like this, let alone seen the like. The sun was there, but it had changed. It appeared as though it were eclipsed by something. It felt as though its energies were corrupted somehow rather than blocked.

And just as soon as the darkness had settled upon the desert it was replaced by an eerie blue glow. Sprites of some kind began to appear and flit about in the sky. The orbs, each as unique in size and shape as Atrethians were diverse, began moving around the skies in an intricate pattern of movements. The orbs danced around the desert in one of the most beautiful scenes Kane had ever seen.

The dim light of the orbs lit the desert in a way he had never seen. It almost made the horrible and deadly Terrei Desert seem peaceful and beautiful. An unfamiliar sense of calm washed over Kane as he watched this nocturnal ballet. The rest of the world seemed to melt away.

A sound that was familiar, but also sounded odd for some reason, echoed in the distance of the desert and Kane's own mind. Kane tried to shake free of the trance that had fallen over him. The sound came again; slightly louder than it was just moments ago. He recognized why it sounded odd. It was panic, or at least what he thought one of these creatures in the desert would sound like if they were to panic. But he couldn't imagine anything that could make them panic.

Kane shook his head, only bringing himself slightly out from the haze that dulled his senses. A roar rang out from the rock fields. He recognized the roar. It was a Behemoth. He couldn't see it yet, but he recognized that roar. He would never forget that sound. Kane oriented himself towards his home ready to retreat quickly if he needed to.

The ground began to quake with each step of the Behemoth as it approached. It was definitely drawing ever closer to his position. The roar sounded again. Kane brought his eyes across the edge of the field looking for the Behemoth; waiting for the moment it would emerge.

But the Behemoth's roar sounded wrong. That much

was certain, but Kane couldn't figure out why that was. There was only one creature that came to his mind that was more threatening than the Behemoth and it wasn't the season for it to be in this area of the desert.

A look of realization snapped onto Kane's face. Nothing in the desert was created to be beautiful. It was all created to be destructive; to kill. This realization was quickly affirmed when the Behemoth emerged from the rock fields with several of the sprites 'dancing' on its heels.

The Behemoth seemed to be pumping its four arms harder than it needed to move as quickly as it was. The beasts powerful legs strained under the force with which it propelled itself. Kane watched in rapt fear as this scene unfolded. Kane was shocked that this massive creature was running from anything at all, but especially from these lights. He didn't have to wait long to find out the reason.

Several of the sprites caught the Behemoth as though they were simply playing with it before that. The sprites darted into its abdomen and passed straight through, but not without showing some signs of resistance.

The smell of burning fur and flesh hit Kane's nostrils quickly. The air seemed saturated by the addition of this new odor. The horror of what he was witnessing struck him even more then the odor. The sprites flashed through the beast burning it inside and out as they went through. It was alive all the while. The huge brute was being tortured to death.

They were killing it with pain alone. Kane took several steps away trying to put some distance between him and this horrible scene as even more of the sprites converged on the suffering creature that had now collapsed to its knees.

Fear bit at Kane for the first time in years. He now knew why no one in history had ever survived an exile. He would have to find a way. The sprites hadn't seemed to notice him yet. He wasn't going to wait to see how this situation turned out.

He turned and ran for his home. He didn't think the rock would stop this new threat, but he would try to think of way to survive. He thought that maybe if he made it to the cave before he was noticed, he could simply hide from them. That was only a hope though and he would come up with a plan if it wasn't true.

Just as Kane came upon the crown of the final hill before reaching his shelter, several sprites fell in behind him. He hadn't escaped notice and he wasn't sure he would escape this one alive. He didn't want to die here in this way, but it seemed his luck had run out.

Jerek Kis'tohl stood with his hands bound behind his back before the High Council. Raven flanked him with a hand on Jerek's shoulder. He wasn't about to give him the chance to get away. Not after all it took to get him here in the first place.

"Jerek!" Grand Magistrate Doe'n's voice didn't hide his anger at all and he didn't want it to. "What were you thinking?! Do you have any idea what you've done?!"

Jerek hadn't raised his eyes from the ground once since entering the Mythril Hall. His resolve had been shaken by being brought in for crimes against Atrethia, but he was right in what he did. He knew he was. Jerek brought his eyes up and held his chin proudly in the air. His voice came out sure of his righteousness, "I've only done what was needed to preserve life on Atrethia."

"You've caused the end of life on Atrethia!"

This statement caused Jerek to flinch back. He couldn't believe that his actions had done anything, but halt the warrior of prophecy from breaking the peace.

"Jerek, our world is going to end! Life will cease to exist! The prophets said something you did has caused it!" The irritation and anger was rising in Doe'n. None of the other Council Members said anything though as their own anger at Jerek Kis'tohl was just as righteous.

"I ... I ..." Shame and fear stained his words. He trembled at the thought that he had caused the end of not only the peace but all life on Atrethia.

"Well?! What do you have to say for yourself?!" The entire Council wanted answers. Raven wanted answers. They all hoped that Jerek would have them.

"I ... I don't understand how this could have happened. I thought it through so thoroughly. The warrior had to be stopped to save the peace. I spoke with those boys to make sure ..."

"Boys? What boys? Jerek, what did you do?!"

Jerek brought his eyes up to meet Doe'n's. The helpless look in his eyes pleading for answers of his own. He wanted to help, to make it right. That much was obvious to Doe'n now. Despite his actions, his intentions were pure, though that didn't change the situation he had caused.

Tieg watched as Aerika solved puzzle after puzzle using only her power. He was in awe of what she could do. She didn't even move like most people did. She just directed the Flow with her mind. Most people had to use a physical motion to direct the Flow but not Aerika. She was extraordinary.

Tieg immediately noticed when Aerika's concentration slipped away. She was suddenly focused on something very far away. He had seen this before. Tieg scrambled to his feet and starting running towards her. He got to her side just as she collapsed. She let out a loud shriek and began convulsing. The pain appeared so intense yet Tieg saw no signs of injury. He looked up for just a moment to find the door, "Someone help!"

Aerika screamed again. Tieg could do nothing but cradle her against him and try to hold her still. She was writhing in agony and screaming out in pain, but he still could see nothing physically wrong with her. He had witnessed this only a few times before. He couldn't imagine the cause and she would never say.

Tieg cried out for help again as Aerika let out another blood curdling scream. Tieg was sure her voice would escape her if she kept at it like that but he doubted she would be screaming like this if she weren't truly in pain.

Aerika fell silent and still though her breathing was ragged and shallow. She had fallen unconscious. Whatever she had been experiencing must have been excruciating. Tieg screamed out for help again. He hoped someone was nearby and heard his cries though he felt alone and helpless to Aerika's plight.

16

Kane closed his eyes to focus through the pain. Several of the sprites had already burned through his abdomen. It was the single most painful experience he had ever had but he had no time to think about how much it hurt. He had to focus on surviving. He pushed his energy out away from his body forming a sphere all around him.

The sprites weren't slowed by the rock like he had thought they wouldn't be. He could feel the energy that flowed around him inside the shield. He pushed more energy into the shield to block out the sprites. They were stopped for just a short while when they changed. Something about them became different and they started squeezing through his shield. They were learning and evolving to get to him.

Kane pushed more energy into the shield and changed the way he had brought it together. He created more layers to it and made them different from the last. He sat silently, focusing on maintaining and shifting the make-up of the shields around him. He would need to continue to do that until this 'season' was over. It seemed his only way out.

He could sustain himself longer if he went to his sanctuary. And so he did. He drew in a deep breath and thought of the place he felt safest. He went through several locations. His old room, his parents room, the entire house; he even tried his cave. But, understandably, right now, he didn't feel safe there.

He blended more energy into each layer of his shield and went back to trying to find his sanctuary. He felt the sprites pushing through the layers of his shield. He had to get to his sanctuary. If he did that, he could separate himself from his physical body to better control the flow of energy around him.

He didn't have a lot of time left. He thought back to happier times. He thought of his times out at Barean Cliffs with his family. He visualized himself standing amongst the flowers. He imagined feeling the winds common to the cliffs blowing around him. He could even smell the flowers.

He looked around at the cliffs and felt at peace. If this was the end, at least he could have that much. That's when he felt the sprites as they were being pushed back out of his shields. He had found his sanctuary. His new one at least. And it seemed, for now, that he had the sprites at bay.

In an Enforcer Barracks in Mi'Tiya, a squad of Enforcers stood in a long formation. Raven paced before them, looking them over. These Enforcers would join him in his search for the young boys that Jerek Kis'tohl had enlisted to stop the warrior of prophecy from breaking the peace.

Twenty-one of the orders best and brightest under his command. He had hunted down and brought back the man that had started all of this single-handed. He would lead these Enforcers in their efforts to get their world back to the way it was.

Raven surveyed the armored group that stood before him. They would need the authority that the armor gave them to complete this hunt. It would not be simple. "Some of you know who I am," Raven started, "But let me introduce myself for the rest of you. I am Raven Mataius. I have been appointed as the lead Enforcer on this hunt, but that doesn't mean we'll be together. You were all chosen because you are the best and you will need to be at your best if we are to succeed."

He looked over the assembled crew to ensure they were all listening. "You have all been briefed on what failure means for this hunt. That means that failure is not an option. For the people … for Atrethia … we cannot fail! We will not fail!"

At his words the chest of each Enforcer pushed out. They were proud now to serve under him. That was important. They would need to follow his instructions if they were to succeed. He had to teach them an almost entirely new way to investigate events that had transpired. Normally, they would just delve into the memories of the people involved. But the investigation techniques they had been taught were for immediate cases and an incident was fresh. They would need to look deep into the memories of each person involved to find out the facts of what happened this time since it had been so long so since the event had occurred.

"This will not be easy. The search will be grueling and may take months or even years to complete it. You will each be given a location and a description. You will need to find out all the young men that live in that area that match that description and ensure that you find the right one. They must be informed of what their actions will do if they carry them out. But you cannot tell the wrong boys … we don't need to spread undue panic. That is what will make our mission much more difficult. Does anyone have any questions?"

One of the Enforcers stepped forward. "How are we to get a clear picture of what happened? Our techniques weren't meant for use years after the fact."

Raven nodded stepping in the Enforcers direction. "You're right. But with the location and description I give you, I will also supply instructions. It will teach you how to probe deeper into the memories. It requires very intense concentration on your part, which is why you all were chosen. Only the best can accomplish the level of concentration required and you are the best."

The Enforcer nodded, satisfied with the answer and stepped back into line. Raven surveyed the formation again waiting for anyone else to step forward. No one did.

"Enforcers … We are the last line of defense here. We have no options. We must succeed. When you fall out you will come up and get your description and instructions and then you are on your own. Once you find the child you will return to me for another description and location."

They all clapped a salute to their breastplates. This struck Raven as odd as he had never been on the receiving end of the salute but put the thought from his mind.

He looked over the group, pausing for a moment. "Fall out!" The Enforcers broke formation moving quickly to get into line to receive their instructions. This would be quick and orderly, but the search would not be easy; nor would it be quick.

Aerika was resting now and she seemed at peace … for the moment. The Academy's Headmaster had sent for her father, Sinal, but he hadn't arrived yet. Tieg didn't want to leave her until he got there. He didn't want her to wake without having someone there.

He put his face down into his hands and breathed out a frustrated sigh. He didn't know what was going on. Aerika wouldn't tell him and no one else seemed to have an explanation. He couldn't help her if she wouldn't share the problem. Magus was no help either. Every time this happened, Magus would just go off and train by himself. He didn't really have friends. He just had people he could exploit.

That was the significant difference between Magus and Tieg. Tieg had friends and he was loyal to them. Magus didn't know what friendship was. Tieg shook the thought from his mind. He needed to keep his mind on the situation at hand. When Aerika's dad got there, he had to explain what happened.

Just then, Sinal burst into the room and moved straight to Aerika's side. He didn't even look at Tieg. Tieg just watched for a moment before getting up to his feet.

"Sir … she … I'm not sure what happened. One minute she was fine and solving puzzles and the next she was in so much pain that she fell unconscious. Her screams … I … I've never heard anything like it."

Sinal just stood there, one hand holding Aerika's and the other caressing the side of her face. Tieg looked down at the ground and started heading for the door.

"Thank you … Tieg." Tieg stopped and looked back. "For staying with her until I got here." Sinal hadn't looked up from Aerika.

"It … It was my pleasure, sir. She doesn't associate with many people so I feel honored that she lets me be around as much as she does."

Sinal still didn't look up. Tieg continued, "If there is anything I can do for you or Aerika, sir … please don't hesitate to ask." Tieg waited for a moment though he wasn't sure for what. Perhaps he wanted Sinal to ask for something but he couldn't image he would need anything at that moment that he couldn't get himself. Tieg turned and walked out of the room.

The threads of The Flow weaved together; Bound tight until they almost became solid. The elements worked in unison as instructed by their master; each amplifying the strengths of the other. The structure formed blocked every advance by the sprites, ensuring that Kane remain safe behind it.

Kane listened to the soft whistle of the wind on the Barean Cliffs. The familiar sounds of the waves crashing against the rocks below. He smiled enjoying the sounds when something odd began to fade in. It was quiet at first but it grew slowly in intensity.

A rumble from within him shook him from his

sanctuary. This was a problem. He needed to eat, but he couldn't stop concentrating on the shields. Kane pushed the shields out farther forcing the sprites out and giving him more breathing room. He needed to come up with a plan to get at the food.

Kane shifted the energy of the shields and started towards the food. Before he could make it more than a few steps, the sprites were breaching his barriers. He stopped almost mid-stride. He called energy from his core to push them back out. He sat back down and tried to think of some other way to get to the food.

That's when it came to him. He didn't need to get to the food. He just needed to get the food to him. He called on the water where he kept his fruits to lift a few bits out. A fount of water lifted several pieces out of the pool and sloshed across the cave floor to him. Once the food got to him he let it fall to the ground.

He focused more into the shields while absently eating the fruit. He needed to keep his strength up otherwise these sprites would get the better of him. And that would mean his undoing.

Aerika had come to, but she hadn't regained her strength enough to get out bed. She wouldn't even eat. Sinal rung his hands almost raw. His face drenched with sweat. He was going to worry himself to death if he kept it up.

"Aerika, you must eat. If you don't, you'll die." His words carried the weight of his worry to any that could hear him. Aerika shifted her eyes absently to her father.

"Father ... why should I eat? Why should I enjoy these comforts when Kane is in such pain?" Sinal flinched as she said this. Mentioning Kane struck a chord that he had tried to keep buried.

"I ... I don't know Aerika. I ... How can you even know if he is in pain?" He had heard her mention this before, but he never got an explanation. She had told no one of her connection.

"We're connected." She said as tears began streaming down her face. "We always have been. When he was getting bullied, I felt every hit; every broken bone; but I could also feel his joy; his happiness. Now I can only feel intense pain every so often and I have nightmares of what is causing this pain. Creature's the likes of which I've never even heard of. Father ... where is he?"

Sinal was stunned by this revelation. He had no idea that any of that was happening between his two children. But it gave Sinal hope that, maybe, Kane was still alive.

"He's in the Terrei Desert. It's where they send you when you're exiled." Sinal got up from his seat and went over to sit next to Aerika on her bed before he continued. "It's a place of great darkness and ... and you've never seen those creatures because ... because no one has ever survived exile to describe them to us. I'm sorry, Aerika."

Tears came renewed to Aerika. She became racked with heavy sobs and leaned against Sinal. The thought that Kane was in a situation that none before him had survived was more than she could take. He placed a hand on her back as her arms wrapped around his abdomen. He sighed and frowned. Kane's exile had torn their family apart. Sinal admonished himself for thinking that. It wasn't Kane's fault all this happened. He was defending his sister and no one could fault him that.

"Don't worry, Aerika. He'll make it back to us. You know his strength more than anyone. Never lose faith in him." Sinal just stared blankly at the wall. He couldn't help Kane and Aerika was all that was holding him together. His hope was quickly fading that he would have a reason to live once she didn't need him anymore.

Raven stood in the shadows, watching a group of children play in the street. One child was sitting off by himself; the child matched the description he had pulled for himself; small framed, dark-shaded eyes, and solitary.

He stepped out of the shadows and moved towards the child. The group that was playing saw him and stopped. Their fear of the Enforcers was well placed, but only if they were doing anything wrong. It didn't change the fact that each Enforcer was an imposing sight in their armor.

He had hoped that the name he had pulled from the memories of the adults in this neighborhood was the right one. He had already checked several children matching this description and none of them had any clue what he was talking about.

"Jereth Loake?" The boy jumped at hearing his name spoken by an Enforcer. "So you are. Good. Listen son." Raven knelt down in front of the boy. "About two years ago you spoke with an older man. He was wearing a cloak so I don't imagine you remember what he looked like. But he may have referred to himself as a 'concerned citizen'. Does any of this sound familiar?"

The boy nodded hesitantly. He hadn't removed his dark blue eyes from the helmet that hid Raven's face.

Raven smiled under the helm. This boy was the one he had been searching for. "Good. Listen that man was a very bad man. He is a criminal and if you carry out his request, some very bad things will happen."

"What sort of bad things? He said I would be a hero." The child was puzzled and rightly so. He had been told that he would be doing a good thing and now he finds out that it would be bad.

Raven looked over at the other children who still hadn't resumed playing. "Go home children." They didn't hesitate. He hadn't even finished speaking his command and they were breaking for whatever doorway they could find.

Raven returned his look to the boy he had come to find in the first place. "This man that he wants you to stop. He's not a bad man. He doesn't know what he's doing. But if you try to stop him, events will spiral out of control. Do you understand me?" The boy nodded and Raven continued, "If you try to stop him … our world will be destroyed. Everyone will die."

The boy's face went pale. He looked sick. Raven placed a hand on his shoulder to try to reassure him. "You haven't done anything yet and that means it can still not happen. Everything will be fine. You just have to remember that we Enforcers are the peacekeepers of this world. We will stop any threats to the peace and to the people. It's why we're here."

Jereth nodded. He was still pale, but he didn't look sick anymore. Raven took his hand back and pushed up to his feet. "Now, Jereth, I want you to run along home. And you can't tell anyone about this prophecy. It's a secret and you're special enough that I was able to share it with you."

The boy smiled, the color returning to his face. He got to his feet and ran down the street and around a corner. Raven sighed. One down, entirely too many to go. He turned and headed back for the barracks to await the return of the others.

Kane's shield held. He sat, undisturbed for the most part, deep in meditation. Something, however, seemed off. Kane dropped out of his sanctuary and pushed out from the haze he had placed over himself to keep his focus off the physical.

The sprites were gone. He tried to remember how long it had been; how long he had been meditating. He looked at what remained of his food and sighed. He had been under for at least thirty days. His 30 day supply was gone now. He would have to go out for more.

He huffed in frustration. 'At least the sprites are gone,' he thought. Kane made his way out through the maze that led to his home. He stepped out raising his arm instinctively to block the sun, but he quickly realized he didn't need to. The 'eclipse' yet continued.

Fear snapped back into Kane's heart. He was unsure as what it would bring now, but he still needed food. He would have to brave whatever terror yet await him to go get food and get back before it found him.

Raven went through the processes in his mind again. Even though he was the one that had figured out how to investigate deeper into memories then anyone had ever thought possible, it was still difficult for him to keep it straight. Its complexity was beyond anything else he'd had to do.

A small contingent of Enforcers entered the barracks. They each clapped a salute to their breastplates. Raven returned it in turn and brought out a stack of papers. Each page in the stack had a location and a description. The stack was substantial and the mere sight of it visibly disheartened the Enforcers.

Raven noticed the change in their stance when it happened. "We are Enforcers. No task is beyond us. You must remember this. It seems insurmountable now, but this stack will only shrink. It will never grow. After a time, it will dwindle and we will complete this task just like we always do. Now, draw from the top and get to your next child."

He understood their distress. It did seem impossible. He needed to keep their spirits up and by the way they walked out with their chests puffed out, he assumed it had worked. That was the last group before he needed to take his next assignment. He grabbed the page on the top of the list.

When Raven read the location on the page he almost fell flat on his face. This one would take him out to a small town out near the Terrei Desert called Loreda. His thoughts went immediately to Kane and Aerika.

He hadn't seen Aerika for some time. He had no time

to check on her like he normally did. Raven wondered to himself what Kane was doing, if he were even alive. He shook the thoughts from his mind. Distractions would do him no good right now. He set out for this village. It would take him two weeks to make the trek and he had no time to waste. Not with all that was at stake.

Kane crept up to the oasis. It was still intact, at least for now. It had survived this long before he found it though so he imagined it would survive long after he was gone from this place. He gathered up enough fruits to last him another thirty days and was preparing to leave when a thought occurred to him. He had no idea just how long the eclipse would last. If he needed more food, he would need to make another trip.

He gathered another thirty days' worth of fruit and dried them all out just to be sure they wouldn't spoil. He would freeze these and put them in the bottom of the pool to keep the others cool and preserved. Once he was satisfied with what he had he made his way back to his home.

Aerika extended her hands out straight and bent forward at her waist. She reached down and grabbed hold of her ankles pulling to exaggerate the stretch further. She was getting rather flexible through this physical defense training. She didn't know how much she would need it, but you never could tell so she took every lesson seriously.

Tieg was in this class with her. So was Magus. He was his normal solitary self, while Tieg was friendly as always. He was always happy to be anyone's sparring partner, but he rather enjoyed being around her. And she liked having him around. It made her feel closer to Kane; being friends with his friend.

She frowned at the sudden thought of Kane. Tieg saw it as soon as her expression changed. "Is everything alright, Aerika?"

She looked up at him and smiled halfheartedly. "Yes,

I am well, Tieg. I just … I thought of Kane, that's all."

Tieg looked down at the floor. He missed Kane too. He had told her as much before. "I see ..."

"Listen Tieg," Aerika tried to come up with the words to explain to him her situation. "I feel like I should be honest with you. You've been a good friend to me and I feel like I owe you as much."

"Aerika, you don't owe me anything. I'm just glad I'm able to be there for you as much as I am."

"I know and that's sweet of you. I appreciate your friendship, but this is important to me, so just listen." She stopped stretching and stood straight up. The act of trying to stretch was hindering her thinking. Tieg had already stopped. He was very curious as to what she wanted to tell him.

"Tieg, those times that I … was in pain." He nodded. He knew what times she meant. "It's because … I can feel Kane. I feel his pain. Before he left, I could feel everything he felt. Happiness, sadness, joy, pain. I felt it all. Now I only feel his intense emotions. Which just so happens to be fear or pain."

Tieg looked rather confused, but more at how it was possible and less that he didn't understand. Aerika continued, "I know what you're thinking and I don't know how I feel it, but we're connected somehow."

Tieg just stared at her like he was still trying to understand. She went back to stretching. She felt embarrassed now, like Tieg had just caught her changing. "You … you don't have to say anything, Tieg. I just wanted to tell you that. So you weren't confused anymore if it happened again."

Tieg just kept watching her as she stretched. He was happy she had thought enough of him to share this with him. "Aerika?" She looked up from her stretch at his call. "Thank you for telling me." They smiled at each other and went back to stretching.

Kane had felt strange the entire trek back to his cave. He felt as though he were being watched, but he couldn't hear anything moving like he normally did when he was hunted here. He just couldn't shake the feeling that something was after him.

He knelt down by the pool of water where he kept his food. He placed the bits in a way that they would each rest close to the block of ice that housed his next supply. Once he was satisfied with how they sat he prepared to stand when he felt something approaching behind him. It was moving slowly for now, but he guessed it would move fast once it knew that he was aware of it, whatever it was.

He shot up to his feet pivoting quickly crouched and ready for the coming assault. It was a stalker, though it wasn't moving normally. It was shambling when it normally scrambled and leapt quickly. And that's when Kane noticed the blue shimmer from the creature's eye-sockets. It was possessed by a sprite; or at least by the energy that the sprites were comprised of.

And behind the one stalker, more emerged. Stalkers weren't the only ones though. Several of the berserkers were among them as well and the ground was shaking like a behemoth was not far off. It had probably gotten on its hands and knees to follow him.

Kane had to think of how to get rid of all of these creatures otherwise he would be quickly overrun and his time to think was almost up.

Kane ran at a stalker, one of an uncountable amount of the deserts inhabitants approaching him. He leapt hard at it and put his foot into its chest. As it fell back he pushed off of it to leap over the small group behind it. But it wasn't enough. There were too many of them and he wouldn't clear them.

He pushed his arms out at them sending a wave of wind to knock them away. When he hit the ground that had cleared for just a moment, he rolled back up to his feet and continued to run. He twisted this way and that skirting the reach of the creatures making their way into his home. He would need to block the entrance to his cave, otherwise this would never end.

He turned a corner to head towards the outside and ran headlong into a Behemoth. Its eyes were filled with a fog the same shade of blue that the sprites had been. It extended out two of its massive arms and tried to grab at Kane. He scrambled back away, but it caught hold of his foot. He pushed his hands out towards the creatures face, summoning flame this time.

His panic got the better of him and the corridor filled with the flames he conjured. The fireball rolled down the tunnel, engulfing everything as it went. Kane shielded himself as it rolled. He waited for the explosion at the end. When it came the beasts around him were knocked to the ground by the shock wave. It stunned Kane for just a moment. He recovered as quickly as he could and got back to his feet.

He looked around trying to orient himself. He could only guess at which way was out now so he picked a way and started running. The maze he had made to protect himself was now his enemy.

Aerika sat upon the hill before the Barean Cliffs. A smile washed over her face. She loved coming here. It was so serene. She closed her eyes and took in a deep breath. Her lungs filled with the salty air from sea that crashed against the rocks below.

A subtle breeze blew past her. The sounds of the waves crashing against the rocks helped to add a layer of depth to Barean Cliffs that could not be replicated anywhere else. The wind whistled softly as it blew by. She let her eyes glide open lazily. She so enjoyed the feeling she got from everything so naturally beautiful about these cliffs. It brought a peace to her heart that was difficult for her to find elsewhere.

She watched as the Barean Halos swayed on a cool breath of the wind. She used to enjoy running through those flowers, though she hadn't done that since Kane had gone into exile. She dropped her gaze from the halos. Her thoughts slipped to Kane and what he might be doing and, in an instant, her feeling of peace had gone.

Something changed in the atmosphere around her. She felt as though she weren't alone. But when she looked around at the hills around her and even towards the cliffs, she saw nothing. She got to her feet and started towards the cliffs edge.

She suddenly felt panic rising in her heart. It felt distant, as though it wasn't really her feeling it. As she approached the edge of the cliff, panic bit at her heart and brought her to a halt. The presence she felt wasn't over the cliff.

The face she saw when she turned was shrouded in a metal shell. Its jagged teeth augmented by the helm fused with its face. A menacing glow emanated from within the head of the beast. Every hole, crack and orifice was filled with a subtle blue light.

The beast shrieked and leapt at Aerika. Its claw tipped fingers dug into her shoulders as it tackled her off the cliff towards the jagged rocks below. Her scream echoed on the wind as she fell. The wind rushed past her and she closed her eyes waiting for the sudden impact and end to her pained existence.

Aerika screamed and sat up in her bed. The dark of her room seemed thicker the normal. Her heart felt like it was going to pound painfully out of her chest. She bit back a sob while wiping away the tears and sweat that were mixing on her face.

She felt so alone in this room. Kane's side of the room had remained the same while hers continued to change. Her father didn't come in to check on her this time. He was used to it by now she guessed. Or he had stopped caring. His once apparent lust for life had been slowly dying since her mother had given up and left them. She had lost count of how many nights she had had a nightmare that caused her to wake her father. It could just be that he was so used to it that he slept through now though she couldn't be sure.

She lay back down to try to fall back into her slumber, but the panic did not subside. So she just lay there staring at the ceiling, her heart pounding so hard it echoed in her ears. It was all she could do until she was able to calm down and fall back into a fitful slumber.

Kane had turned several corners and found he was no closer to getting to the outside. At least he had lost the shambling hordes for now. He reached out with his energy looking for the open air. He had marked the entrance for just such an occasion. He felt it straight to his left but he had no way of getting there.

He thought for a moment and decided it was better to

get to the entrance now to block it then to maintain his maze. Kane placed his hand on the rock wall that stood in his way and it turned to dust before him. Directly before him stood more of the beasts, between him and the exit. Kane reached out past them with his energy.

He stretched his arms out towards the open air until he found what he wanted. Once he had it he lifted his arms slightly towards the sky and jerked his arms back in hard to his chest. Kane struggled to look past the amassing horde as they moved towards him.

They broke for a moment; just long enough for him to see the boulder he had called flying towards the entrance. Kane turned and dove back away to avoid the carnage that was about to ensue. The boulder hit the face of the cliff, collapsing the entrance and sending large chunks of debris flying through the gathered bodies. Chunks of rock tore through stalkers and behemoths alike. And bits of them tore through others. The violence of the act was exactly what Kane had needed to stem the tide in his favor.

Kane collected himself and got back to his feet. He would need to start clearing the caverns of what remained. Once they were clear, he would be safe, at least for now.

The Bubble. It's what the Council had named the shield constructed around the Terrei Desert. It kept all of the nasty things inside from spilling out. And it was very close to where Raven was now. Close enough, even, that he could see it very clearly.

Raven sighed. He had hoped that his first time seeing The Bubble would be from within when he brought Kane back from his exile. But he guessed it would be the next. He closed his eyes and tried to sense anything behind the shield. He could feel the life all around it; the grass, the trees, even a bird that had perched for a rest on The Bubble itself, but he could feel nothing beyond its shell.

Raven shook his head. It was no use. The power of

that shield had held against everything, in- or outside of it, for thousands of years. His senses wouldn't penetrate it. He turned slightly to the east of The Bubble and sighed. He still had another few days walk before he was at the target location and he would need to keep moving to make good time. He had his mission to carry out and he would see it done. Just as Kane had seen his done.

Kane lowered his arm as the last of the beasts burned to ash. He made his way back to his home. He wondered just what would be the next thing thrown at him here in this forsaken place. Whatever it was he hoped that he could overcome it as he had all of the other obstacles.

Every time something new came along, he figured out a way to survive it and he would keep doing that with everything else that came. Survival was all he had. Every moment he spent thinking about his life before was a moment he spent preparing to die.

He got back to his little cavern looked around. At least he had kept the horde from being in here when they turned to ash. A thought occurred to him that if he had the cave entrance blocked now, he didn't need the maze any longer. He would have to change that around at some point.

Of course, he had plenty of time to go about that. It had taken him nearly two weeks to clear out the creatures that invaded his home. He would still have another two weeks or so, if he was right, until either the next thing came along or the eclipse ended. But, for now, he would rest. He was exhausted and needed to sleep.

The sun was beginning its descent towards the horizon when the village came into view. Raven only had another three or four hours walk until he would be in Loreda, the village in which the boy he was looking for lived.

He had been traveling for nearly two weeks and he would welcome the rest, however fleeting it would be. As he continued on, he continued to glance at The Bubble. The menacing form that stood so near to the north. It was hard to believe anyone wanting to live near that dead spot on their world, though he imagined that they didn't choose to live here. He imagined they probably all inherited their homes from family that lived their long before The Bubble even existed.

Everything seemed bleak when he saw its figure resting in the distance. It was almost as though its mere presence drained the hope out of any that looked upon it, though he supposed one got accustomed to its sight. But he could finish his task quickly and get back to Mi'Tiya and away from this dreadful place. There would surely be Enforcers waiting for his return when he was through finding this child.

His thoughts drifted to Nih'al. He wondered what she was doing to at that moment. He hadn't seen her since her expulsion from the order. A pain began rising within him. He swallowed hard trying to suppress the pain, but it continued to rise.

It felt to him like something was missing within him. Like there was a wound inside that had not quite healed. The pain grew, extending out of his abdomen into his limbs. Before long, his entire body ached merely at the thought of how much he missed her. He couldn't imagine going another day without her and yet he had to. He had promised her he would go on.

He pushed that thought from his mind. If he gave in to those thoughts, if he sacrificed everything he believed in to be with her, then he did not deserve her. He loved her. That much he knew, and she knew; He would do what he needed to do to one day be back with her.

He pushed the pain back down into his gut and steeled himself. He had a long hard road ahead before he would be with her again and he had to keep moving to get to the end of it.

Though Raven wasn't the only one thinking of their lost love. Nih'al pushed a broom across the floor. She had once thought it easier to just call on the winds to clear the floor, but then she would spend the rest of her day with nothing to do. Plus the manual labor kept her muscles sharp.

She had gotten a place to stay and a job to do from this man and his wife. The orphanage they ran seemed an appropriate place for her. She didn't remember her parents and she had essentially been abandoned by the order. She lived with the children and kept the place as tidy as possible though the couple that ran the place had said she worked too hard.

She thought the rest of the world would do good to get as much done in their days as she did. But it wasn't her place to try to change their minds. She would just smile and get back to work. There was no point getting attached. Eventually, she would leave, just as the children would.

This job kept her close to Raven. It was only a few blocks from his home. He hadn't been there for some time but she had seen him leave the city. He must have had a task that took him far away. He would be back and she would see him safe again. She knew she would. But until that day came, she would just keep working.

Aerika slid her left foot forward slightly easing her weight so it was even between her legs. She raised her hands up into a guarded position. She dragged her eyes across her three sparring opponents. The rules were simple enough. Subdue your opponent without the use of the Flow and without hurting them ... too much.

She was one of the best in the class so facing three wasn't difficult for her. The first attack came from the student to the left. She noticed a slight twist in his hips and shoulders indicating an incoming jab with his lead arm.

Aerika's reaction was standard when facing multiple opponents. She twisted her body with the punch taking his wrist and forearm and pulling him. She used his momentum to launch him up and over her tossing him onto his back before delivering a kick to his side and pivoting back to face the other two. They were already moving in.

The first threw up a kick aiming for her side. She stepped in; closing the distance between them and moving too close for the kick to hit her. She grabbed his leg and the top of his thigh. She stepped out with her right foot and twisted her upper body holding his thigh close. This gave her the leverage she needed to pull the other student off his planted foot.

The twist allowed her to swing him hard enough that when she let him go he tumbled into one leg of the remaining student. He pulled his foot up and back to avoid getting knocked off his feet. But he sacrificed his balance when he did this, which allowed Aerika to put him down hard with one quick kick to his stomach.

She surveyed her opponents, ready still, in case they wanted to continue, but they weren't going to. She snapped her attention to the instructor when she heard him clapping. She didn't know who he was. He had insisted that they all refer to him simply as Instructor.

He was as anonymous as all of the other Enforcers, except for Raven. She knew him every time she saw him. After her father had stopped teaching the physical defense class, they had asked the Enforcers to step in and teach the class. They were more than happy to supply a temporary Instructor until they could find one that was a suitable replacement for Sinal. Their instructor's armor was as shiny and well-taken care of as every other Enforcer. There was nothing to distinguish him at all.

He stood against the wall, as he always did when they practiced. He pushed away from the wall and walked towards her.

"Very well done Aerika. You would have made an

excellent Enforcer." He thought this was a compliment, but Aerika thought it was a horrible idea.

"Thank you, Instructor." She wiped the sweat from her face and returned to her seat next to Tieg on the mats.

"That will be all for today. Conduct your stretching and then you may retire for the day. Good job, everyone. I'm glad you haven't forgotten what you learned last year."

He made his way out of the training room as everyone began stretching in their normal groups. Aerika went through the motions of her stretching while letting her mind wander. She thought of Kane and what he might be going through. She wondered if maybe the creatures from her dreams really were things he was seeing.

Kane dragged his hand along the wall of the cave while he walked towards the entrance. He just wanted to make sure everything was closed off. So far he had closed all of the corridors and filled in all the rock making it solid again. He didn't want to take any chances at something breaking through.

He was almost to the entrance when he heard something behind. It was such a soft sound he almost hadn't heard it. He turned quickly and looked over the tunnel. He didn't see anything. It was strange. He was at the last leg of the second thirty days of the eclipse. Maybe the next phase was starting. He listened carefully, but heard nothing. Maybe he had imagined the sound.

He drew his eyes over every inch of the tunnel. Nothing was out of place. Everything was perfectly still. He turned back towards the entrance and continued until he got there. Once there he turned drawing his hand still across the wall.

As he came to the end of the tunnel entering into his home, he heard the sound again. It sounded like something shuffling around on the ground. He turned quickly, but, again, found nothing. It was perplexing. He couldn't figure out what was making the sound, but he was certain he had heard it.

Kane scanned every detail of the tunnel. Every rock was unmoved. But something was out of place. The dust on the ground. There were footprints in the dust. Kane raised his arm before him, calling a gust of wind to blow up the dust in the corridor. When it did, he saw it. The dust now coating the creature that had, until now, remained hidden.

The creature was so large it almost filled the entire tunnel. Its massive arms were almost as big as Kane was around. It was hunched forward leaning on its long arms as though they supported it as much as its legs. At the end of its arms were massive, three fingered claws that looked enough to cleave a behemoth in two.

It had its legs tucked tight under its body as though it were ready to spring forward at any moment. Atop its massive torso sat an equally large head. The narrow eyes were framed by two coiled and menacing horns that aimed towards anything that happened to be unlucky enough to have this beast looking at it.

Below the eyes and flared nostrils was a massive jaw full of fangs that measured almost a half a foot long. It had two, much larger, fangs at the ends of its lips. Those two fangs extended up between its horns and stopped just shy of reaching its line of sight.

Kane felt out with his energy, trying to gather what he could from this creature, but there didn't appear to be anything there. Kane took several steps back, but it would do no good. The creature did as it had appeared it was ready to do. It leapt forward at Kane, moving much faster than anything Kane had ever seen.

The creature drew in close. Kane flinched completely on instinct though he knew it would do him no good. The beast impacted Kane, though the impact did nothing. It merely disappeared when it passed into him. The dust crashed apart as the creature disappeared. Kane's eyes rolled back into his head and he collapsed, unconscious.

Aerika screamed in horror at the creature she saw. It was like nothing she had ever seen, even in her nightmares. It was like the embodiment of fear itself. And, in her vision, it had pounced on Kane. But that was all she had seen. The creature jumping at him and then she had woken up.

She noticed that she couldn't move. The fear this beast had instilled in her was paralyzing. Her heart was pounding so hard it caused her entire body to ache and her ears to rind so loud she thought it might wake her father. All she could hear was the shrill whistle. She didn't even know if she had actually screamed aloud. She thought she had but there was no way she could be certain.

Her head hurt. Her lungs burned. Her chest ached from her heart beating so hard. She tried to slow her breathing, but she just couldn't seem to calm herself. Panic bit at every ounce of logic in her mind. The thought of what she had just seen. The memory of the dust covered invisible creature rose a terror in her heart that was near palpable.

She closed her eyes and bit her lip to try to help compose herself. She tried to think of other things; to focus her mind elsewhere. She couldn't get the image of that creature out of her mind. She couldn't forget the fear that she felt emanating from Kane. She couldn't block out the memory. She could not forget.

Raven locked the door to the room he was given to stay in. He flipped the lock on his helm and slipped it up from atop his shoulders. As it cleared his head, he sighed and set it down in the corner. He unsnapped the spaulders and slipped them off his shoulders next as per the ritual for removing the armor. It was easier to remove other pieces first, but the ritual for doffing their armor was meant to signify how simple things could still be difficult.

He did the same for the rest of his armor and sat down

on the bed. He needed to rest after that long march he had. Two weeks of walking from Mi'Tiya all the way out here to the edge of civilization without so much as making camp for the night. His calves were beyond the point of burning. His legs felt as though they had rotted off days prior.

He kicked his legs up onto the bed and lay down finally feeling a bit of a release after that exhausting trek. He placed his hands upon his chest with his fingers interlocked and closed his eyes. He took in a deep breath and let his focus slip away.

His mind went to Nih'al and what she might be doing. He hadn't heard from nor seen her since that night in her temporary home. She disappeared the day after that. He missed her so much it hurt. He let the pain spread in his body. He wanted to feel the pain of her absence. The loss of her as a part of his life; as a part of him.

A knock came at the door. The harsh sound pulled Raven out of his thoughts. He looked towards the door even though he couldn't see who was there.

"What is it?" Raven asked as the knock came again.

A feminine voice came from the other side of the door. It was the tavern owner's daughter, Helena, or something like that. Raven couldn't quite recall exactly what her name was. It didn't matter. He would finish his business here and be and his way. Most likely he would never see this family again. "My father wanted to know if you needed anything."

"No. Thank you. The only thing I need is to remain undisturbed until morning."

"Of course. My apologies." Footsteps trailed off away from the door.

Raven looked back up at the ceiling and let his mind wander back to Nih'al and into the pain of being without her. He brought a memory of him and Nih'al together to the forefront in his mind and then he drifted calmly into sleep.

Kane stood silent among the flowers on the Barean Cliffs. The wind blew around him. He heard the wave's crash against rocks below. He shook his head, trying to shake away this place. He knew in his heart that he wasn't there but he couldn't remember what had happened. He heard footfalls on the hill behind him.

Kane turned to see Aerika standing on the hill across from him. Her eyes were locked on his. She looked shocked to see him.

"Kane? Is it really you?" She swayed slightly and it almost looked like she was going to collapse, but she gathered herself.

"Aerika? Am … am I really back?" He was almost as shocked as she was. It felt so real. The smell of the salt air. The breath of the wind on his skin. He wanted to run and hug her, but he couldn't make his legs work. He couldn't even think of how he gotten back here. He strained and struggled to no avail. No matter how much he tried nothing came to him. He couldn't recall anything before standing on the hill.

"How … how dare you come back? Do you realize what you did to this family?!" Her shock and surprise had quickly turned to anger. She even advanced a few steps like she was ready to strike.

"I … what are you talking about?"

"You left us! Mom gave up hope! She left us too! Dad quit working! He's giving up hope too! It's only a matter of time before he leaves me too!"

"Aerika, 1 …" This was all too much for him. It was too difficult to process. Her anger seemed so sudden and burning though after all she had been through, he could hardly blame her that much. "Aerika, I don't know what to say."

"You can leave, Kane! Go away and never come back! I don't want you back! I don't need you anymore!"

She stormed off away from him and the cliffs. Kane just stood there, completely dumbfounded. He couldn't make his mind work.

He felt a haze over his mind. He knew this wasn't real but he felt like Aerika was right, real or not. His mind went to a very dark place. He thought of what it might be like to just give in. Let it all end. Just give his family the peace that they could have had if he had never been there in the first place.

18

Aerika slipped her feet from her bed down to the floor. She could hardly move. She couldn't even seem to catch her breath. Her heart was beating so hard it felt as if her chest would explode out at any moment. Fear still gripped her mind.

But at least she could move, if only a little at a time. She had to find her strength. She knew what she had to do but she wasn't sure how to go about it. It wasn't as though it were something she had tried before.

She closed her eyes and drew in as deep a breath as she could manage. Her lungs burned with the effort. She was in so much pain, she couldn't imagine being able to focus through it. But she had to try. She had to do something.

She let her mind slip from reality. She wandered to the Barean Cliffs. She sighed as the wind blew through the grassy fields and swept by her. Her mind went white for a moment as a sudden shock of pain shot through her body. She let the sound of the water crashing against the cliff-face below calm her mind. She took in a few deep drags of the salty ocean air. Another bolt shot through her, but this one felt less intense.

She let her mind float. She left the sanctity of the cliffs, crossing landscapes she had never even seen in person. The ache in her body felt more and more distant. She slipped through towns and forests and river valleys. She weaved her way across the land until before her stood The Bubble. The pain she had felt only moments before seemed only a whisper now. The Bubble was more ominous and foreboding than she had imagined and even more so than she had been told.

She walked up to the massive shield and reached out to touch the shell. The enormous amount of energy it took to construct and maintain this prison was like nothing she had felt before. Her eyes washed over it, examining its every detail. She would breach it this day. She would save her brother. She had to.

She pressed the palm of her hand against the face of the structure. She let her energy mix with it; she let the shield become a part of her. She leaned forward slightly and pushed her hand through the surface. She drew the rest of her body through as her arm moved forward.

She inched ever farther through the shield. She felt its energies beginning to push against her, trying to keep her out. It knew she was foreign and wanted to expel her. She pushed onward against the growing force attempting to impede her.

Aerika raised her hands out trying to pull herself forward through the shell around the desert. And just when she felt like it may just be too strong; that she may be unable to push through the shield; she felt her hands breach the inside of the structure.

She pulled on the inside of the structure to draw herself the rest of the way through. As she entered for the first time into the Terrei Desert, she felt the most terrifying thing she had ever felt; death, all encompassing, and all around her. The only living thing in the desert was her brother and his energy was faint already and growing more dim by the minute. She was running out of time. She couldn't even stop and be amazed by the fact that she was the first being to ever breach the walls of The Bubble without being sent by the Grand Magistrate.

She kept moving towards him. She paid no mind to

the strange energies around her that were intrigued by the new life moving through their domain. It wasn't as though there was anything they could do to her. She wasn't actually there after-all, she had only sent her mind. She continued through the strange, dead land until she found where her brother's energy was, but it was beneath the ground. Or rather behind a cliff-face. She continued to move through the rock and into the caves hidden behind.

She found him deep within the caverns. His body lay in a lump on the hard ground of the tunnel. He was motionless save for the subtle rise and fall of his even breaths. She recognized the feel of her brother's energy though it was altered. She could only assume the desert was to blame for that. His features were scared and he had grown. She would have to stop thinking that her brother would emerge as he was. But there would be time to reflect later.

Aerika dropped down to her knees beside him. She choked back her tears. She would have time for those later also. For now, she needed to stay focused if she were to bring him back. She placed a hand upon his cheek and the other on his chest.

She felt him, but he was very far away. He was almost gone and it seemed as though he were just giving up. She needed to draw him back out.

She dove down into his mind. He was lost in a world of nightmare creatures and horrors beyond imagining. He was living in the desert even in his dreams. She called out to him. She would need his help to find him.

"Kane ..." Her voice echoed in the nothing that he was lost in. "Kane, it's me ... its Aerika! Please come back to me!"

She waited a moment, but there was no response. "Kane! Please come back!"

The echo of her voice was almost painful. The

nothing around her seemed to be closing in on her; trying to choke the life from her. She had to find him soon otherwise there might be no hope for either of them.

"Kane! You promised me! You promised you would come back! You can't break your promise, Kane! You have to come home!"

Her voice echoed off into the distance, but she still got no response. She sighed and let her gaze drop down. The hopelessness of it all closed in around her.

"Aerika …" Kane's voice was almost inaudible, but it pushed the darkness back. "Aerika? You came for me?"

She looked up to see Kane standing only a few feet from her. "Kane ..." Her voice shook. She was happy to see him again, but they were both in a bad place.

"Aerika … I'm sorry. I'm sorry I did this to you. I'm sorry I did this to mother and father. I'm just … I'm sorry."

"You didn't do anything except protect me! You promised me before you left that you would make it back to me! So let's get out of here!"

Kane just stood and stared at her for a moment. "You … you're right."

Aerika stepped over to Kane and took him by the hand and pulled him out the way she came in. When she exited, she looked down at his still unmoving body. His heart began to gain in strength though it was still very weak.

Kane lay in the darkness of the tunnel. His breathing was still even. His power fluctuated, mixing with the world around him. His eyes frantic beneath his eye lids. A soft groan escaped his throat and his eye lids fluttered.

As his eyes opened he only partially saw Aerika. She was crouched next to him brushing his hair from his eyes. He knew it was her, though he could hardly see her. She gave him the softest smile before disappearing from his sight. The fuzzy image of her that he had seen was gone.

Kane sat up quickly and immediately regretted it. He

184

swayed from the rush and closed his eyes again. He put a hand to the side of his head while steadying himself with his other. After a while he opened his eyes slowly letting them adjust as he did. He looked around the tunnel for any signs of his sister, but it was as though she had never been there. He pushed up to his feet and stumbled down the tunnel to his home.

He got to where he slept normally and collapsed back into a huddled mass on the floor. He was still very weak from that ordeal but at least he was alive. He wasn't even really sure if any of that had actually happened. He thought he remembered seeing Aerika but, through the haze, he couldn't be sure. Whether it was real or not, he was happy to have seen her.

He curled himself tight into a ball. He tried to make himself as small as he could, like tightening up small would make it all hurt less. He grit his teeth against the ache in his bones and let his exhaustion take him.

Aerika, back in her room, opened her eyes which were now brimming with tears. She broke down crying. Her father must have heard her. He stepped up to her from her doorway and sat next to her. She put her head into his shoulder and just let the tears flow. She felt a lot of peace letting it out. It had been good to see Kane but it hurt so much to see him like that.

"What happened, Aerika? Did you have another nightmare?" He spoke soft enough that she only barely heard him over the sound of her own sobbing.

She shook her head against his shoulder. She tried to find the words to tell him what had happened but she couldn't think of how to explain it. The link was hard enough for him to grasp; she could only imagine how he would react to hearing that she had gone into The Bubble to help Kane survive. She thought it better to just tell him part of the truth.

"I saw Kane … in my dream, I guess. But it felt so real … it was … it was so good to see him. Even if it was a dream."

Sinal closed his eyes and thought of what it must be like for her. He couldn't even imagine what losing a twin must be like. It was nice for him to hear that she had a happy dream for once. He hugged her against him and just let her cry.

Raven woke to the silence of his solitary room. He sat up in his bed and went about methodically polishing and donning his armor. Once he was done, he opened his window and slipped out into the night. It was time to go to work.

He crept to the first house and slid up to the first window he saw. He took hold of the window and pulled it open without a sound. He had gotten good at this. He slipped his body quietly up in through the window into the room beyond.

He scanned around in the dark as he made his way through the dark home. He crept into the master bedroom. The man and woman of the house still slept. He moved up next to their bed, turned his hands, palms down, towards them and let his mind slip to the place he needed to go.

He hated doing this. It was so much more invasive then the normal technique, but it was necessary to get to the truth. Asking questions just didn't get the results he needed to get.

Raven focused his thoughts on the task at hand and poured his energies over the man. His energy weaved into the man's mixing and melding as if it were his own. He pushed his energies deeper and deeper until he reached the man's core.

Once inside the core he branched his energy out into the rest of the man's energies. He used his connection to the man's core to access his thoughts. Raven felt the man's love for his family and friends, his hopes and dreams, his fears and his pain as he had many times before. It was a technique he had developed during his search for Jerek Kis'tohl. He skillfully slipped into the man's memories.

He searched through the surface memories hoping he wouldn't need to delve very deep. He saw one of a disagreement with a neighbor. The neighbor's child had done something upsetting to him but that wasn't important. He searched the memory for the child. Disappointment struck. It was a boy with blonde hair. He needed a boy with brown hair.

He pushed deeper, searching further, hoping to find a memory of the town's children playing, maybe at a festival or party or something of the like. Raven could find no such memory so he slipped back out the way he had come in.

He would go over and check the neighbor's child at least. The boy would definitely have memories of the boy he sought. Maybe even memories of the direct event that he wanted to find.

He slipped back out of the house and made his way to the neighbors. He approached a window, quickly and quietly opened it and made his way inside. It was all becoming entirely too routine. Raven was a little disconcerted by how easily he had taken to breaking into people's homes while they slept and leaving no evidence he had been there. He slid stealthily through the home and made his way into the child's room.

These small homes made it easy to find who he wanted to find. He stood next to the boy's bed and turned his hands, palms down, as he had done many times before and would certainly do again. He let his energies pour into the boy and found his way into his core.

The boy's memories were easily accessed. Children were more free with their minds and much less reserved about what they thought. Raven searched for memories of the other children. He found what he wanted. The town's children playing happily in the square. They were all running around and laughing while chasing one-another.

Through the chaos of their game, Raven saw one boy off by himself. A small boy with short-cropped, light-brown hair sat alone, watching with intense gray eyes. The boy's small frame didn't betray the power within him. Anyone merely looking at the boy would not see his true capabilities, but Raven did, even in this other child's memory.

He had what he needed now. As he pulled back out of the boys memories he heard footsteps in the hall behind him. He moved quickly off to the side and hid himself in the darkness of the room's corner. He would not like to have to injure someone over something like this, especially an innocent but duty was duty and he would carry out his task no matter the cost.

The boy's father peaked into the room just to check on him. He was only there for a moment before he turned around and returned to his room. Raven was relieved but he would show that relief when he was back in his own borrowed room and safe from detection. After waiting a few moments for the man to return to his own bed, Raven slipped out of the home and back to his own temporary dwelling.

He closed the window to his room and slipped out of his armor and as quickly and quietly as he had donned it. He placed it lovingly in the corner of the room and lay back upon the bed to get some rest. He would find and confront the boy in the morning. He closed his eyes and let his mind drift off into the subtle rhythms of sleep.

Morning seemed to come quickly. He felt as though he had just gone to sleep and he was suddenly waking to the sounds of breakfast being prepared. Raven pushed up from the bed and grabbed his breastplate from the floor. He sat back upon the bed and took to polishing it, as he did every morning. It was his way. He would wait for his attendants in this home to bring him a wash basin and his breakfast. By law, they could not see his face. He knew that and so did they.

Once he had finished polishing each piece of his armor, a knock came at the door. His breakfast had arrived. He waited for the footsteps to fade before opening the door and picking up his meal from the floor. He closed and secured the door again before going to his meal.

He ate it like he hadn't eaten in days. Truth was that the rations he ate during his journey weren't very tasty, but they gave him the strength he needed to make the distance. He ate each real meal like it was his last, because it had more flavor than anything he normally had.

Raven finished his meal and went back to the door. Sitting on the floor was a wash-basin, a rather large bowl full of water with a cloth. He went about the small task of washing himself before donning his armor. These people were kind enough to give him a room to stay in and even afford him the courtesy of his orders rules and laws. The least he could do for them was bring them their dirtied dishes.

He grabbed the wash-basin and plate and made his way into the common room at the end of the hall. The family was sitting, still eating their own meal. They stopped when he entered.

"Everything was to your liking, I trust?" The man of the house regarded him with a truer respect than most did. Most feared any from his order and that was the only respect they received.

Raven smiled, though he knew the man could not see it. "It was delicious. Thank you for your hospitality. You have done much more than was asked of you. I am only sorry that I have no way of returning your kindness."

As Raven walked the dishes to counter-top that held the cooking utensils of the mornings meals, the man made his reply.

"My parents were both of your order. They met while among the Enforcers and I was conceived. They were both released from the order with the High Councils blessings. They settled out here and I stayed here after they passed, taking a family of my own, but never forgetting the morals instilled in me by my father. You and the rest of your order are always welcome in my home."

Raven hadn't heard of such events happening before. It lightened his heart to know that one day he might be released with the High Councils blessing to be with Nih'al. "I am humbled still by your kindness. My business will likely be concluded before the days end. If it is, I will be off before nightfall. If that is the case, I bid you farewell and wish good tidings upon you and your family."

The man nodded his head in respect to Raven before returning to his meal. Raven turned and made his way out the door. He still had a job to do and it would be easy to find the boy in this small town. He found his way into the town's main square where he had seen the children playing.

They hadn't arrived yet, though it was likely they were still finishing their own meals. He didn't have to wait long before they started arriving. He stood against a wall off to the side waiting. Finally, the boy he was searching for came out.

He made his way over towards him before he even sat down. The rest of the children saw Raven moving and stopped. Raven approached the small boy whose intense gray eyes remained locked on him. There was no fear in his eyes. Raven respected that much from this boy.

"Young man, what is your name?" Raven dropped to a knee before him to get on eye level. It would make the conversation easier and less intimidating for the boy, though it hardly seemed an issue at the moment.

"My name is Tak. Who are you?" The boy didn't

flinch or shy away at all. He wasn't just hiding his fear from Raven. He truly wasn't afraid.

"I am Enforcer Raven. I'm here to speak with you about an event that may have happened a few years ago."

19

The dim light faded from the center of the room as the prophecy came to a close. Flames flickered back to life atop the torches on the walls. The Twelve stirred only slightly as the light returned to their eyes.

They each scanned around to see the reactions from the others. They had all seen prophecies that were rather unnerving, but this one trumped them all. They all pushed up to their feet. They would not like to see another prophecy today so they decided, almost as if of one mind, that they would retire for the day.

They began moving towards the Prophet's Hovel where they slept. They would send for the Grand Magistrate. It had been his order that any prophecy pertaining to this specific chain of events be brought to him first.

As they left the Vi'jal Rotunda the torches lost their light. The torches within the Prophet's Hovel came to life. They each in turn sat upon their beds except for the youngest of them. It was his duty to inform the Enforcers of who was to be brought in.

He walked out into the Chamber of Visions and approached the Enforcers standing guard. "Bring the Grand Magistrate at once. This prophecy is urgent."

The Enforcers clapped salutes to the violet eyes upon their breastplates and marched from the room. They made their way through the weaving corridors that connected the Mythril Hall to the Chamber of Visions.

The two Enforcer's marched in step. These two had

served The Twelve for most of their time as Enforcer's and they were almost perfectly in tune with each other. They walked past the Buorthian Chamber and stepped forward to the Mythril Hall. The Council deliberated within on matters well above the status of these two. They ceased their conversation when the Enforcer's entered.

"What is it? Has there been a prophecy?" The Grand Magistrate obviously recognized these two. He had been there often enough to notice the subtle differences in their energies as compared to the others of the order.

The two Enforcer's clapped a salute to the violet eyes and spoke in unison, "The Prophets call you, Grand Magistrate."

Doe'n nodded and looked around the room. "Continue to deliberate in my absence. Theana, you will update me upon my return."

She acknowledged the order with a nod. Doe'n stepped from his spot at the head of the Council and followed the two Enforcer's, as he had done many time before. These corridors were growing more and more familiar to him. Despite their snaking nature, he felt he could walk them with his eyes closed without missing a turn.

They found the door to enter the Chamber of Visions and Doe'n entered without hesitating. He paused for a moment when he saw a prophet awaiting his arrival. If they were waiting, it must truly be an important prophecy. Doe'n approached the waiting prophet.

"Grand Magistrate, a prophecy has been shared and you shall hear it." No matter how many times he went through this, they never broke this tradition … or was it protocol.

"Speak and I will listen." He would play the game so long as they desired him to. It was how he got what he needed from them so he kept them happy.

The glow from beneath the prophet's hood shifted its

hue. The color began to mix as though his eyes were changing color. The glow now held a myriad of colors ranging from yellow and red to blue and green. Every color eye that existed mixed with the color of this man's eyes. When the prophet spoke his words sounded as though a dozen people were speaking all at once.

"Upon the crossroads The Warrior will fall to the Betrayer. His heart will be shattered, but his resolve will not falter. The Warrior will ascend from this defeat in a new form. The Warrior will bring change."

The many voices fell quiet. The glow from beneath his hood returned to its normal shade. This man was a member of The Twelve. His platinum eyes betrayed the power within him.

"If this prophecy is true, then nothing we are doing is changing anything." Doe'n was disheartened by this revelation. It seemed nothing would stop this from happening.

"I'm afraid not, Grand Magistrate. But your efforts have changed how the events themselves unfold. Take heart that you are making changes and continue in your efforts. You may yet save us all."

Doe'n stared into the eyes of this young prophet. He was wise beyond his years, though Doe'n imagined that was a product of the connection to the other prophets. The Grand Magistrate stood silently watching this prophet. He was perplexed. None of the others had ever said more than was necessary. This one still had his compassion. It was refreshing.

The platinum-eyed prophet nodded to Doe'n and turned to return to the Prophet's Hovel. He had taken only two steps when his legs gave out from under him. The prophet groaned as he fell to his hands and knees.

"Somebody help!" Doe'n ran to his side while several of the other prophets entered to see what the commotion was

194

about. He had only just gotten to his hands and knees when he collapsed further to his side. He convulsed in what appeared to be a torturous ordeal. Doe'n dropped to his knees beside the prophet.

He had barely gotten to his knees when the torches within the chamber flickered out. The color faded from beneath the hood of the fallen prophet. The other prophets stood in mute shock. A prophecy occurring, unconnected and outside of the Vi'jal Rotunda.

The dim light grew over the prophet. An image of a Grand Magistrate appeared. Doe'n noticed immediately that it was not him and it must be a future Grand Magistrate as it was a female and that had not happened yet.

The Grand Magistrate in the vision raised her hands up to her the sides of the violet hood shrouding her face from sight. She pulled the hood back and let it rest upon her back. Doe'n recognized her as soon as the hood was removed and he knew what the prophecy was foretelling.

The image disappeared and the light returned to the prophets eyes. The torches came back to life with the Chamber of Visions and the other prophets shook themselves of their shock to help their fellow prophet to his feet. They began to carry him to the Prophet's Hovel.

"Wait!" Doe'n's words halted the prophets. "Prophet … the woman in that vision … who was she?"

The Prophet looked to the Grand Magistrate and locked his eyes in his gaze. "I think you already know the answer to that question. Don't you, Grand Magistrate?"

Doe'n simply nodded as they took the prophet to rest. He turned and made his way out of the Chamber of Visions. He had never witnessed an actual prophecy before. He had only heard them related. And this one told him who would succeed him when he felt his term was done as Grand Magistrate.

He made his way back to the Mythril Hall, lost in

thought the entire trip. Like he thought, he made it without really looking. His thoughts had kept him from really paying attention, but making that walk as often as he had, helped him to make it by instinct alone.

Doe'n entered the Hall which brought the High Council to a halt in their conversation again. Doe'n glanced around at them and thought to himself for only a moment longer.

"I must think on what I have been told. Retire to the Buorthian Chamber until I send for you again." They each nodded and stepped out past him for the chamber. Doe'n returned to his own room as the last entered. He had a lot to think about.

Raven walked back into the barracks to see how many, if any, of the other Enforcers were waiting for their next assignment. Instead, he found Grand Magistrate Doe'n awaiting his return. Raven clapped a salute as he approached.

"Grand Magistrate, the mission is going very well. I believe that we shall be through with this list in a matter of months." Raven sounded very pleased with the way the mission had been going thus far. Doe'n was almost heartbroken to be the bearer of this news.

"I know. You've done an admirable job. However ..." Doe'n paused to find the right words to break this as easily as possible.

"However?" Raven was confused. If things were going well as it was, why would they change it?

"Listen, Raven. You really have done an exceptional job, but a prophecy was seen. The works we have undertaken aren't changing anything. I don't want to continue to waste our efforts if it isn't going to stop it. We need to think and refocus. I am sorry."

Raven dropped his gaze to the floor. After all they had done, it would end like this. "The other Enforcer's?"

196

"They've already been told. You were the last to return."

Doe'n placed a hand on Raven's shoulder. "Keep your head up, Raven. You performed well and it has not gone unnoticed. We will figure something out and you are at the top of our list for solving this problem."

Raven looked into Doe'n's eyes. He seemed so resolute; so certain that they would succeed. Raven found strength in that. He clapped another salute before Doe'n made his way out of the barracks. The Grand Magistrate didn't have that far of a walk from the barracks back to the Mythril Hall.

He had a lot on his mind, but he kept thinking back to the cause of this whole mess. The one person at the center of it all. The man that was the cause of the end of their world. All of this was set into motion by Jerek Kis'tohl.

He tried to make it right, but he only made it all worse. Doe'n made up his mind. Jerek would pay for his crimes, well intentioned or not. He would pay the highest price their laws allowed. Doe'n hastened his walk to the Mythril Hall. He would pass judgment immediately upon returning.

It was not long after Doe'n had returned to the Mythril Hall that Jerek was brought before them. "Jerek Kis'tohl!" Grand Magistrate Doe'n's words echoed throughout the hall. His anger highly apparent in his tone.

Jerek stood before the Atrethian High Council with his head hung in shame. He would finally receive punishment for his crimes. He hoped that he had at least done something to stop the tragedy that was foreseen.

"You stand before us, because your actions have set into motion events that will lead up to a break in the peace that we have all worked so hard to maintain and eventually, the end of our world as we know it."

Doe'n paused, partly to let the gravity of this

statement to sink in and partly to quell his own anger before continuing.

"Jerek Kis'tohl, your services to the people of Atrethia are overshadowed by what you have done since being removed from your station. In light of what has transpired and what will happen because of your actions, you are sentenced to the highest punishment that our laws will allow."

Jerek knew all too well what this punishment was, as did everyone else in the room. None of the Council Members would look at Jerek, or at the Grand Magistrate. They may as well have been the only two people in the room.

"Jerek Kis'tohl! You are hereby sentenced to twenty-five years exile in the Terrei Desert! Enforcer's! Remand the prisoner until preparations are complete for the ritual!"

The two Enforcer's flanking Jerek took him under his arms and led him out of the Hall. He looked pitiful, but everyone knew just how deserving he was of this punishment. It didn't make it any easier to carry out, however.

While Jerek was awaiting the ritual to send him to the Terrei Desert, Kane struggled to get his eyes open once again. He had been slipping in and out of consciousness and he wasn't even sure how much time had passed since he saw Aerika. He clung to that memory trying to push his way back from the darkness that had been consuming him.

He dimly noticed the pain coursing through his body, though it seemed like someone else was feeling it. He pushed at the darkness, attempting with every ounce of strength he had to re-enter some form of awareness.

Kane tried to use the pain he felt in his body to pull himself back into the conscious world. He tried to feel the pain though he only felt it as though all his muscles were sleeping.

The darkness around him began to creep back in upon him. His mind slipping back into the comfortable dreamy world he was getting to know very well. An idea came to him. He bit as hard as he could into his lip, trying to use this new pain to push back the sleep that was coming for him. It worked, if only slightly. The pain jolted him out of the darkness for a moment. Blood trickled down the side of his face from his now pierced lip.

Before he could latch on to the small bit of light that he had found, the darkness came back in for him. Kane slipped back into unconsciousness again, the nightmares of the desert only a dim reality to him as he slept in his home.

Aerika sighed looking at her father sleeping nearby. He had fallen asleep while comforting her. He looked so peaceful in his own dreams. She wished that she could sleep peacefully like that, but her dreams were haunted by the nightmares that were hunting her brother.

She walked out into the quiet of the rest of the house. It all seemed so lonely every time she saw it. The light that her mother used to bring to the house was gone. She walked over to the window to look outside. The sounds of rain broke the silence of the house.

It grew from nothing to a low drone. It wasn't raining heavily. The amount was strictly controlled to just maintain the environment and keep the climate stable. The sound of the rain beating down on the roof of their house though was soothing. It made things seem almost right.

She stared out the window at the rolling plains just outside of Mi'Tiya. Out there, a long ways off, was The Bubble. And inside that, was a massive desert that threatened to steal away one of the last people that mattered in her life. She didn't know what she would do if he didn't come back but she would keep pushing on until he did and she would worry about it when it happened if he didn't return.

Jerek Kis'tohl sat on the stone slab they called a bed in his cell. It was uncomfortable, but he knew it was more than he deserved. He would wait however long he needed to for his just punishment.

The sound of footsteps echoed in the hall outside. The sounds stopped outside his cell and the sounds of muffled voices slipped under the door. The lock clicked open and one of the Enforcer's standing guard opened the door. The familiar violet of the Grand Magistrate robes slid in through the open doorway, flowing about the feet of Jerek's successor.

Doe'n motioned for the Enforcer to leave them. He did as ordered but not before clapping a quick salute to his breastplate. The door slammed closed behind the armored warrior. Doe'n's brow creased; he had so many things he wanted to confront this man with he really didn't know where to start.

"How! … What were! ..." Doe'n stuttered before stopping himself. He took a deep breath to calm himself while Jerek just sat there silently awaiting the rebuke he was sure was on its way.

"Jerek … What were you thinking? After your removal from your position, you should have stopped trying to change things. You know that without the use of prophecy it is impossible to change things. And all you did was make it worse." Jerek flinched at Doe'n's words. This statement, though not very harshly toned, appeared to have struck a very deep nerve in the former-Grand Magistrate.

"Doe'n … I don't have an excuse for my actions. While my intentions were pure, I did not think of what the consequences might be."

"And what did you think you would be doing? You were knowingly asking these children to commit a crime and that crime has now set our end in motion! And we can't do anything to stop it either!"

Jerek dropped his gaze to the floor. His shame bared plainly for the world to see. Doe'n couldn't even force himself to be angry with Jerek now. He had always been a reasonable man. And these actions seemed reasonable on the outside. Doe'n couldn't say for certain that he wouldn't have done the same.

"They are preparing the Mythril Hall for your exile as we speak. You will be brought in once it ..." Doe'n's words were interrupted by a knock at the door.

The thick, heavy-looking door slid open and the Enforcer standing in the door seemed to look straight into Jerek's eyes. "It's time." Those simple words seemed to shatter Jerek's world. He struggled up to his feet. His legs just didn't want to work. He had had to go through this ritual before, though never on this end and the terror of what lie before him set upon him. Doe'n put a hand under Jerek's arm.

"I will escort you personally ... since I'm here already."

The Enforcer's took up their flanks as Jerek and Doe'n began the march from the prison block to the Mythril Hall. It wasn't that far of a trek, but Jerek was barely able to stand, let alone walk, even with Doe'n's assistance.

They finally made it to the Mythril Hall. Being on this side of the black doors halted Jerek in his tracks. He knew what lay beyond for him. He would accept his punishment, though, much to his dismay, it would not be with grace.

He brought his gaze over to Doe'n who was giving him a moment. Doe'n still respected Jerek enough to let him contain himself before going to what would certainly by his final moments in this society.

"Just tell me when you're ready, Jerek. Your punishment awaits behind these doors and though it is deserved, I'm in no hurry to send my mentor to such a fate."

"Doe'n," he choked back the fear before continuing. "I'm glad that it's you that is sending me. If it must happen, I would have it no other way."

"Let's get to it then, shall we?" Jerek nodded at this and they stepped up to the massive doors marking the entrance to the Hall. The doors pushed open on their own beckoning Jerek and the Grand Magistrate to enter.

The scene, familiar to both men, lay before them. Jerek found strength in his legs and made his way to the center of the symbol. He stepped carefully avoiding the sand that formed each design drawn upon the ground. Once he made his way into the center, Doe'n took his place as did the two Enforcer's needed for the ritual.

"Jerek Kis'tohl," Doe'n spoke softly, not really ready for this himself, "are you ready for your punishment to commence?"

Jerek nodded and blinked long trying to hold back the tears that threatened to emerge. He bit back his fear. He wasn't really ready, but there was no turning back from this now. It was a fate he knew he deserved and he would accept it willingly, even through his growing fear.

Doe'n began the chant and one-by-one the small, white, deliberately-drawn symbols solidified and lifted into the air around Jerek. Each one going to a very particular height. The glow they gave off was beautiful and something that Jerek had never seen before. The sight from outside the symbol was far less spectacular.

They began to spin in place as if dancing to the tune of the chant. It changed as Jerek had known it would. These were words he had spoken himself before. The blue square lifted into the air about his head and began spinning in perfect unison with the speed of the chant. The glow emitting from that symbol seemed like that of the sun itself.

Doe'n's words echoed louder in the chamber and again changed. The red line of sand split beneath Jerek's feet to form a circle around him before lifting to chest height on the two Enforcer's. The ends of the line extended to meet the chest of the Enforcer's, joining them to the symbol and lifting them from the ground.

The light from each of the symbols began to sift down into the circle that still rest upon the ground. The power of Doe'n's chant was almost deafening already to Jerek. He could hardly make out the words though he knew them well enough. All Grand Magistrate's had to memorize this ritual.

As the last of the light drained into the circle beneath him, Jerek looked down to notice it wasn't the symbol itself absorbing the light, but the area within the symbol. The floor was alight with every color Jerek could think of. It danced and flowed together making it difficult to pick out any one color to hold on to.

The floor flashed bright white showing an image for just a moment. The chant grew in intensity, though Jerek hardly noticed it. He was mystified by a side of the ritual he had never seen before.

The floor flashed once again leaving the image for just a moment longer showing Jerek his new home for the foreseeable future. The sound of the chant boomed to its highest point causing the image to flash again. The light faded out from beneath Jerek, save the outer edges of the image he now saw. A hill of sand beneath his feet.

Jerek looked up to Doe'n and made eye contact with the man for what they both knew would be the last time.

"Tell everyone that I apologize for my actions. Tell them I wish I could take it all back."

Doe'n nodded at Jerek. "Qui'l vanie … TERREI!"

A power took hold of Jerek. Terror filled him and he closed his eyes. He didn't want to see what happened next though he knew what it would be. He felt the ground slip from beneath him and he fell into suspension for just a few moments before he found soft earth beneath his feet. His feet slipped from beneath him and he began rolling down a hill that seemed to last forever.

20

Kane stirred in his sleep. The air felt wrong. There was a static to it; a charge that was not there normally. He pushed up to a seated position and felt out at the energies around him. His cave felt as it always had. Empty, save for him and his safeguards that would alert him should anything breach the walls.

He reached out beyond the entrance to his cave. The energies were stirring; however, the source was just beyond his sight. Kane felt out further, scanning out among the dunes and even beyond the stone fields. He scanned in all directions to find the source of this disturbance of the norm.

After searching for only a while longer, he found the source. It sat atop the highest dune he knew of. The one he had fell onto when he had first arrived. The beginning of his exile over three years prior had begun on that very hill. And it struck him what this must mean.

Kane shot to his feet. Whoever was coming to join him was in great danger. It was the season of the worm. He needed to get there and save whoever it was before their life, however cruel it would be in this unforgiving place, was cut short.

Kane flew as fast as his feet would carry him. His muscles still hurt from whatever that creature had done to him weeks prior, but this person, whoever it was, needed him. He threw his arm out as he approached the boulder blocking his cave and it shot out away from him. He leapt from the rocky floor using the wind to boost him up to land on the boulder as it flew through the air.

He pushed off of it as hard as he could towards the dune and the portal that would soon open atop it. He pulled slabs of rock up to meet his feet as he ran staying as far from the sand as he could manage while trying to save time. He could see the dune and the circle forming above it that would become the portal.

He could see the multicolored lights shining down upon surface of the dune. He was running out of time. He pushed his legs as hard as he could and then he pushed them harder. The burn in his thighs was almost too much to bear, but he pressed on. His need was greater than the pain.

Truth was, Kane was longing for some company, any company. And if he could save this person, he could have it. The light disappeared and the portal formed. A rift in space and time opened to the outside world. A one-way door to the Mythril Hall that would send Kane's new companion in to meet him or the worm if he couldn't get there in time.

Feet appeared through the portal as the newcomer descended through the hole. As the whole of this person finished his journey through the portal, Kane recognized him immediately. It was the former-Grand Magistrate, Jerek Kis'tohl.

Kane ran with renewed vigor. He would have answers at the very least. A reason for all that had happened. Jerek made ground atop the dune and collapsed down the side of it, much like Kane had the first night. He turned to meet Jerek at the bottom. Before Jerek came to a stop at the bottom the ground was already shaking. The worm was coming.

Kane turned the stone on which he had just stepped and launched himself toward the worm's target. He caught Jerek in his mid-section just as he got to his feet at the bottom of the dune. They cleared the worms exit just in time. Kane pulled Jerek in to him and rolled through the impact in the sands pulling his charge to his feet and into a dead sprint.

"Don't think just run! We have to get to some solid rock!" Jerek was lagging, he still wasn't oriented, but they had no time to wait. Kane pulled him along and Jerek ran absentmindedly along with him.

"Kane … is that you, boy?" Jerek's words betrayed his shaken wits.

"Yes! It's me! Now hurry or we'll be the worm's next meal!" At his urging, Jerek seemed to put a little more effort into his running.

Kane ran, dragging Jerek along with him, zigging and zagging; swerving this way and that way to avoid setting a pattern the worm could follow. They were in the middle of the dune sea and the nearest rocks that would provide safety were his home.

The pain in Kane's legs was becoming almost too much to push from his mind and his charge was breathing heavily and obviously not cut out for this sort of activity. He wouldn't survive long if they didn't get to shelter soon.

Jerek plodded along as quickly as his aged body could carry him. He had allowed himself to grow weak and he would suffer for it now.

Kane saw the top of the cliff that held his home at the bottom as they crested the last dune. They were almost there. Kane summoned a strip of water down the opposite side of the dune. He cooled it as quickly as he could, but it was freezing just in time for them to slide on it as they went shooting down towards the cliff.

The makeshift slide let them fly down the dune with ease and it curved up shooting them into the air towards the cliff. Jerek's screams echoed through the land. It was annoying, but at least Kane wasn't alone anymore.

"We're going to miss!" Jerek screamed when he saw they would over shoot the edge of the cliff.

"I wasn't aiming for the top of the cliff! We're going

to the bottom of the cliff!"

Once they had cleared the edge, Kane summoned a gust of wind to slow them down before they reached the sand below. Once they had Kane pushed off dragging Jerek along towards his cave. They were almost there!

But suddenly Jerek's hand slipped free of Kane's grip. Kane turned to see that Jerek had pulled free and stopped moving. His gaze fixed on Kane, he obviously had just gotten his wits back about him and wanted answers but it wasn't a good time.

"Kane, you will tell me what is going on before I take another step!"

"I'll explain once we get inside the cave, but we must get inside otherwise we'll die!"

Kane started running back towards Jerek as the ground began to shake. Jerek stumbled and fell back into a seated position before meeting Kane's eyes. He mouthed the words 'I'm sorry' before the worm shot out of the ground beneath him swallowing him whole. Kane ran headlong into the side of the worm and was sent flying towards the cliff-face.

He used a gust of wind to orient his flight towards the open cave and called a boulder to block the entrance. He flipped back and slid to a halt in the tunnel leading to his home. He stared longingly at the now covered entrance.

Kane fell to his hands and knees. Tears began streaming from his eyes. They had almost made it. Once again he was alone and the pain of that realization was almost unbearable. Painful thoughts were racing through his mind. 'Why had the worm chosen Jerek and not him? Why had Jerek not just followed him to safety? Why didn't Jerek just trust him for a few moments more?' He worked over thought after thought after thought, but no answer would stop the agonizing loneliness that was consuming him.

"Why him and not me? Why must I continue to

suffer so ..." he closed his eyes and bit his lip against the pain, against the loss. Kane screamed at the top of his lungs, more in anger than sadness. "WHY!!"

Kane screamed again, this time his instincts added a force of energy to his scream which caused the tunnel to expand and crack under the pressure. His lungs burned from the exertion. His legs didn't want to work anymore. He had pumped his arms so hard they felt like they would fall off any moment. And on top of all that, he had lost Jerek Kis'tohl to the worm.

He was so close to getting answers; so close to not being alone. He had almost saved the man that had condemned him to this fate so long ago. He had almost gotten answers for everything that had happened. Kane reluctantly pushed up to standing and made his way back into his alcove. He had failed to save the one person that could give him at least some semblance of closure.

He sat down to wallow in his anger and sorrow. He would remain alone for the rest of his time here it seemed. But at least he had the little amount of conversation he had had with Jerek before he died. He could take solace in that much. At least he had gotten to speak, even as quickly as he had, with another Atrethian.

Aerika felt like she was in shock. Her emotions were going crazy. She thought it might be more accurate to say that Kane's were going crazy. In a matter of minutes she had felt joy, fear, anger and sadness. She couldn't even remember which one she had felt first, but she knew that the anger was consuming her brother.

She sat in her room staring at her brother's old bed, terrified of what that anger might do to him. If he let the anger take control of him, he could become something worse than anything their world had ever seen.

The thought of her brother becoming something like that, some kind of monster, it was more horrifying than anything she could imagine. She knew he would conquer his anger. He was too strong to let it take over. At least, she thought he was too strong for that to happen.

Tears began to stream anew from her eyes. She lay her face down upon her pillow and let the sobs overtake her. It felt good to let out the sadness she was feeling, but the release wasn't always enough. She would speak with Tieg when she stopped. He had become her confidant in all things.

She trusted him to keep her pain from everyone, including her father. If he knew she suffered as she did, he may not be able to control his own emotions. Tieg was a good friend, both to her and to Kane, despite all that had happened and surely would happen.

Her tears soaked her pillow. It became almost uncomfortable for her to continue to lay on it so she pushed the pillow away and just cried into the bed. Her heart felt as though it were breaking for her brother. She wanted so badly to help him more, but that last trip out there had distanced her from what was real.

She had become plagued with visions of what lie behind that barrier, though she had never seen them save through her connection to Kane. Interacting with The Bubble as she had must have altered her energies and somehow connected her to that place.

She couldn't decide which emotion she needed to feel. She was scared of what Kane might become and what that place had done to her. She was filled with sorrow at what her brother was going through because of her. And then she felt all of his emotions. And she realized that she hardly knew him anymore and that thought alone brought her more pain than she had ever felt.

A knock came to her door. Her sobs kept her from hearing it. Moments later, another knock sounded through the room. Aerika slowly lifted herself up from her bed trying to contain herself, but she was too deep in her own emotions. She couldn't stop crying now.

She swallowed hard, containing what she could so she could speak, "Who is there?" Her words were shaky despite her efforts.

"It's Tieg." His voice betrayed his worry. It was almost as though he was getting cues from somewhere to when she needed someone. She thought that he must be gaining a sense of when things were wrong with her.

"Tieg ..." His name had barely broken free of her lips when she became racked with sobs again. Tieg heard her only barely and pushed open the door. He slid it closed behind him before he moved across the room to her. She lay back down against the bed, consumed by her emotions.

Tieg just sat next to her with his hand resting on her shoulder. This was how he comforted her. He would always just sit with her and let her know he was there. That was really all he could do and, considering the situation, it was enough.

Kane sat with his legs crossed, his eyes closed tight. His energy roiled with the anger that was now feeding it. He was starting to like the way it felt. He let his eyes open as he pushed up to his feet. He walked with purpose to the end of the tunnel leading into his home. He raised his arm to push the boulder from its resting place.

Once the entrance was clear Kane pushed off with his legs lifting into the air. He caught himself with a powerful wind that carried him from his cave all the way to the rock fields. He landed atop a boulder and pushed off leaping from rock to rock.

He felt out with his energy to find if anything was near. There was something at the other end of the fields. It was just what he wanted and he felt like he would make short work of it this time.

Kane pushed himself to run across the top of the

boulders as fast as he could. He could see the beast that he searched for. It noticed his approach and turned to wait for him to arrive.

He got to the last boulder before reaching the Behemoth that stood waiting for him, hunger in its eyes and rage twisting its face. Kane pushed off of the rock flying over the beast, just barely slipping from the grip of the massive creature.

He flipped over the Behemoth and, pulling his hand in knife's edge cutting motion across at it, summoned wind to do as he desired. The wind cut through the legs of the Behemoth as if it weren't even there. It twisted in the air as it fell, legless.

Kane made two more cutting motions with his hand, separating the beast's arms from its body as well. The look of rage upon its face didn't change, though fear was now in its eyes. Nothing except the worm had ever challenged it and won and now it was at Kane's mercy.

He walked slowly up to the beast that was staring up into the sky. He climbed up onto its huge torso and sat down on its head, fixing its eyes with his own. He reached down and took hold of the beast by the fur on the side of its head.

A sinister grin crawled across Kane's lips before being quickly replaced with the fury in his own heart. He slammed the creatures head against the rocks on which it now lay. The knots in Kane's stomach loosened. His anger was fading out from within.

The behemoth flinched at the hit and had no time to recover before Kane did it again and again and again. It roared out in the pain it was feeling, something it had never known outside of the eclipse. Kane beat its head continuously against the rock until the dull thunk of skull against rock became nothing more that the sickening sound of sagging flesh slapping against stone.

The brutal scene continued long after the unnatural

life had left the behemoth. Kane continued to relish in the sound and feel of slamming the creature's lifeless head against the rocks. The beast's blood was splattering onto him, but Kane didn't mind it. The rage; the pain; the anguish he felt, was released. He felt comfort in the death he had just caused.

Aerika stood unmoving amid quickly thickening brush. Flowers sprouted from the vines as they slithered up and around the massive trees that were growing around her. Wind and rain blew through the forest, weaving its way between the thick foliage. Cones grew on the coniferous trees and fruit sprang from the fruit-bearing.

The sweet scent of new life overwhelmed Aerika's senses. The rain washed over her and soaked her training robes. Her hair whipped in the frenzy of life blossoming around her. She looked to her left and raised her hand towards the sky calling a brand new tree to spring from the ground as if it had been there the whole time.

The deepening forest continued to grow and flourish. She conjured life at her slightest whim. The training room in which she stood was now completely filled with grass, flowers and trees of all shapes and size. Every sight, scent and sound you could imagine in a forest was found in this one room. The room expanded to welcome in what was conjured by the user within.

Tieg stood in awe of what Aerika had created. He had never seen anything quite so wonderful. Her control of the energy around her allowed to create life from it simply by changing its nature. He had only heard of one other person able to do that in the past and that person was dubbed the 'Malicious One'.

Aerika didn't have the means to make it permanent though. It would only remain so long as she maintained her concentration. She let the trees wither and shrink into nothing. The grass receded next and the flowers simply shrank once more into the floor from where they had grown. She opened her eyes to survey the room.

She smiled when she saw Tieg. "You're still here." she said. "How long has it been since I started?"

Tieg shrugged. "I'm not sure, but it was absolutely amazing. Your control is unlike anything I could ever imagine. How did you make all of that?"

Aerika shook her head. "I don't really know. I just think it and it happens." Her eyes met his then she nervously dropped her gaze to the ground. "The energy just does what I ask it to do. I'm not sure why."

Tieg looked away feeling that he had embarrassed her with his questions. "I ... I'm sorry for asking you so many questions all the time."

"No, Tieg." she replied. She took hold of his chin and turned him back to lock eyes with her. "You're my friend. I like having you around and your curiosity is part of who you are. Don't ever change, Tieg. Ever."

A smile crept across Tieg's lips. The few moments of true joy he got to share with Aerika made all of the other times worth it. Aerika laughed a little to lighten the mood up and walked out of the training room. Tieg shook his head, laughed a little himself and followed her out.

The two friends made their way through one of the many halls of The Academy. As they turned a corner an unassuming man almost ran headlong into them.

"Whoa!" He slid to a halt and bent forward at his waist resting his hands on his knees. His chest heaved as he drew in several deep breaths trying to catch it. "Aerika?"

She looked at the man for moment trying to place how he knew her, but she definitely didn't recognize him. She looked over at Tieg to see if he did. He looked just as puzzled as she did. She decided it was best just to answer him. "Yes? How may I help you?"

"Aerika," his voice sounded relieved, but dire at the

same time. "You need to come with me." he continued, "It's your father."

The dire tone in the man's voice when he mentioned her father sent a shock down her spine. The man's tone had escaped Tieg as he stood still confused as to what was going on.

"Take me to him." The command didn't really hold much authority, but the man nodded none-the-less and turned taking off at a dead sprint. Aerika followed close on his heels without missing a beat. It took a moment for Tieg to realize they had started moving. He stumbled for a moment trying to get his legs to follow.

They seemed to be running forever. Every corridor looked the same as every other. Each stairwell just as blurry as the last. Aerika couldn't focus on anything except her father at the moment and details around her were understandably escaping her notice.

She was almost outrunning the man leading her. Her mind was racing with what could possibly be so wrong that they were taking her out of training. She wanted to push harder, but she knew that it would do no good; she didn't know where her father was.

They raced into the entry hall of The Academy. There were Enforcer's waiting to open the doors for them and when they saw the pace at which they approached they pushed the doors open as quickly as they could. Tieg, Aerika and their guide barely squeezed between the doors. Aerika would have seen to it that doors were opened for them had they not been prepared.

They raced down busy city streets. They blew through the busy market. Tieg and the guide took great care to dodge everyone around them. Aerika just ran without bothering. She caused a few to stumble and even ran headlong into others, but she never fell and never slowed.

They took turn after turn after turn, weaving their way

through the thick of Mi'Tiya. When Aerika realized they were headed for her home, she pushed her legs as hard as she could. She blew past the guide almost as if he were standing still. Tieg sped up trying to keep up with her, though he knew that he couldn't. She had a much more important purpose for her pace.

Aerika sped up to the door to the house she had grown up in. There were a pair of Enforcer's standing outside the door. They opened the door for her as she ran up. She slowed as she approached the entrance and came to a halt just inside. She looked around the familiar home. Aside from looking unkempt everything was in place.

Without further pause, Aerika walked to her father's room. He was lying on the bed, comfortably under the covers. He drew his gaze over to her. A weak smile crawled across his lips.

"Aerika," he whispered, "my lovely daughter."

"I'm here." she said out of breath. She made her way to the side of his bed and sat down beside him. "What's wrong father? Are you sick? Hurt?" Her panic was evident no matter how she tried to hide it.

"You've always been so strong. You were stronger than me and your mother both. You dealt with all of this the best out of us."

Tears welled up in her eyes. She shook her head in defiance. "No ... you can't"

He put his hand atop hers and shushed her. "Aerika," he continued, "I need you to be strong again. I need you to keep moving forward. You need to be here when your brother comes back."

Tieg walked into the room still trying to catch his breath. He looked at the scene and just stayed near the door.

"So do you, father! You can't leave me!" Tears streamed unhindered down her cheeks. "Kane will need us both! He will need a family when he comes back!"

"Aerika." he tried to make his tone as soothing as he could. "You will be all the family he needs. You two only ever needed each other. You never needed your mother and I much. I know this isn't easy for you, but I must go to be with your mother. It is where I belong."

Aerika closed her eyes against the tears, but they still pushed through. Her chest heaved with the sobs that came unbidden. She clenched her teeth trying to hold it all back.

"I know it's not fair, Aerika. You've already lost so much, but I don't have a reason to stay any more. It's just my time. I am sorry. I'm so ... so ... sor ..." His hand fell slack on hers and his eyes slid closed.

Aerika slid from the bed down to her knees and let the sobs take her. Tieg knelt beside Aerika and put a hand on her shoulder. She fell against him and cried into his shoulder. He slid his arms around her and just held her there while she mourned.

21

Kane let his hands slip from the fur at the side of the Behemoths head. His joy in the carnage he perpetrated slipped away. He looked down at the blood coating his hands and much of his body. Kane pushed one hand down the other to try to clean the blood from them, but both of his hands were so covered that it really didn't change. A frown washed over his face and fear of what he had just done crept into his heart. He continued to frantically wring his hands together trying to clean them of the blood he had just spilled.

He shook his head at the grizzly scene before him. He fell to his knees beside the beast and stared unblinking at his hands. "What have I done?" His words, barely a whisper, were more thinking-out-loud than a plea for answers.

Kane pushed away from the ground and ran off towards his home. His mind raced and raced over what he had just done. The memory of what he did had burned itself into the forefront of his mind. Once he got back to his cave, he pulled the boulder in to block the entrance and fell into a ball on the floor.

Kane lost control of himself and began to weep. The guilt of his vicious act had caught up with him. A sound somewhere in his cave brought him out of his haze of sorrow. He clambered to his feet, preparing himself for whatever may be lurking within his home.

He waited silently, listening for whatever was about to make another noise. When it did, Kane's heart jumped into his throat. It was behind him. He turned slowly to see the bloody head of the Behemoth before him, attached to its body with arms and legs restored. It roared and brought its fangs to bear on him.

Kane screamed as he awoke from the nightmare. Sweat drenched every inch of his body. It had been several days since he had killed the Behemoth. The guilt was eating away at him; eating away at his resolve. He struggled to catch his breath. His heart beat wildly. The nightmares had started the following night and they were getting worse.

His muscles were tense. They kept his body stuck. He could only look around. He was frozen in the terror of his dreams. It was hard enough to deal with the desert as it was. To add this to it would make it nearly impossible to survive.

After a while, Kane felt his muscles loosen up. He sat up slowly as if he were unsure if his muscles would work and wiped the sweat from his brow. He pushed slowly up to his feet and stretched. His muscles burned at the strain. The air in his cave was thick with energy. Kane must have released it during his dream.

He thought hard, searching his memory for what he had dreamt, but to no avail. He couldn't remember what had woken him. He never could with his nightmares. He tried to stretch out his muscles again, but it just hurt too much. Kane lay back down and just stared at the ceiling. He wouldn't sleep anymore this night. He would just have to wait until morning.

In the silence of the cave, the slightest noise made it impossible for Kane to relax. He would hear something scrape against the stone or a breeze would blow through and move a small stone. At least that's what he thought he was hearing, though he really couldn't be sure. And even when he went to investigate, he found nothing.

Morning finally came but he had gotten too little rest. The days were getting harder and harder to process through the exhaustion. His reflexes would slow and his awareness would slip … eventually.

Kane let the boulder simply roll out of the way this time. He was too tired to want to do anything more than that. He wanted to stay in and rest, but he knew he needed to stay active to survive. Though, death seemed more and more welcoming with each passing moment without rest. At least in death he could rest.

The desolate and unwelcoming landscape of the desert stretched on and on in every direction. Kane decided he would just go for a while. Maybe he would get tired enough that he could just sleep through without dreaming. That was a hope he wouldn't dare hold on to.

Kane simply chose a direction and started walking. He had become rather adept at moving in the sands over the years so he scaled the dunes with ease in spite of his exhaustion. His descent of each dune was much more graceful than his first day. He pushed his way on and on. A strange rock formation blocked the horizon from view. He decided he would find his way to this formation and see what it was.

He walked for hours and hours. The day seemed to go on forever, or at least he felt like it did. It was probably just exhaustion tricking his sense of time. Kane crested yet another dune and found the base of the rock formation just ahead. This particular formation stretched as far as he could see into the sky and as far to his left and right as he could see as well. It seemed to go on forever.

Kane couldn't tell for sure, but he thought he saw an opening near the bottom of the formation. Only a few more hours of walking and he would be at its base and he would find out for sure. He pressed on, pushing through the harshest lands yet. Jagged rocks, narrow walkways with sheer falls, uneven and loose terrain. His path was treacherous but he was determined to make it.

He pushed on through to the base of the massive mountain. It indeed stretched far up into the sky and went unending in both directions as if to serve as a barrier for everything within. At the base of the massive structure was an opening big enough to fit a Behemoth.

Kane stepped in without hesitation. If he truly cared about survival now, he probably would have turned back, but his care for his own well-being was becoming more and more non-existent. He pushed on through into the unknown. It felt much like his own cave, though the jagged walls proved just how natural the creation of this cave was. He moved deeper and deeper through the winding cavern.

Just when he thought it couldn't get any darker in the cave he spotted a strange glow at the end of the corridor in which he found himself. When he rounded the next corner, he entered a large antechamber that stretched up into the blackness. If there was a ceiling, Kane couldn't see it. But the glow of The Bubble filled the room with a dim golden light. He had never seen it before. Even living within it, it stretched so far into the sky that you couldn't see it and he lived too far from it to see it from his home.

He lost himself in the gravity of his predicament. It now dawned on him that there was an end to all of this. And now, he had seen it. He took a step towards the wall of the bubble trying to take in all that it was. He heard scratching against the rock walls. Lots of it. There was an uncountable number of creature's here.

The sounds echoed through the chamber. He couldn't tell where they were and that did not bode well for him. His hope temporarily renewed drove him to run as hard and as fast as he could out of the cave. He threw an arm out cutting a path straight through and out back to the dunes. He wouldn't stop until he was safe back in his home.

Aerika knelt atop the hill her mother had been buried. Now her husband had joined her in her resting place. He had said he wanted to be with her and now he was, in body and in spirit. She couldn't bring herself to cry, to mourn her father's passing. So much had happened that to cry even one more time seemed too daunting a task.

Tieg stood on the hill across from her. She had asked him to let her say her goodbyes alone. Kane was in exile, her mother passed in her grief and her father followed all too shortly after. Now she was alone. The last of her family left unless Kane returned from exile, which by all accounts seemed an impossible event. Aerika admonished herself for such thinking; 'Until' Kane returned. She had to have faith that he would keep his promise. Otherwise she had no real reason to continue on herself.

She placed her hand atop the small boulder afforded her for her parents monument. Their names, Sinal and Liana, already inscribed upon its face. She had yet to decide upon the epitaph. It would be hard to choose the words to describe the lives of her beloved parents.

Aerika brought her eyes around to fall on Tieg. When she saw he was still watching her, she smiled. Tieg made his way across to stand beside Aerika. He looked at the monument for a moment before looking back to Aerika.

His words broke through the silence atop the hill in what felt like a hostile manner though that was just the serene nature of this place. "Did you decide what the epitaph would be?"

She shook her head. "No," she said almost dejected. "It's not easy to reduce all that they meant to me to just a few sentences."

Tieg nodded. He didn't really understand, because both of his parents were still alive, but he did understand how hard it could be to describe just what they meant to him.

Aerika stared at the boulder for a few moments more. Her thoughts drifted to Kane and how she viewed him. A genuine smile fell upon her. She knew how to describe them. She would use the way she had seen her own brother as an inspiration for the epitaph. At least how she viewed him the last time she had seen him.

A light breeze blew through the hills overlooking Mi'Tiya. The fresh scent of the morning dew carried to Aerika by the wind filled her with a sense of calm. She closed her eyes and drew in a deep breath. She had laid her parents to rest atop this hill many year before. She had thought this an appropriate place because of how much time her family had spent there while they were still together.

A single tree stood atop the hill before her. At the base of the tree stood a single stone monument. It was a simple enough monument that, at first glance, could easily be mistaken for a plain boulder. At the top of the face of the monument two names were inscribed; Sinal and Liana. Below the names was an epitaph for the two that had past.

In life, their love brought light to the world around them; In death, let them serve as an example of love eternal.

Aerika had chosen the words herself. She thought it best described their lives before the tragedy that had befallen their family. Kane walked up next to her and looked across at the grave site. His parents had both left this life during his exile.

"This is the place?" Kane had been hardened by his experiences but he still felt a pang of guilt, as though somehow he knew they would still be with them had he never been sent into that forsaken place. Aerika didn't speak; a slight nod was her only answer.

Kane stepped off making his way to the monument marking their graves. He could at least pay his respects. He stood before the stone marker, reading the inscription and trying to come up with words to say. His mouth opened for just a moment, but he bit back his words. They wouldn't do, he knew. Nothing he said could make up for what was lost.

"Mother ... Father," his whispered words broke the

solemn silence of the grave site. "I'm sorry." He raised his hand up and brushed his fingers across their names above the epitaph. Blood trailed behind his fingers marring the beauty of the monument.

Kane stepped back in shock and flipped his hands up to look at the blood dripping from his hands. He tried to draw in a deep breath to calm his nerves, but his lungs caught as if there was no air to breathe. He closed his eyes and concentrated on slowing his heart-rate. It felt as though it would explode through his chest at any moment.

He knew it wasn't real. He only had to regain that connection to reality. Kane finally found his breath. He slid his eyes open to see the monument and his hands clean. He took another deep breath in and looked back across to Aerika. She still stood on the hill he had joined her at before. Perhaps she thought it was his turn to mourn them; she had already gone through all of this after all.

Another breeze blew over the hills. Aerika hugged herself against the chill and locked eyes with Kane to let him know it was time to leave. He nodded in response to her silent plea and turned back to face the monument, but it was gone. Replaced by the massive form of the fallen behemoth.

Its severed arms and legs lay nearby. Its head looked more a fleshy, blood-soaked mass then the head of a fearsome creature. The hills before him were now hills of sand and the ground on which he stood was stone though you could hardly see it through the blood pooled upon it.

Terror crept into Kane's heart. Not fear of the fact that he now knew he was in a nightmare, but fear of himself; Fear of what he was capable of, of what he had already done. Kane closed his eyes and took in a deep breath hoping to get fresh air. All he could smell, however, was death; the dead, rotting flesh of the Behemoth that lay at his feet.

He rose slowly from his sleep. It wasn't deep at all and it was hardly as restful. He hadn't slept well in weeks.

The nightmares had gone from bad to worse. He was beginning to feel as though the desert had corrupted him into becoming one of the monsters that lived within it. The rage he felt that drove him to kill the Behemoth still smoldered within him and the knowledge that it was a part of him frightened him more than anything he had faced. The thought of what he might be capable of brought out that fear.

He bit back at the fear rising up in himself. He swallowed hard to get the feeling back down into the pit of his stomach. Once he felt the tight knot collect in his gut, he chided himself for that fear. He knew better than to fear anything. Fear would give him pause and that pause would get him killed. And that would break his promise to return.

22

All around Magus, the air itself ignited. The conflagration spread through the air about him and until it had surrounded him completely. The flames formed a complete sphere around him. He focused on maintaining the control. He had gained more and more control over the power of his fire.

Magus gritted his teeth, focusing more on controlling the fire. Suddenly, the flames around him lifted him from the ground. The air all throughout the training room sizzled from the heat he was creating. It had become almost unbearable to Tieg who was watching his brother for the first time in a while.

Magus let the heat recede and he lowered to the floor. The flames had left scorch marks on the floor and ceiling more from the heat than from contact with the fire. Magus let the flames die down until there was barely a spark remaining. The single remaining spark floated before Magus' eyes. He watched it for a moment before he closed a fist around allowing it to finally dissipate.

Tieg finally caught Magus' eye. Magus' gaze fell upon his brother for a moment before a look of disgust crawled across his face. "What are you doing here? Shouldn't you be with that shameful girl?"

"Don't you call her that!" Tieg stepped quickly across the room stopping within inches of Magus. "She has lost everything in her life because of the actions of others and you know it!"

The righteous fire of Tieg's anger was evident in his

eyes. The angers target stared, unblinking, right back. A sinister smile crawled across Magus' lips. "That anger ... This is the first time I actually believe that we're brothers, brother."

Tieg checked himself and blinked long while backing away from Magus. He fought back the anger and let the fire die; No matter how righteous. Tieg was not like his brother. He was the compassionate one. He would never raise a hand in anger to anyone, even if it were righteous.

Magus chuckled under his breath. "That's what I thought. It never lasts. Go back to your girlfriend and stop interrupting my training. I have a great destiny ahead of me and I'll not let you stand in my way. Leave me and don't come back. You don't deserve to be my brother."

Tieg looked into the eyes of his twin for only a moment longer. "Magus, I don't know what's wrong with you that you can't see the pain of others. Or maybe you do and you just don't care. Either way, I pity you. Take care, brother. I can't allow myself to be around people like you ... for my own sake."

Tieg walked to the door and paused for a moment. He wasn't sure if he wanted to look back or if he had just paused hoping that Magus would suddenly change his ways and ask forgiveness for his cruelty. Neither happened. Magus returned to his training and Tieg disappeared down the many winding corridors of The Academy.

At this point in their training, Tieg and the other students his age could come and go from The Academy as they pleased. It was merely on them to train further. The instructors had all taught them everything they could. Tieg made his way to the main doors and exited out onto the busy streets of Mi'Tiya.

Tieg thought he would wander for a bit. He needed to think. He had just been told by his brother that he never wanted to see him again. It was a lot to deal with. He let his mind wander to other things.

He thought of Aerika and how she must be feeling. Her father and mother both gone from this world. Her brother, Kane, long exiled, if he even still lived. He thought of how horrible it must be to have lost all of that and not even know if her twin was still alive.

But, he thought, she had been having those nightmares. Seeing creature's that couldn't possibly exist in their world. Perhaps they were visions of what Kane were seeing. Or maybe, he had died long ago and those were visions of the things that had killed him. There was no way to be sure.

He shook the dark thoughts from his head and looked about to get his bearings. He was a bit shocked to find himself standing before Aerika's home. Though, it sort of made sense when he thought about where his mind had been.

He knocked on the door. He may as well see how she was doing since he was there. After waiting a moment, he knocked again. Once again, nothing. She must not be home. He turned to head back into the city and to his room at The Academy. Just as he did the door opened.

Aerika stood in the doorway rubbing her eyes. She looked as though she hadn't slept in days, maybe longer. The dark circles only made her pure white eyes stand out more in contrast. A small smile crept across her lips though it seemed forced to Tieg.

"Aerika, are you alright?" The look of worry was plainly evident on Tieg's features.

She shook her head. "I'm fine, Tieg." she lied. She knew he worried and she hated to worry him about something he couldn't help. "I've just been awake a lot dealing with family affairs. We have distant relatives that need to be notified of my parents passing."

Tieg knew the whole thing was a lie. He had helped her to find and inform all of her family. There was no one left to notify, but he went along with it anyway. He knew what she was trying to do. "Alright then. I was out walking and thought I would see how you were doing. Do you need anything? I can make a stop in the market."

Aerika absently fiddled with the teardrop pendant hanging at her neck. She shook her head just the slightest bit. "No, I'm just going to try getting some sleep. It's been a long day."

Tieg nodded. He wanted to say more, but pressing the issue wouldn't do any good. Aerika was stubborn. He smiled, hoping maybe it would improve her mood a little bit knowing that someone was still around for her.

She stared off at nothing while pushing the door closed. When all the light from the open door had gone, she made her way back to her bed.

She flopped down onto the bed. The softness of the pillow was something she had become intimately familiar with over the past days. She hadn't even moved from the bed until Tieg had knocked. That's not to say that she had slept however. A vision of a giant, hairy beast covered in its own blood had been haunting her when she closed her eyes.

She had no idea what it was, nor what had killed it. But she knew that she had never seen it's like before and something that massive had to have been exceedingly difficult to kill.

She had thought that maybe Kane had killed the beast, but she didn't want to think her brother capable of such a brutal act. Somehow though, she knew deep down that he had done it; that Kane had killed it. And, furthermore, she somehow knew that it hadn't been in defense of his own life. That thought terrified her more than the image itself.

The arm of one Scythe cut through the air at Kane. He leaned back letting it pass over him before he twisted to avoid another that followed from a second source. He calmly calculated each move; Ducking cut after cut, slash after slash. He dodged this way and that.

His movements were fluid and deliberate; He wasted no energy; He wasted no movement. He was getting better at survival in these situations than he could have hoped. As one of the blades stabbed at him he spun to the side grabbing hold at the creature's shoulder. Without stopping he twisted the arm back around and pushed it through into the chest of its source.

Another blade arced across at his shoulders. Kane ducked under the one before pushing off the ground to flip over the next as it swung low. He gripped the arm of the beast mid-flip and twisted it off at the elbow.

As Kane's feet hit ground he thrust the blade as hard as he could into the back of the remaining Scythe. He paused to let the creature die before letting it fall to the ground. He surveyed the bodies that litter the tiny battlefield. He had run across these Scythes as he had been hunting for food.

It had gotten easier for him to handle these creatures. His cold, emotionless gaze crawled across the lifeless forms before he stepped off once again to continue his search.

It had been nearly a year since he had killed the Behemoth in cold-blood and it only seemed to get easier to do it. He had completely cleared out the area surrounding his home. Now the creatures of the desert knew to fear going near the cave in which he lived.

It had taken him a while to get used to the idea of killing, but he decided these things that lived here weren't worth the time it took to mourn them. With every death following that first, it got easier and easier to do what he needed to survive. He had even started to enjoy the rush of the fight. The euphoria of the battle for survival.

Kane had gotten so used to the desert itself that his footfalls left minimal tracks to follow. The creatures could no longer follow him. He had even taken to stalking the

Stalkers when he had nothing to entertain himself.

He would hunt them for days without them knowing he was there. He would watch them hunt, feed and even sleep. When he grew bored of the hunt, he would kill them, sometimes while they slept. It had all become something of a game to him.

This calm that he felt while killing the different inhabitants of the desert had frightened him at first, but as he learned to swallow his emotions, it became less and less a chore to deal with. Survival felt almost a certainty though at this point he could hardly imagine life outside with others.

The cold disdain he felt for all life in the desert crept across his heart again. It normally stayed away longer after a kill. He figured he would have to find something else to play with.

Aerika sat upright quickly. Her breath caught in her throat. The bitter taste of bile stained her tongue. Her nightmares lately had been only of Kane. He was viciously killing these otherworldly creatures without the slightest hint of remorse. She had even had a few in which he had been hunting them for no other reason than to hunt them.

In these nightmares, he had felt cold; He had felt detached, even hateful. She couldn't figure out why she was having these dreams of her brother, but she refused to accept that it was actually happening. Her brother was far too kind to do the things he did in her dreams.

Sweat beat at her brow. She cringed at the bitter taste in her mouth. She slid her feet off the bed onto the floor and coughed trying to catch her breath. Just as she did, a knock came at the door. It had to be Tieg. No one else came to see her. She thought it was probably out of fear.

So much misfortune had plagued her family; people must think her blood cursed. She rose to her feet and made her way to the door. When she pulled it open she saw the pain on his face.

"Tieg?" She said, "What is it? What's happened?"

"I fought with Magus ... He said he never wants to see me again."

"But, you're brothers ..." Her words seemed more a question than a statement. She felt as if she had been pleading for herself more than for Tieg.

"I know, but he's just ... intolerable!" The anger in his voice made her flinch. Tieg saw her and closed his eyes before drawing in a deep breath. "I'm sorry. I shouldn't shout at you. You did nothing wrong."

She smiled her soft, comforting smile. "It's alright. You're upset and understandably so." Tieg opened his eyes again to look at her. "What did you fight about anyway?"

Tieg averted his eyes. As soon as he did, she knew exactly what had happened. "Tieg ... I'm so sorry. You should not suffer for my sake."

"Maybe not, but you don't deserve any less than a loyal friend that cares about you! I'll not suffer anyone to speak ill of you or your family! It's not fair to you!"

She saw, for the first time, the righteous anger burning in his eyes. He had been standing up for a long time, obviously. The fire burned bright and deep and Aerika could see no end to it. She just smiled at him hoping to cull the flames at least a bit.

Tieg blinked away the anger. In the brief moment that his eyes had been closed Aerika's arms had wrapped around him. He kept his eyes closed just relishing in the embrace of his friend. Her compassion was amazing given all she had been through.

She held her friend hoping to push away both of their problems. The cold feeling she got when she tried to reach out to her brother and his brother's clear disdain for him. It felt like it were linked somehow, but she couldn't place it. Maybe spending time with a friend would diminish her problems somehow. And maybe she could help him to bear his own burdens.

As she stood there in silence with her friend, sharing in his grief, she couldn't help but think of Kane and what he must be going through. She wondered what trials he must really be facing in exile. She shook her head a bit to bring it back to this moment. "So, when did you fight with him?" she asked.

"Yesterday … Just before I knocked on your door." She was confused as to why he only now brought it up, but she imagined that she must have looked terrible for him to care more for her than losing touch with his own twin brother.

"Tieg, why didn't you say something?" Her worry for him was evident in the sound of her voice.

"Because you looked like you needed me more than I needed you."

She smiled. She had grown to expect no less from him. He was a good friend and far better than she thought she deserved. But he seemed to know better than her.

23

Magus sat in silent meditation. His blood still boiled from his confrontation with Tieg days before. He couldn't believe his own brother would be so weak. Heat began emanating from his very skin causing the very air around him to sizzle. Just as his anger were about to reach its peak, a knock came at the door.

He ignored it thinking whoever it was would get the hint that he didn't want to be bothered. His thoughts began to trail back to his destiny and what he would one day accomplish. He smiled his arrogant smile, but that quickly turned to a frown at the sound of the door opening.

"Oh I'm sorry ... I didn't think anyone was in here." It was a shy boy, maybe a little younger than Magus. The boy was so skinny it seemed he wasn't fit for his skin.

"How dare you interrupt me! Who is it that you think you are just walking into a room with a closed door?!" Magus now had an outlet for his anger and this child was in the wrong place at the wrong time.

Fear was grossly apparent in the soft blue eyes of the boy. He had never seen such rage before, let alone had it directed at him. "I ... I don't know what to say. I'm sorry! I knocked first and came in when there was no answer ..."

Magus closed the distance to the boy causing him to back up against the wall. "And you thought that was acceptable?! Closed doors mean people are training! Explain yourself now, you simple fool!"

The boy was at a loss for words. He opened his mouth, but he couldn't find his voice. Fear gripped at the boys very heart-strings. He fell to the ground and curled up into a ball. Magus enjoyed that this boy was now cowering at his feet.

"You are very lucky that I don't kill you for such insolence!" Magus thought he would bask in his feeling of power for a bit longer before sending this boy on his way.

"Is that so?! And you think threatening other students is appropriate?!" The deep voice echoed through the training room. Magus' eyes were drawn to its source. Standing in the door was exactly what he had feared. An Enforcer had overheard the entire exchange. Magus knew he wouldn't get out of this one.

"You have a lot of nerve, boy!" The Enforcer marched up to stand over Magus. "You think that you are special?! That you are exempt from the rules at The Academy?!"

Though Magus couldn't see the eyes of the Enforcer, he could feel them staring right back into his own. And his fear of this imposing figure kept him from looking away at all. The gaze from behind the Enforcer's helmet kept Magus frozen.

"No answer, then? Fine! We'll just see what the Headmaster wants to do with you!" The Enforcer took hold of Magus' shoulder and ushered him out into the hallway. They seemed to walk forever. Magus tried to think of a way out of this. His mind went over all possibilities, but it seemed that his fate lie in the hands of the Headmaster.

The winding halls of The Academy seemed to go on forever, though Magus thought it was just his current predicament that made it feel that way. The Enforcer continued to angrily push Magus towards the Headmasters office. It was only a matter of time before they arrived and his fate would be decided.

After walking for what seemed like forever, they came to a hallway that ended at a very elaborate door. The engravings were of trees, animals, people, and buildings. Everything about the door depicted the beauty of Atrethia. The heavy-looking door was made of some type of wood that Magus couldn't identify outright.

The Enforcer shoved Magus hard against the wall next to the Headmasters door and held him there with one hand. With his other hand, he knocked three times upon the Headmasters door.

The Headmaster called from behind the closed door, "Be gone. I'm busy."

"Headmaster. It's Enforcer Dro'Ven. I have an urgent matter that needs your judgment." The Enforcer hadn't taken his eyes from Magus for even a moment.

"Fine, fine. Come in. And be quick about it." The Headmaster sounded agitated and rushed.

The Enforcer pushed the door open and shoved Magus into the room. "Sit." He said pointing at a chair against the wall. He continued to walk towards the Headmasters desk.

"What is this urgent matter, Enforcer?" His tone lacked any sense of patience and seemed more agitated at this intrusion than should have been warranted. Magus was certain now that he wouldn't get off easy for this one.

"Headmaster, I caught this student here threatening the life of another. He very obviously lets his anger and arrogance guide him in his use of The Flow. As he is still a student in The Academy, I thought it better for the matter to be brought to you rather than brought to the High Council."

The Headmaster sat silent for a moment before nodding, his irritation from earlier was gone now that he understood the situation. He also seemed less impatient. "Very good. Thank you, Enforcer Dro'Ven. You did the right thing bringing this matter to me. There is certainly no need to bring it before the Council. They have much more important matters to attend to after all."

The Headmaster stood from his seat. "You … boy! Step up here!"

Magus got to his feet and rushed to stand before the Headmasters desk. The Headmaster appraised him for a moment before continuing.

"What do you have to say for yourself?" The Headmasters tone was authoritative. It came easily to him though Magus thought it was more through practice than anything else.

"Well, Headmaster. The other student had interrupted my meditations."

"And you thought this sufficient reason to threaten his life?"

"I ..." Magus dropped his gaze to the floor. He wasn't ashamed; he just didn't want to look into the Headmaster's eyes while he came up with a reason.

"Whatever your reasoning was … it was insufficient. You should have learned better in year one, but apparently that lesson didn't stick. An infraction like this would have been little more than a slap on the wrist before the incident twenty years ago, but now, I'm afraid I have no choice. You are hereby expelled from The Academy and condemned to banishment from Mi'Tiya. Should you return to this city, your fate will be decided by the High Council."

Magus was taken aback. He hadn't expected expulsion. Not for this. It seemed a tad severe though he supposed he understood why. While the headmaster's calculation was about four years short, it was an accurate assessment of why things had changed. After everything that happened with Kane, punishments were heightened when it came to student interactions. Understanding didn't quell his anger at this situation, however.

"You think that expelling me is going to halt my destiny?! You have no idea who I am, or what I am destined to become! When next I come to Mi'Tiya, I will be greeted as a hero!"

Magus turned on his heels and stormed towards the door. He had hardly taken two steps when Enforcer Dro'Ven took his mind with a bit of The Flow and Magus fell unconscious.

It had been a great many years since things in Aerika's life had taken that turn for the worst. First her brother had been sent into exile for her crimes. Then, her parents had decided they no longer belonged and left her all alone.

Tieg walked beside her. They were headed for the Barean Cliffs ... to the site of her parent's graves. She hugged her cloak tightly around her as a cold gust of wind blew through the hills. It was another chilly day. She smiled weakly at her friend.

She was happy for his company, though it wasn't a happy occasion. It always pained her to visit their grave site. She thought, however, it was more because she feared she would be adding a name to the list on the monument when it came time to seek her brother's return.

Her and Tieg had both completed their training at the Academy and were trying to find their way in the world. Tieg had taken to controlling water flow in Mi'Tiya for the farmers. It was a simple task for him and one that he had become able to do without even being there. She had still not found her own calling. So few things interested her. She wanted only for her brother's return.

She had tried to contact Magus for Tieg. To attempt to smooth things over and get them back together. They were brothers after all. She couldn't stand for them to hate each other. When she searched for him, she had found out that he had threatened another student at the Academy and had been thrown out without completing his training.

She thought maybe she would find him doing some menial labor or something nearby, but he had simply disappeared. And he had done well in covering his tracks. He certainly did not want to be found, wherever he had gone.

She and Tieg came to the top of a hill. It sloped down again and back up to a hill with a tree and the stone monument. This had become a very solemn place. Her eyes were already beginning to fill with tears and she wasn't even to the monument yet. This would be a tough visit.

Kane stood at the edge of a steep rock overhang. The desert stretched out before him. A gentle wind whistled by blowing his now shoulder length hair to the side. He closed his platinum eyes and drew in a deep breath.

He had grown a lot since arriving in exile. He still remembered that first night. His first encounter with a Stalker. He recalled how he had cried himself to sleep that night. And now he couldn't even remember the last time he had cried.

Now, he stalked Stalkers for entertainment. The Scythes weren't even a nuisance anymore. They were too slow to even touch him; even in numbers they were easily dispatched. The Lurkers were simple enough to spot and the Behemoth's ... Well they were a slight bit more difficult but he could handle them in single combat.

The worm was simple enough to avoid. All he had to do was stay on the rocks when it was around and it slept the majority of the year. Kane had grown into quite the warrior. 'Father would be proud,' he thought to himself.

He watched as the few denizens of this horrid place that dared tempt his gaze scurried from hiding place to hiding place. Though it did little good. He had not only grown in strength and his physical ability. His control over The Flow had grown with him. Now, if he had no time to take enjoying the fight, he would simply cut them asunder with whatever he fancied at the moment.

He had complete control of every bit of energy that

surrounded him. He could conjure fire hot enough to turn sand to glass. Wind so harsh and precise he could flay flesh straight from bone. At this moment, reflecting on just how far he had come, his thoughts found their way to Aerika and his parents. He wondered how they had been doing.

Aerika stood before her parent's graves. The simple monument stood in stark contrast to the world around it. She placed a hand upon the face of the monument and sighed. Her raven hair flowed along as the wind blew by.

She had grown into a beautiful women though quite scarred with all she had been through. With her twin brother in exile and her parents both gone under the circumstances that they had chosen, she was hard pressed to find anyone that didn't think her bloodline was cursed.

Tieg stepped up beside her. He looked down at the monument for just a moment, and then shifted his gaze across to Aerika. Her fair skin and white eyes stood out against the black of her hair. She returned his gaze and smiled.

"Thank you for coming with me, Tieg." Her voice was very solemn. Tieg knew that it was difficult for her to visit her parent's graves. He hoped that in another year or so it would be Kane that accompanied her to this site.

Kane walked slowly, surveying what had become a land under his dominion. It was only a short trek back to his home and he wanted to enjoy this relaxing day. He came to a halt atop one of the many dunes in the desert. It was one he knew well. The dune he had set foot on first when he arrived that fateful night.

He wasn't sure exactly how long he had been in the desert anymore, but he knew one thing. His time in exile was drawing to a close.

24

The dirt within Kane's cavernous home stirred. His energies twisted and mixed with that of the world around him. The myriad of colors that Kane saw through his mind's eye danced together in such a way that no color truly stood out amongst the rest.

He pushed and pulled at the different strings of The Flow, bending the energies around him to his every whim. He worked the dead energy of the desert that surrounded him back to life and used it to create whatever it was that he needed; Food, water, clothing. His very desire became reality as he saw fit.

At this moment, he was merely toying with the energies. He practiced almost continuously to maintain his proficiency with The Flow. He didn't want his death to come, because he forgot something important.

A familiar sensation cast itself upon the desert. The creatures of the desert were afraid. It had been almost ten years since this had happened last. Kane was not afraid. He pushed up to his feet and walked calmly to the mouth of his cave. He watched as the strange blackness covered the sun.

He maintained his calm as the terrors of the desert ran from the blue orbs. Kane pushed out a shield of energy to block them from getting to him and began walking about his domain. The orbs tested his shield and changed to get through them, but Kane's deft mind stayed one step ahead of them without even the slightest effort.

He took in the sights of the dead and dying corpses of the horrid creations that stalked the desert. He knew they would not stay that way though. The desert always saw to reviving the dead in some disturbing and gnarled fashion. That was its very nature after all.

After he had satisfied his curiosity at the sights and sounds of the eclipse, Kane made his way back to his home to prepare for the second phase. It would arrive without fail, but he would be ready for it and the horde that would come with it.

As he lowered himself to sit and meditate, he wondered at what his sister might be doing. 'Was she still training in the Academy? What of their parents? Was there truth to the dreams he had had or was he just punishing himself?'

He pushed these thoughts aside. They would do him no good and they hardly mattered anymore. They were just idle thoughts of fancy at this point. He wasn't even sure that he would truly ever make it out of this place, let alone see his sister again. And even if he did, would she even accept the man he had become?

Half a world away, Aerika was having similar thoughts. What had her brother become, if he even lived? She pushed the thoughts out of her mind. They would do her no good. Since completing her training at The Academy she had become a steward to the Atrethian High Council. Her duties were minimal as they had little need of a servant but she observed and learned from them and was even allowed to sit in on the less sensitive matters the Council had discussed.

When she had left the Academy, Grand Magistrate Doe'n had taken her in to learn what the Council did. He knew that someone of her talents would be best suited for leadership of the Atrethian people. She observed everything he did; Learned from his every choice.

She would groom herself to the position she desired. She would make a difference in their society. She felt Tieg's familiar energy coming into the Buorthian Chamber. She stood and removed her hood as he entered the room.

"Tieg, my friend. It's good to see you." Aerika smiled as she embraced her friend. They didn't see each other as often as she would like. He spent most of his time ensuring the flow of fresh water to the surrounding farmlands.

"And you, Aerika. I came to see if the rumors were true." Tieg hadn't even tried to hide the excitement in his voice.

"What rumors are you talking about?"

"They say that one of the Councilmen is passing on and that you are to take his seat."

A confused look washed over her face. She wasn't at all sure how a rumor like this would circulate without her having heard it first. After all, as steward to the High Council, she had direct access to the Council members at all times.

"I hadn't heard that, but I suppose it's possible." Tieg lost the excitement from his face. He was clearly hoping it were true. "But," she continued, "If it turns out true, you will be the first to know."

His smile returned. "You don't need to go out of your way to let me know. I'll just stop by to see you again when I get the chance."

"Of course. You are always welcome."

"Besides, we have a date to keep. Your parent's memorial site needs tending."

She nodded at the reminder. She had almost forgotten; A product of being so busy with studying the rules of the Council and laws of Atrethia. She went to embrace her friend once more to bid him farewell.

"Be well until then Tieg."

"And you, Aerika."

Tieg made his way back out the way he had come.

Aerika was a tad confused still, but she thought better of taking stock in rumors. It never brought about anything good. She had better just keep to her duties and continue her studies of the laws.

"Steward Aerika," One of the Enforcer's that tended to the High Council had stepped out of the Mythril Hall. "The Grand Magistrate requests your presence immediately." She had become familiar with these Enforcers, but they never lost their formality.

"I'll be in at once, thank you."

"Of course." He withdrew back into the Mythril Hall. Aerika didn't wait long to follow. By the sound of it, it was a matter of importance. She would get back to her studies later.

Aerika made her way into the Mythril Hall. The sight of the hall didn't take her breath away as it once had. She had grown so accustomed to walking through its doors that she hardly realized the grandeur of the place anymore. This time, however, it felt much more imposing.

The air was thick with tension and Aerika took note of the stern looks on most of the council member's faces. Grand Magistrate Doe'n's eyes had locked on her the moment she crossed the threshold. This was a tad unnerving, but she thought better of showing her unease.

Aerika approached the lit circle before the Council, ready to be addressed. The Grand Magistrate didn't wait for her to be set in place. He was sometimes impatient like that when it was a pressing matter.

"Aerika, do you know why you have been summoned?" His voice boomed throughout the chamber. Some of the Council Members flinched at the sound. He had apparently forgotten the Flow would boost the volume of his voice in the chamber. Aerika stood her ground showing a calm expression despite his words hurting her ears.

"I have heard rumors, Grand Magistrate." Her voice

was but a whisper compared to his but it was loud enough that she was heard. "But I don't know for certain."

He contemplated her words for a moment. "Rumors, eh? No matter. That might make things move more quickly. You have been summoned, because one of those among the council has chosen to pass and has named you as successor to their position upon the Atrethian High Council."

He waited a moment to appraise her reaction to his words. She showed none. A smile touched the edge of his lips before he spoke again. "I've always been fond of your family and despite what has occurred in your life, you have persevered. I want to ask you a question before we continue, if you would permit me."

She merely nodded as she was mostly unsure of what to expect at this point. The silence throughout the hall was almost too much to bare, though Aerika remained unshaken by the situation.

"Aerika," he continued, "what is it that has driven you to this point?"

She was taken aback by this question. She had always been driven. She never really gave anyone reason to think she had ulterior motives, at least none that came to mind. She paused for a moment to gather her thoughts before she answered.

"Well Grand Magistrate, I suppose the answer to that question is rather simple and one that everyone in this room is familiar with, if not intimately so." She felt that she had the room's attention if they hadn't already figured out to what she was referring.

"The exile of my twin brother Kane has driven me to this point. I strive to attain a position where I can ensure that no one is ever put into that position again. I wish to make certain that no other child is sent into exile for defending the life of his or her sibling, or anyone for that matter. In my own opinion, justice was not served that day."

While Grand Magistrate Doe'n appeared unaffected by that bold statement, many of the other Council Members exchanged nervous glances. She paused a moment to let her answer thus far sink in before she continued.

"Under the circumstances given to you Grand Magistrate, you did the best you could with what you had and while I feel that the laws of our land can and do uphold justice, I still believe that certain situations may call for a bit more deliberation then was given and I would thus strive to make changes to allow that to happen."

She had thought long and hard about her own motivations before this day. She had always questioned herself to make sure that she was not driven by selfish thoughts, but instead was putting justice and the good of Atrethia before her own desires.

In fact, she had questioned her motives so much that she almost didn't accept her current position. She would have moved on to something else if she had even the slightest doubt that her motivations were for anything but the good of all Atrethia and its people.

The Grand Magistrate stood silent for a moment letting the answer fill his mind. He gave a satisfied nod. "I had thought as much myself. Thank you for that answer. Now that I've been indulged, I think it appropriate to continue in the way intended."

The tension noticeably eased at this seemingly innocuous statement. Grand Magistrate Doe'n continued without pause. "Aerika Malacor … Do you swear to place the needs and well-being of Atrethia and all its people above your own until such time as you depart the Atrethian High Council?"

His words seemed to hang on the air as if threatening to materialize into solid objects right above them all. The power of this oath was undeniable. It was something she had studied and learned, but it seemed all the more profound now that it was the only thing standing before her and her future.

"I do." Her answer, though simple, held a profound grip upon the rest of the Council. Given what they had just heard of her motivations, some were, at best, unnerved at her joining the council at this juncture.

"Do you swear to uphold the laws of Atrethia to the best of your understanding and always serve as a moral standard to those of lesser standing?" She almost took a step back at this question. She had studied the oath many times and he had changed it.

Given her prior statement, there was no way she would be able to take the oath. He should have asked, 'Do you swear to uphold the laws of Atrethia as they are written,' yet he changed it. She thought maybe he did that because of her answer to his question, but she thought better of delaying her answer. "I do."

He continued immediately as to not allow protest at the change. "Aerika Malacor, I hereby instate you as a member of the Atrethian High Council. Please retire to your new room within the Buorthian Chamber and don the robes of your new station. You will be summoned when you are needed for deliberation. Please feel free to keep your appointment as I don't think we'll need you so soon that you can't pay respects to your parents."

"Yes, Grand Magistrate. Thank you." She bowed slightly before spinning on her heels and walking from the Mythril Hall. It took every ounce of her will to keep her emotions in check. She was finally going to get the opportunity to make a difference as she had desired for as long as she can remember.

She marched to the door to enter the Buorthian Chamber, the power behind which she could hardly fathom. When one opened the doors, the chamber could send you to the personal dwelling of any council member granted you were invited by that person.

She stepped through the pure white smoke of the door to enter into her home at the edge of Mi'Tiya. Upon her bed sat the robes of her station. The brilliant red robes that marked her as a member of the Atrethian High Council.

She slid the plain brown hood from atop her head and shook her raven black hair from within it. She drew down on the knot holding the robes about her shoulders and let it slip down her slender curves. Her form beneath the robes was unassuming and plain, but when uncovered, she was a beautiful sight to behold. Her pure white eyes etched a sharp edge upon her face that forced anyone peering into them to catch their breath.

Her raven black hair fell down to her upper back and stood in stark contrast to her eyes. Her fair skin denoting just how little time she spent outdoors. Her pale features, however, didn't hide the sensuality of her curves. She gripped the silken hem of her new robes and lifted them over her head. She let the fringe fall and slide down her near-naked frame.

She sighed happily at the feel of the robes against her skin. She ran her hands up across the robes relishing in the moment of finally being on the council. A knock interrupted her celebration. She quickly tied off the robe and pulled the hood up while walking to answer the door. She assumed she was being summoned again though she thought it a bit soon given the Grand Magistrate's statement.

When she opened the door, she stood face-to-face with Tieg. He gaped at her in her new robes. His mouth hung open at the mere sight of her. That's when she realized that these robes weren't quite as unassuming as her old ones. These complimented her figure and Tieg had certainly taken notice.

She blushed a bit at this but decided it better to change the subject so he could get used to them. "So the

248

rumors were true. I'm on the council. I was sworn in only moments ago." Her beaming smile brought him out of his daze.

He smiled in return obviously not wanting to let on what he had been looking at and hoping she would not want to admit that either. "That's great, Aerika! I'm so happy for you! … Oops, I mean Councilwoman."

She shook her head so hard that her hood almost fell from her head. "No, Tieg. You will always call me Aerika. I would accept nothing less from my oldest friend."

Kane moved as though he were one with the world around him. Bits and pieces of the creatures he'd faced already littered the sands behind him. He had no need to hide anymore. He was so in tune with the Flow, he could all but control these beasts.

He conjured fire, ice, wind, whatever destructive force he wished. The elements were at his command. A behemoth lay, torn asunder by gusts of wind. A stalker was frozen and shattered. Entire groups of beasts burned until only ash remained.

The desert resembled a battlefield, littered with bodies and parts all killed or dismembered in different ways. But the battle did not end. The battered and the torn reassembled by the foul energies of the Eclipse. Wave after wave returned to the fray. Kane paid no mind to the endless mobs. He just continued to unleash destruction.

Kane paused for a moment to draw in a heavy drag of the acrid smoke from the charred remains of a group that was indistinguishable from what it once was. Just as he was about to be struck from behind a fount of flames shot into the air around him throwing back his attackers and shielding him from harm.

The flames expanded out around him torching and charring everything they touched. When all was clear, Kane calmly made his way back to his home. He had grown bored with the fight and wanted now to meditate and wait for the next phase of the eclipse.

The walk back to his cave was uneventful. Save for a few stragglers, he didn't see any of the deserts inhabitants. He pulled the entrance closed as he crossed into the sanctuary. He made his way deep into the cave.

His home was something of a miracle. He had created a small pond for his drinking water. He'd even managed to shield this place against the desert itself to bring a garden to life for food. Everything he needed to survive was at his fingertips.

Kane walked out atop the spring, creating a thin sheet of ice to stand on with each step. Just as he got to a seated position he conjured gusts of wind to lift him into the air above the water. He floated unmoving above his source of fresh, clean water, ready to begin his meditation.

In his meditations, he broke down the walls of his cave, his new sanctuary. He found the world anew every time, its living splendor seemed unnatural after all this time living amongst the death and destruction in the desert. His own energies seemed to pollute everything that he came into contact with, though he hardly noticed. He had grown so accustomed to the feeling of the desert that death was no longer a shock.

He recalled the last time he'd experienced the Eclipse. The last time he'd felt Aerika's presence in earnest. She had saved him that day. He somehow knew he could never repay that, though he felt that his time here more than paid that debt.

His thoughts went right back to the task at hand. He visualized the threat that would come with the third phase. He would be prepared to face that shade, the creature or energy or whatever it was that had assaulted him the last time. He would be ready for it and he would defeat it. His goal was survival and it was one he was confident he could achieve.

Raven sat silently, staring at his Enforcer helmet resting in his hands. He had spent a long time contemplating his existence. Nothing was going easily for him. He hadn't even heard from Nih'al and, for all he knew, Kane was dead and never to return from exile.

Ever since that search had been called off, he'd lost his sense of purpose. His mind was always racing with what-if's. He even found it hard to focus on his day to day duties. He had requested post as the personal guard for the newest member of the Atrethian High Council, Aerika. He hoped that being close to Kane's sister would help him focus, but word hadn't come back to him yet.

The sound of footsteps echoed down the hall. He lifted his helm into place and latched it down. Just as he pushed up to his feet, another Enforcer walked into the room. The golden spaulder that adorned his left shoulder marked him as an Enforcer Commander. Raven clapped a salute to the violet eye at the center of his breastplate.

"Enforcer Commander Loreth … To what do I owe this honor?" Raven's words were a mere formality. Loreth and he had all but trained together and they shared a common link in having been a part of Kane's exile. Loreth returned the salute before offering his hand to his friend.

Raven returned this show of friendship. "Raven, your request was granted." He offered him a slip of paper. "Your orders." Raven took the orders and gave them a once over. Everything was in order. "Thank you, Loreth," he said.

Loreth clapped a salute to his chest, which Raven quickly returned. Loreth spun on his heels and made for the door. He stopped just short and looked back over his shoulder. "You know, the time draws near." Raven knew what he was referring to, but he was surprised that Loreth was keeping track.

"If he yet lives, we'll be called to bring him back,"

Loreth continued.

The two friends shared a knowing look that betrayed a meaningful connection. At that moment, Raven knew that Loreth wanted to find Kane alive, just as he did.

"If he yet lives," Raven replied, "He'll make his own way back." Loreth nodded to Raven and shared one last breath before marching off down the hall.

Kane descended to his feet upon the water in his home. It was time. The third phase had begun and the beast, whatever it was, was coming for him. His fight would begin again soon. He summoned gusts of wind to kick up all of the dust in his cave so when the beast arrived, he would know.

He extended out his energy, feeling for any changes in the sanctuary that was his home. He would attack first. He would not give the creature the satisfaction. Not this time. He would have his revenge and he would be victorious.

After a wait that seemed to pass in an instant, Kane heard a shuffling sound within the cave. He opened his eyes to find what he already knew to be there. The same creature from fifteen years prior. The one that seemed an absence within the Flow.

The creature was as large he remembered, almost reaching the roof of his cave. Its massive arms weren't quite as big as they had seemed before, but Kane was bigger himself. It was hunched forward leaning on its long arms. At the end of its arms were those same massive, three fingered claws.

It had its legs tucked tight under its body as though it were ready to spring forward at any moment, as it had during their first encounter. Atop its massive torso sat an equally large head. The narrow eyes framed by two coiled and menacing horns that aimed towards Kane.

The beasts jaws were exactly as he remembered them,

full of fangs that measured almost a half a foot long and two, much larger, fangs at the ends of its lips. Those two fangs extended up between its horns and stopped just shy of reaching its line of sight.

Just to be sure, Kane felt out with his energy. He wanted to confirm that this was, in fact, the same creature. It was. He felt nothing where it stood. An absence of anything; No energy what-so-ever; No life; No death; No nothing. And just as he had planned, Kane made the first move.

25

Aerika and Tieg stood before the memorial to her parents. The solemn site always seemed so appropriate. Even in death they would remain together. She sighed and placed the simple bouquet of white flowers she held atop the stone. She knew the words she wanted to say because she'd rehearsed them so many times before, but she just couldn't find the moment she wanted.

"Well," she said finally, "I guess now is as good a time as any. I made it. I'm a member of the High Council. I'm on my way to achieving my dream. I just thought you would like to know."

Tieg looked off towards the Barean Cliffs. He knew they already knew she had. Where they were, they could see everything all at once. They knew the moment she had become a Councilwoman. But he also knew that she knew it too. This was more for her than it was to let them know.

"Mother. Father. Kane's time in exile draws short and I can no longer feel him. My ...," she choked a bit on her words. Tears welled up at the edges of her eyes, but they never fell.

"Our," she corrected, "connection has failed. I don't care if I can feel him or not, I know he's alive. I just want you to give him the strength to come back. Please ... Keep him safe."

She finally gave in. She let the tears flow free down her face. Tieg turned her towards him and she buried her face into his shoulder. Her body quaked and convulsed with each sob. All her pain, all her sorrow, seemed to pour itself into this one moment. Tieg just held her against him and let her cry.

After a few minutes of crying, Aerika started to regain her composure. She choked back the pain and fought back the tears. She lifted her head and looked up at her friend. "Thank you, Tieg. I just hope that he returns to me. I don't have anyone else."

He winced at her words as though she had struck him. Her expression changed to confusion. She had seen him. He sighed and made a quick decision. "Like you said, I guess now is as good a time as any."

"I've wanted to tell you this for a long time, but no moment ever seemed right and though now doesn't feel right either, I don't see any other option. Aerika, I love you. I've loved you for a very long time. Almost as long as I can remember."

She just stood staring at him, barely blinking, if at all. Her mouth stood agape. She couldn't find the words to reply. She gathered herself and thought for a moment that maybe she should have known already. She thought that the signs must have been there. She just never saw it.

"Tieg …" He heard the pity in her voice and looked down. "Tieg, I'm sorry, but I can't say it back. You are my oldest and best friend, but I just can't afford to have that sort of connection to anyone."

Tieg shook his head. None of this was going the way he had wanted. He was supposed to say those words and sweep her off her feet. He was supposed to take all of her pain away, to protect her from all of it. Yet she was the one that pitied him. The look in her eyes and her words said it all.

"I … I'm sorry, Aerika. I never should have said anything. It's my fault. I … I'll see you later." And without missing a beat he walked off towards Mi'Tiya.

"Tieg wait!" Her words got lost in the wind. He kept

on his way and disappeared behind one of the many hills that rolled towards the cliffs. A cold wind washed passed her. It seemed to chill her more to the bone than any other wind she'd ever felt. She wrapped her arms tightly around herself to try to warm up, even a little. Now, more than ever, she felt alone.

An Enforcer marched as fast as he could without running. His feet carrying him through the many halls that separated the Vi'jal Temple from the Mythril Hall. At this dire moment, he thought it a bit strange that the two places that housed two groups so connected, The Twelve and the Atrethian High Council, were so far apart.

But he put his mind to the task at hand and marched on. His footsteps echoed through the hall and off into the distance, heralding his approach to any that happened to be in his way. He pressed on. This was a walk he was familiar with, but the way the prophet had given the command demanded haste.

Finally, the doors to the Mythril Hall came into view. Mere moments and he would be at his target. And two Enforcer's stood outside the doors. That either meant the Council was in session or the Grand Magistrate was inside. Either way, he knew where he needed to go.

As he approached, he clapped a salute to the eye at the center of his breastplate which they returned in kind. "I come on business for The Twelve." The two Enforcer's didn't move to stop his approach. Instead the doors swung open as if they feared even his touch.

He crossed the threshold into the black of the hall and saw the familiar violet robes of the Grand Magistrate at his station. He moved to the light, as was custom, and voiced the commands of the prophets.

"Grand Magistrate, the Twelve summon you to Vi'jal Temple. They said it was dire and that you must make haste."

Doe'n didn't wait for the Enforcer to finish voicing the command. He had already stepped from his station and was making his way towards the huge black doors. "Let us make haste then, as commanded."

Doe'n and the Enforcer walked swiftly through the halls. He had only gotten a summons such as this once before and it was to herald something horrible. He would like to run there, but one miss-step could prove fatal. The slick floors were designed to ensure those within did not rush needlessly.

Doe'n wondered what it could be that was so dire that he was summoned like this. Normally the summons was sent and he could arrive at his leisure, but when The Twelve summoned, you came quickly.

They made the trip as quick as possible and Doe'n pushed through into the Vi'jal Temple. The Rotunda seemed grown out of the very earth and disappeared into the blackness above. The light itself seemed to want nothing to do with the ceiling.

Standing in the center of the room, a familiar prophet waited. Doe'n approached with haste, leaving the Enforcer to guard his station at the door. As Doe'n took his place the familiar words found their way from the prophet.

"A prophecy has been shared and you shall hear it. Listen close and hear my words."

"I shall hear it." At times like this, Doe'n found this ritualistic repetition useless, but he would indulge as it made it go faster.

The glow from the prophet's eyes shifted its hue. The color shifted and mixed as though his eyes were becoming all colors at once. The glow now held a myriad of colors ranging from yellow and red to blue and green. This was a sight that Doe'n had grown familiar with over the years but it was still rather unnerving to see someone's eyes change like this. When the prophet spoke his words sounded as though a dozen people were speaking all at once.

"The one in violet that sent the warrior into exile must pass the torch. A new Grand Magistrate is called to stand in service to the people of Atrethia; One that will herald peace and is the first of her kind."

'Her kind'? Doe'n had heard correctly. This prophecy was calling for him to step down and relinquish his position to a woman. Someone that would 'herald peace.' The first female Grand Magistrate. And he knew exactly who it would be.

By the time Doe'n spoke, the glow beneath the prophet's hood had returned to normal. "I understand what you wish of me and I know exactly of whom you speak."

The prophet gave Doe'n a solemn nod knowing what this meant for him. Doe'n turned and without hesitating, made his way back into the winding halls leading back to the Mythril Hall.

The violet robes marking Doe'n's position as Grand Magistrate draped down his body. He stared down at them, the heavy fabric designed to keep out the cold, but also to breathe so that the wearer didn't overheat. He had grown accustomed to wearing these robes. They were familiar; they were safe.

Now, though, he would have to turn them over. He would have to give up his position, because prophecy demanded it. He swallowed hard trying to fight back the emotion threatening to overtake him.

He would do this for the good of Atrethia. It was what was demanded of him. He must obey. And, as if on cue, the members of the Atrethian High Council joined him in the Mythril Hall. The huge black doors slid closed as the last member stepped through.

None spoke. They all just exchanged sidelong glances, wondering silently to themselves why they had received such an urgent summons. They each took their positions flanking Doe'n; he in turn waited for them to get into place.

He drew in a deep breath when they had all arrived and steeled himself for what was to come. He wasn't sure how he was going to tell them what the prophecy said. He wasn't even sure he fully recalled the words spoken. He knew the message that needed to be delivered. The one thing he was certain of was that he would find the words.

Doe'n looked around the chamber and the words came as if they were sent from somewhere else completely. It didn't even feel like his words. "Members of the Atrethian High Council. Much has transpired of late and many of us have seen more than our share of trials during our tenure here in this council chamber."

Some were only more confused by his words while others nodded understanding at least of what he spoke. He continued, "I have summoned you here today with an urgent message given by The Twelve. This message is not one in which we can take any deliberation and it does not offer room for interpretation. It is absolute and a command we must follow to the letter, without argument and without delay."

The Council Members all nodded their agreement without even knowing the command. It had been their collective experience that any word from the prophets, if not followed, brought dire consequences. Doe'n surveyed the hall before continuing.

"That is why, with the greatest of sadness, I offer my resignation as Grand Magistrate." Every member of the Council gasped aloud at this. None of them could have guessed that this was what he had summoned them for. The room was completely silent for what surely had to follow and not a single eye left Doe'n unwatched.

"And with my resignation, comes the ordered appointment of a new Grand Magistrate. As per the prophecy, this Grand Magistrate has a great destiny ahead of them and will be the first of her kind."

Many in the Council took note and whispered amongst themselves when he said 'her.' He paused for a moment to let his words sink in.

"The Twelve have commanded this appointment through their vision, though I expect it goes without saying that we will follow this command. With that, by the authority granted through The Twelve, I appoint Councilwoman Aerika Malacor as Grand Magistrate."

Aerika's already shocked expression changed to confusion. There was no way she could have heard that correctly. She shook the confusion from her face and put on her most resolute expression.

"Grand Magistrate Doe'n, surely there must be some mistake. I've only just joined the Council. They must have meant someone else."

Doe'n shook his head. "No. As I said, there was no room for interpretation. Prophecy clearly stated that you would succeed me as Grand Magistrate. I am sure that, young as you are, you will preside with great wisdom and grace. I am also sure that your time as Grand Magistrate will be of great benefit to the people of Atrethia."

She nodded understanding at his words. She took great pride in this man's praise. He was, after all, her father's oldest friend and a man of great influence and import in their society. His words and his wisdom meant a lot to anyone lucky enough to garner them.

"And Aerika, I want you to know that you can always call on me for advice, so long as I remain among the people." She offered a nod of gratitude, unable to find the words to thank him properly for his praise and support.

"With that, I ask that you all, as is customary, return to the Buorthian Chamber and await summons for the next point of deliberation. Aerika, your new robes are already waiting for you in your home."

Enforcer Commander Loreth walked swiftly through the halls of the barracks. He wanted to get there before Raven had packed up everything. Once word had gotten to him that Aerika had been named the Grand Magistrate, Raven had to be notified that his orders to guard her had been rescinded.

Loreth weaved his way through the many convoluted halls. When he arrived, Raven was still packing up his things. Loreth paused for a moment to catch his breath. Raven stopped when he felt the presence in the room and clapped a salute once he saw who it was.

"Enforcer Commander Loreth, to what do I owe the honor of this visit?" That same formality that was always required, though Loreth seemed annoyed by it.

"I'm glad I caught you." Loreth had gone over exactly what he had wanted to say to them. "I have some bad news for you, Raven. Your position protecting Aerika has been declined at the last minute."

Raven, though his expressions were hidden behind his helmet, was visibly taken by surprise by this. "What? Why?" He sounded obviously frustrated.

"She is no longer a councilwoman. Doe'n has stepped down from his position as Grand Magistrate and she has been elected to his position, so her protection detail falls on the Shades."

Raven had already put that together in his mind when he mentioned her election. The Grand Magistrates were protected by an elite group of Enforcer's known as the Shades. The Shades were originally established to take down the Malicious One and assumed protection of the Grand Magistrate following his execution.

The first group of Enforcer's selected to become Shades was almost entirely wiped out during their attempt to capture the Malicious One. Enforcer Gale Noral was the last surviving member and the hero that brought the Malicious One to justice. He was also the originator of the training regimen that the Shades endure and too this day remains the primary overseer of training for the Shades.

"I understand." Raven sat down and slumped down resting his elbows on his knees.

"I wasn't done, Raven." Raven perked up a bit when Loreth said this. "I also have some good news. After a review of your record, and a recommendation from myself and every other Enforcer that has ever worked with you, and not to mention a very kind recommendation from the, now, former-Grand Magistrate, you've been selected to go through Shade training."

This was more than Raven could have ever hoped for. And it was a great honor and one that he would not waste. Not for anything.

26

Kane's eyelids fluttered lightly. He grit his teeth and cringed at the pain he was feeling. His head ached as though it had been smacked against the stone wall. He opened his eyes just the slightest to let in a bit of light, but it only caused the ache to worsen while blinding him in the process. He wasn't entirely sure where he was; let alone which end was up.

He brought a hand up to the top of his head and felt around the slope of it. He was relieved to find no blood. At least none that was wet. He was confused. He had lost time. He was hungry so it had obviously been a few hours. He felt weak. There was really no telling just how long he had been out.

He felt around trying to get his bearings. He felt at least a rock nearby so he pulled himself to it and pushed up to a seated position against it. His entire body hurt so much he felt like every inch of him had been torn apart and put back together. His skin felt like it was on fire.

He grit his teeth and let his eyes open. He figured he may as well just take the pain and let his body adjust to the light again. He couldn't see anything through the white. Then, slowly, his vision returned; blurry at first, but it eventually began to clear.

He was still in his cave and, luckily, not far from the spring. He fell over onto his side and pulled himself to the water's edge. He lowered his head down to the water to sip at it. When the water touched his lips, he realized just how thirsty he was. He drank from the pool greedily.

With each gulp, Kane felt his strength returning. He must have been severely dehydrated. His headache started going away almost immediately, but he would need food and rest to get back to his full strength. At least the creature wasn't around.

He couldn't fully recall what had happened. He remembered bits and pieces of the frantic battle. In the beginning he was on the offensive. He sent balls of rolling flames, founts of water, and gusts of wind. Everything hit and everything passed through. Nothing he did had an effect on it.

The tide of the battle quickly shifted. It was all he could do to not get hit himself at this point. He jumped and dove and slid, but then everything went blank. He couldn't remember what happened next. He knew that he had lost that fight, but he was alive, at least, and he seemed to be in one piece.

Kane pushed up to his feet. His legs felt brand new, like they'd never been used. And his muscles felt so weak they could hardly hold him up. He got over to his garden just in time. His legs gave out beneath him and he tumbled into the soft dirt. Lucky for him it was still moist.

He picked what he could reach and chewed on it slowly. He was starving, though he knew if he ate too quickly he would just throw it back up. After just a few bites, he let the creeping darkness take him again, slipping back into unconsciousness.

Aerika waited patiently in her place. The Grand Magistrate robes felt very comfortable to her. She knew she was meant to wear them. The huge black door to the Mythril Hall opened, as silent as they were massive, and in walked the members of the Atrethian High Council.

The members of the council each paused a moment when they saw Aerika. She was the first female Grand Magistrate and the way the light hit her position and shown on the violet robes was quite striking.

The robes covered her entire body with the hood sitting neatly upon her shoulders. Her long raven hair hung down low on her back.

The smooth appearance of her jaw and chin accentuated her soft, pinkish lips. Her lips hanging naturally open only the slightest bit, barely showing the white of her teeth behind them, betraying the natural beauty of her feminine features.

Her pure white eyes sat just below her smooth brow occasionally smoking with the power that lie beneath. Even her beauty couldn't hide the frightening abilities she carried with her.

Around her neck, the amulet that Kane gave her the day he was exiled hung with great care. The amulet, a small red jewel, hung from a thin silver rope and rested at the center of her chest.

Every member of the council paused to take in the imposing sight and then continued to their designated positions. She stood silent as they took their positions. She had waited this long, moments didn't matter much more at this point.

"Council Members," she finally said as the last took their place. "I summoned you to do as I promised the day I took my place on the council. I propose that we alter the rules of deliberation on laws. I think they are far too lax and offer entirely too much room for justice to be left undone or outright denied."

Most of the men and women on the council were either privy to what had occurred within her family or had actually been a part of the deliberations involved. No one spoke for what felt an eternity. Then, someone spoke.

"I second the motion." It was Council-woman Theana. Aerika knew from her time with the council that she had been there when everything involving Kane had happened. "I agree with you and am sad to say that I was part to the case with your brother, Grand Magistrate. I agree with your assessment that justice was not served in that case and probably would have, had we had the deliberation rules that you propose here today."

One after the other, the members of the High Council gave their agreement. The basic consensus was that the new rules would allow for the greatest chance of justice truly being served in every case.

"Now that we're all agreed," Aerika pushed to move the gathering forward. "I propose that, in each case, we, as a collective group, be given all of the facts of the case, from both sides, before we deliberate and make a decision. Then, when we have the facts, we can have a discussion on how everyone feels about them and how everyone views them, and then we will vote and collectively make a decision."

Everyone simply nodded. It sounded like a simple concept and many whispered amongst themselves wondering why no one had come up with it before. Aerika continued, "I take your reactions as affirmation that you all approve of this method."

There was a resounding and unanimous agreement from the council members. Aerika smiled at this. She had achieved her primary goal. "Now that we've concluded that business, I think we should call it a day." They all nodded their agreement and made their way out of the Mythril Hall.

She was pleased with how that went. It was unanimous. With that out of the way, she now only had to wait for Kane to return from his exile. Somehow, with her new position, she could feel him for the first time in a long time.

Raven stepped through the door he had been directed to. This was the only part of the Enforcer compound that didn't have the distinct smell of polish. The Enforcers were known for the care they took to make their armor presentable, but it wasn't something the Shades were known for.

The Shades didn't wear the armor that normal Enforcer's did. They wore hard leather armor dyed black. It was the signature of the Shades. The black was a symbol of their method; remain unseen, if possible, until the very last moment.

While the Enforcers were a common presence in society and most people recognized them, the Shades were widely unheard of unless a person took the time to study history. And even if someone knew of the Shades, they certainly didn't want to ever see one.

Raven looked around the bare room. He wasn't sure this was even the right place but he had been told to go here. There was another door at the opposite end of the room so he started making his way towards it. Just before he reached the door, one of the Shades stepped through the door into his path.

"Raven Mataius?" The man's voice had a no-nonsense feel to it. Raven simply nodded at the man. "Lose the armor. Place it on the table over there. You won't be needing it any longer."

Raven looked directly to the table as if this man had turned his head for him. It all felt controlled even down to the smallest detail. He went about the ritual of respect for the armor. He may not be wearing it any longer, but it was still something he thought was important. The armor was sacred to the Enforcer's.

He unhooked his helmet and placed it on the right hand side of the table. His spaulders followed next. This large piece was difficult to unhook while still wearing the breastplate, but it was the way the ritual dictated.

Raven placed each piece with the greatest of care; the greaves; the sabatons; and finally the breastplate. As per the ritual, each piece was placed the same exact distance apart.

The table was built specifically for this ritual. The entire suit of armor fit the table perfectly. Once he was done, he stepped away from this armor for the last time and went on to his new life as a Shade. Things were finally coming together for him. He had a renewed purpose.

Kane sat, suspended over his spring as he did every time he meditated. The water was never disturbed and he maintained perfect control of all of the energies around him throughout his meditations. This time was no different.

His many arms reached out and felt everything within his domain. The beings of the desert had returned to normal in the weeks since the eclipse ended. He still couldn't remember what had happened with the beast, but he was certain that it had left his energies untouched after he had fallen unconscious. That was the one thing he was certain of.

He could feel each creature as it went about its normal behaviors. Each beast moved cautiously from rock to rock avoiding the sand as one false step would cause them to become the prey of the worm that stalked beneath the sands. He could even feel the worm as it hunted for anything that happened upon the dunes.

Suddenly, something felt different about the energies of the desert. There was a sudden surge and the creatures all ran from their hiding places. Some became prey to the worm that didn't mind the change in energy as it was granted a boon for the disruption. That's when Kane realized where he knew this energy from. The shock of this realization caused him to fall from his meditation into the waters of the spring.

On the opposite side of the continent, Aerika stood before a symbol drawn in sand of different colors; The outer circle, drawn entirely in a dark brown; A square drawn in blue sand met at four points with the circle; A red line dissected the circle completely cutting through one corner of the blue square and exiting out of the other.

Within the circle were several symbols drawn with white sand. Each symbol had a distinct deliberate shape. At the ends of the red line that dissected the symbol, stood Enforcer Commander Loreth and the newest recruit of the Shades, Raven Mataius. Aerika reached deep into her memory to pull the ancient Atrethian words from her mind and pronounce them correctly. If her brother lived, a portal would open and the two Enforcer's would be allowed to go in to retrieve him.

Kane crouched silently at the closed entrance to his cave. He extended his energies out feeling the now tense air of the desert. The static charge that had fallen over the place was one he had felt before, but this one was different somehow. It felt as though it were drawing energy into it rather than pushing energy out.

He thought about how this felt to him for but a moment before he realized what it could mean. He started counting moons. He had missed many the time he had been struck unconscious, but, if he was right, it was time for him to return home.

Aerika's voice echoed in the chamber as she spoke the final words. Loreth and Raven now stood beside one another ready to enter the portal should it open. The Flow moved them to this position during the ritual to allow for the maximum time for someone to be found and returned safely.

Both men stood mute waiting for the portal to open. The echo of the words from the ritual died out. Loreth let his head drop in disappointment. He had hoped that Kane yet lived, but he also knew that no one had ever returned from exile. It had never happened in the history of their world.

Raven and Aerika remained hopeful, their eyes locked on the center of the room. A sudden and thunderous impact hit them all, almost knocking them to the ground. The symbols had all collapsed into the center of the room to form what can only be described as an arch. It expanded, opening up before the two Enforcers, but the inside remained empty.

Loreth let hope return, as this was not something he had ever heard of happening. He and Raven both prepared for the portal to open so they could go in to retrieve Kane and bring him back from his exile.

Kane still waited, checking and rechecking his math. He couldn't believe it was that time. He needed a straight shot to the portal if he were to make it back and if anyone were to come through it, they would be in a very bad position on the dunes.

He turned and ran back through to his home and summoned wind to cut through the stone carving a path up and out to the sands above. He had to work fast as he didn't know how long he had until the portal opened.

He worked carefully and quickly, carving away the rock between him and his freedom. As he reached the end of it he found a dome of sand before him. The rock didn't go all the way up above the dunes. He would be exposed and vulnerable, calling the worm to him with every step. But he knew he could make it, he had to.

Aerika held a stern look upon her face, though her emotions were in turmoil. Inside, she screamed at the top of her lungs, commanding the portal to open now and deliver her brother back to her. Inside, she cried, hoping that she wouldn't be disappointed by having nothing happen.

Her heart sank and rose with every breath she took. It beat so hard she felt like it would pound out of her chest and fly across the room. The pain she felt compounded with each moment that passed and her excitement grew into a lump in her throat until it became difficult to swallow.

She didn't even want to wait for Raven and Loreth to go get Kane out of the desert. She wanted so badly to just dive through the portal when it opened to get him herself.

She imagined pushing the two Enforcers out of her way and running out onto the sands and finding Kane waiting, but she knew that wouldn't happen.

The portal would allow only three people through, the two Enforcers used and the one summoned or sent. It was made to keep out any who might try to go through when it wasn't their time.

Raven remained completely still. He knew that the portal would open. He knew that Kane would be brought back and that this part of his life would be brought to a close with a happy ending. The one thing he didn't know was if he would find Kane or if Kane would find him.

Loreth could hardly handle the anticipation though he didn't show it. He fought the urge to bounce on the balls of his feet ready to run through as soon as the portal opened. The moment seemed to last forever and it was eating them all up inside.

The air in the Mythril Hall was charged with static. Aerika's hair would have floated up from her head had she not been wearing the hood up on her Grand Magistrates robes. The static subsided without warning and a loud pop resonated through the chamber. An image began to appear within the frame of the arch.

Kane felt the static in the air around the dunes intensify. With each moment that passed he felt the energies of the desert grow and change from the amount of energy being distributed. His patience was certainly being put to the test in this moment, but he had waited for twenty-five years so he could wait another few minutes.

He sat on his heels waiting for the moment he would charge from his shelter and make for the portal. It was almost time and he would be home. He could make the run. He had to make the run. He had to keep his promise to Aerika. He had promised her he would return and for the first time in over twenty years, that promise was the only thought in his mind.

The electricity hanging in the air over the dunes disappeared as though it were dismissed from existence in a single moment. The portal was opening. This was his chance; he summoned a gust of wind forth and pushed it through the sand pushing everything that blocked him from the dunes out in a burst. He followed it with all his might out onto the sands and into the threat of becoming the worm's next meal.

With each step on the sands Kane gave his position away to the worm beneath him. On top of that, the creatures of the desert were driven into a frenzy by the energies of this portal. He pushed himself harder and harder as Stalkers, Scythes and Behemoths converged on him. If they had their way, he would not make it out alive and he wasn't going to let that happen.

Kane pressed on, his every footfall as deliberate as the last. He jumped as hard as his legs would allow and called wind to carry him forward just as a behemoth and several stalkers got to where he was. The worm crashed through the sands beneath them swallowing them all whole before slithering back down into the safety of the sands.

The silence inside the Mythril Hall was nearly unbearable for Aerika. The image within the arch became more and more clear with every passing moment. The dunes of the Terrei Desert stood out against the golden backdrop of the Bubble. Her, Raven and Loreth were frozen. Even Aerika was shocked that the portal had opened. It was a well-known fact that none had ever returned from exile and they had never known what actually happened if someone had survived their exile. All that was happening was new and would be passed down for future generations of Grand Magistrates and Enforcers to learn and be aware of.

The now clear image of the horrible place that Kane had called home for twenty-five years flashed white for a moment and then shimmered before them. The portal was open. Raven and Loreth shared a look and nodded to one another. It was time to go in for Kane.

Raven thought to himself that he wasn't going to return if he didn't have Kane and Loreth felt the same. This silent pact drove their first step towards the portal and every subsequent step. Just before the two Enforcers stepped through the portal, Aerika shouted at them, "WAIT!!"

Kane pushed as hard as he could, dodging and diving and sliding out of the way. The worm devoured many of his attackers, but there were just far too many. It seemed the entire desert was following him to prevent him returning home. He pressed on regardless, determined to keep his promise … to make it back to Aerika.

He drove himself forward. The heat emanating from a behemoths mouth as he just narrowly missed being bitten blew across his cheek. A scythes blades came down together just behind him cutting the stalker that was in pursuit into three separate pieces.

More and more assailants came. More and more were felled by the worm, by a behemoths crushing hands, by a scythe that was trying for Kane. Every beast tried for him and none could succeed. He escaped their reach if only by a hair.

Kane looked through the encroaching mobs towards the tallest dune where he knew he was headed. He found exactly what he was certain he would find: a portal. He could not yet make out what the image was within the portal, but he was sure it was the Mythril Hall. He pushed harder.

Raven and Loreth stopped themselves mid-stride and looked to Aerika. "What is it, Grand Magistrate?" Raven asked. He was anxious to get through and he knew she was just as anxious for Kane to be back so he thought it must be important for her to stop them.

The look of terror in her eyes was enough to cause a

chill to run down the spine of even these two hardened Enforcers. Her screams were so loud that it hurt their ears nearly to the point they couldn't hear her, "Get out of the way, both of you! He's coming to us!"

Kane barreled up the dune as quickly as he could, but it wasn't nearly fast enough. The beasts chasing him were slowed just as much so they were hardly a worry. His concern lay with the worm lurking beneath. It would be upon him in moments and he could hardly make his feet move any faster in the loose dirt.

Just as he knew would happen, the worm burst from the sands just behind where he stood, it had misjudged his speed and that gave him the time he needed to reach the peak of the dune. He kicked hard without looking back but knowing that the worm had locked him in and was now hunting him, not just the other food that ran about the sands.

Kane threw himself hard into the air towards the open portal. He summoned one last gust of wind to accelerate towards the portal and, he hoped, to freedom. The worm followed behind him. Its deep maw agape as it prepared to devour its greatest conquest. Kane reached the portal first with the worm not a moment behind him. Both passed through, but once the portal felt something coming through that didn't belong, it closed, slicing the worm's mouth from its body.

Raven and Loreth had only stepped away from the portal when Kane came into sight within the image. He looked very different from what she remembered. His hair had grown down to his shoulders. And his body was much more toned than he had been as a boy. But that wasn't the only thing she noticed. She spotted a horde of unnatural creatures followed up over the dunes edge with a gigantic worm closing in quickly behind him. And she wasn't alone. Loreth and Raven noticed them as well.

Aerika's heart jumped into her throat. All of the

beasts from her nightmares were real. They were the only things keeping her brother company for his long time in that horrid place. She knew at this moment that something in him had to have changed. That there was no way he could have survived his time there without adapting.

She wasn't sure how he had changed, but that wasn't the concern now. At the moment, she just wanted him to make it out of that hell. She watched in mute horror as Kane took to the air in a last ditch attempt to make it through the portal with the worm close behind him. Just as he made it to the portal, she realized that the worm would hit it too.

"The portal's going to close!" Her words had hardly escaped her lips when it happened. A brilliant flash of light that forced them all to avert their eyes and the room went dark. The portal gone and the arch collapsed.

The multicolored sand that made up the arch dissolved into a billowing smoke that filled the room. Everyone within broke into a coughing fit. The smoke began to clear quickly as it all found its way back to the floor. Aerika, Raven and Loreth all jumped back when they saw the open mouth of the worm that had been chasing Kane. It had made it partially through the portal before being cut off.

Aerika knew then that Kane must have made it too. She started looking around the hall while Raven and Loreth began inspecting the worm. They had never seen anything like it and, they thought, probably never would again. Aerika ran from beside Raven and Loreth. She had found him.

Kane was pressed back against the wall. His eyes were fixed on the worm; he hadn't even noticed Aerika, Raven and Loreth standing there. He just stayed frozen where he sat. He could hardly believe that he was out of the desert.

Aerika gripped his shoulder and shook him trying to

break him from his trance. Kane scanned blankly to Aerika. Her hood had fallen back in her rush. The look on his face told her that he didn't recognize her. He got a confused look on his face for just a moment before his eyes dropped down to the pendant hanging around her neck.

Realization washed across his face and he looked back up into her eyes. "Aerika?" His words were hardly a whisper, but she heard him. Tears began streaming down her face. She nodded before wrapping her arms around him. He felt like she might squeeze the life out of him, but it was just nice to be back with her; to even feel the warmth of another person.

Kane put his hands against her shoulders and pushed her back away from him. She looked at him puzzled. "Can I stand up, Aerika?" She nodded and pulled him up to his feet. He bounced a little testing his legs to make sure it felt real. When Kane was satisfied that it was real and he was back, he put his hand on her cheek.

His words were calm and hardly seemed real to her. "I told you I would come back." She threw her arms around him and let the tears take over.

27

Aerika woke with a start. She looked around in her room. She was home in bed. She wondered to herself if it had all been a dream. If her brother was, in fact, dead and she had imagined the whole thing. She shook the sleepy haze from her mind and resolved that it wasn't a dream. It had been all too real.

She slid her legs off the bed and pushed up to her feet. Her body still wasn't fully awake. Her legs tingled a bit. Her muscles felt weak beneath her. The smell of a fresh rain crept into her nose. She didn't remember it having rained the day before.

She heard a soft droning sound in the distance. There was some sort of celebration going on in the town. She wasn't sure what it was for, but her concern was finding Kane first. She stepped out into the kitchen and dining area, but it was empty.

"Kane?" Her words echoed in the eerie silence of the empty house. She worried that maybe he had been gone so long he had gotten lost. She made her way over to the door as quickly as she could, but, with the way her legs felt, running wasn't an option.

She pulled the door open and let out a sigh of relief. Kane was standing beside the tree near their house. 'Their house' she thought. They were a family again. This thought brought a smile to her face. She took her time walking up to him. He made no move to look at her, but she knew he was aware of her presence.

She stood back a few feet looking out to the rolling

hills leading out to the Barean Cliffs, which Kane had been looking at. She wondered just how long he had been out here. Just how long had she been asleep?

Kane spoke without taking his eyes off the hills, "It rained this morning … I haven't seen rain in twenty-five years."

His words held a sound of wonder and appreciation of something he's gone without. She couldn't help but feel sad for him. He'd been through so much; And for what? Because some child thought he could be better than him by beating him up? No. It wasn't that simple. He had gone through everything he went through for her … to protect her from the same thing he himself endured.

"Did you sleep?" It was a weak question given all she wanted to ask him but it was all she could come up with. He didn't answer, he just shook his head. "I don't sleep much anymore …"

She thought she heard fear in his voice, but she could just be mishearing him. She had so many questions that she wanted to ask him. 'How had he survived all these years? What were those creatures chasing him? What had happened to Jerek Kis'tohl, whom she knew to have been exiled as well?' But she couldn't find the words. Or maybe she just thought better of asking them.

"Kane … I …" Her words caught in her throat and she fought to not break into tears again. She was just full of emotions about him being back from his exile that she couldn't contain them.

He must have realized this because he took the conversation into his own hands, "Can you take me to their graves today? I would like to see them, if I could."

She realized now how he felt. He didn't feel connected to their world anymore. Like he needed to ask permission to see the resting place of his own parents. She felt a pang of sorrow for him. She couldn't even imagine how horrible it must have been for him that he was this far disconnected from them.

"Of course we can go. You don't ever need to ask to go, you know? You can go see them whenever you feel the need." He looked at her for the first time since she had seen him in the Mythril Hall. She could see the distance in his eyes, the scars of his exile. This pained her more and she could hardly hold back the tears at this point.

His expression softened a bit when he saw her fighting the tears. He stepped over to her and wrapped his arms around her to draw her head against his shoulder. When he did that, she let the tears flow. Her body wracked with sobs, but he kept her held against him. He was a far cry from the small boy she remembered.

She pushed back the tears. There would be other times she could cry. "Are you alright?" His words were barely a whisper. He was so calm; so collected. She couldn't imagine how he had become that way. She thought she knew but she also thought it better not to ask such questions.

Kane lifted her head up and looked into her puffy eyes. She just nodded, because speaking at this point seemed too daunting a task. He kept one arm around her shoulder while she led him across the hills towards the cliffs where their parents were buried.

Aerika looked up at him and didn't even see the desire to speak. She couldn't imagine that he had nothing at all to say. He had to have something to say. Although she wasn't very talkative herself. She wanted to say something, but everything just felt so unimportant now that he was back.

Kane kept his eyes fixed on the horizon like he was looking beyond everything to see something very far away. She knew he was walking right next to her, but she didn't feel like he was with her. She felt like she was alone walking to visit their parents.

The hill with the single tree came into view as they crossed yet another hill on their silent walk. Not a word was exchanged between the twins. Aerika didn't mind. Just having him back was good enough for her. Kane's eyes were locked on the memorial stone now.

Aerika led him the rest of the way. It felt almost like she were carrying him at this point. She ushered him forward to stand before their memorial. He looked down at and ran his fingers across their names.

He mouthed the words written upon the stone, '*In life, their love brought light to the world around them; In death, let them serve as an example of love eternal.*' He smiled at the thought that it brought to the front of his mind. "That's beautiful. A perfect thought."

She smiled at this. She was pleased that he thought it was good. She knew he would think this was perfect. She was glad that she was finally able to share this with him; glad that he was finally back with her at home. At least there was that much. Days and even weeks passed. He never really seemed to reconnect to their world. And one day, almost a month after he had returned, on a visit to the Barean Cliffs, Kane seemed even more distant. He looked off towards the horizon.

"Aerika?" His words broke her from the daze she was in.

"Yes, Kane?" She still could hardly believe that she was actually talking to him again, even after he had been back so long. It was hard to accept the reality of it all; that he was actually back from his twenty-five year exile.

"Can I ..." He seemed like he was having trouble finding the words. "I know we've been apart for a long time, but could I have some time alone? I just need time to figure things out."

She sort of understood what he was saying. She nodded before answering, "Of course, Kane. Whatever you need." She hugged him one more time before stepping away and making her way back to their home. He stood silent, watching her go before turning back to look out beyond the Barean Halos to the Barean Cliffs.

Kane's mind was stuck on how still everything felt. The calm of this place was almost too much for him. He hadn't felt anything like this in so long. This calm ... this peace was so foreign to him it was almost hard to grasp.

Without even realizing he was moving, he stood in the center of the field of Barean Halos. He looked around at the sight of the flowers he used to know so well. Now they were such a distant memory that it all felt brand new to him. He knew now what he needed in his life.

The silence in the house was less deafening now that Kane was back from his exile. Her world seemed a little less bleak. She smiled at the setting sun as she plucked away at their dinner. It was nothing special, but she imagined it was a far better meal than he was used to, though he never really made mention of it.

A knock came at the door that brought her thoughts back to reality. She made for the door and practically laughed out her words, "You know you don't have to knock before entering. It's your hou-" She was frozen in place for only a moment before regaining herself. "Oh, Tieg." She only just realized that she hadn't seen Tieg since Kane had returned. She wondered if he even knew.

He looked a little confused at what she had been saying. "Hello, Aerika. Who did you think was here?" And right on cue, as if summoned by Tieg's question, Kane stepped over the hill coming from the cliffs. Aerika's eyes slipped from Tieg's to watch Kane as he approached. Tieg followed her gaze, his own finding Kane on the horizon. The shock was evident on his face.

"He's alive?!" It sounded more like a realization than a question. Aerika could only smile and nod. A few short moments passed before Kane arrived at the door and Tieg and Aerika moved aside for him. "Kane … How … um ..." Tieg couldn't manage to find the words he wanted.

Kane was quick with his own thoughts though, "Hello, Tieg. It's good to see you again." Kane's smile seemed genuine, if a tad unnatural. Though Tieg and Aerika both thought he had had little to smile about before returning. Tieg and Aerika followed Kane inside.

Aerika went about finishing dinner while Kane asked Tieg about his life since the start of Kane's exile. It was a long story and Tieg seemed a little uncertain with every question. He wanted to ask about the exile, but didn't know how to ask such questions and Kane wasn't exactly forthcoming with the details himself so they all thought it better to leave it alone.

After they finished catching up, they sat in silence until dinner was ready and then they sat down to eat. The silence was uncomfortable for Tieg, but Aerika seemed contented to be back in her brothers company and Kane seemed content in general if a tad uncomfortable. No one made an attempt to start conversation though there were several occasions in which Tieg was caught staring at Kane and quickly looked down to his food.

Kane finished eating and excused himself. He went to back to his room, which used to be his and Aerika's, but she had moved into their parent's room a long time before. Tieg didn't say much while he and Aerika finished eating, but he said one thing before he left. "I'm happy for you, Aerika." She went off to bed herself.

Aerika woke with a jolt, sitting up quickly in her bed. Something had woken her, though she couldn't tell what. She got up from bed and went to the living area. Kane was sitting on the couch staring out of a window. The moonlight reflected in on his face. She could see the mental scars of his exile as if they were painted upon his face. He shifted a bit to let her know that he was aware of her presence.

She moved over to sit next to him. They sat in silence for a long while, what seemed hours to Aerika. Kane was the first to break the silence, "Aerika ... I can't do this. I feel confined." His words were confusing to her.

"What are you talking about, Kane? Do what?" Sobs threatened to break from within her, but she fought to control herself. The pain in his voice was almost more than she could bear. He waited only a moment before answering her. His thoughts came quickly and it seemed he knew what he was going to say before he said it. "I can't stay here, Aerika. After being in that ever changing environment where things were never calm. The routine of this place is just too much."

She still didn't understand. "What ... Kane, I don't understand." Emotion started getting the better of her. She knew what he was saying; she just didn't want to admit it to herself. Tears pooled up in her eyes.

He sighed before continuing, "Aerika, I'm leaving. I know I just got back to you, but I just can't stay here when it's this calm." Her tears began flowing free from her eyes. His words struck a harsh cord within her. She had only gotten him back and now he was leaving again. "I'm sorry, Aerika. I'll be gone before you wake up in the morning. Try not to worry. I'll come back eventually. I just need time."

Epilogue

The exile was only one of the many painful things I had to endure. There was much more strife and heartache to follow. And I didn't make it easy for Aerika to live with either. I'm surprised she could even look at me after what I had done to her.

I had only gotten back to her, the one who I had sworn I would return to, and left hardly a month later. But fate, or should I say the Flow, had other things in store for me and Aerika both. It wasn't easy for me to do, but, at the time, it was all I could think to do to keep myself sane.

In hindsight, it wasn't exactly the best decision. I mean, had I stayed with Aerika, things may not have turned out the way they had. There are always if's and there are always but's. In this case though, I think that things could not have happened any other way. When I look back, I see better choices; Things I could not see at the time. But then I feel like even if I had seen them, something would have driven me to the same outcome.

I don't know how to explain it. I just have this inkling that I didn't really have a choice in the matter. I'm more than certain that everything happened just as it should have happened. The loss of life, the pain and destruction; It was all for some twisted purpose. What that purpose is, I don't know, but I can only hope that telling you my story will keep the same thing from happening here. But I think you've heard enough for the day. Perhaps you should retire for the night and we can pick it up again tomorrow.

www.ingramcontent.com/pod-product-compliance
Lightning Source LLC
Chambersburg PA
CBHW021951170626
46808CB00001B/104